BLACKMAILED BY HER BULLY

EVERNIGHT PUBLISHING ®

www.evernightpublishing.com

Copyright© 2019

Sam Crescent

Editor: Karyn White

Cover Art: Jay Aheer

ISBN: 978-0-3695-0108-0

BLACKMAILED BY HER BULLY

DEDICATION

To all of my amazing readers. You guys are so awesome and thank you for your love and support. I hope you love this book as much as I loved writing it.

BLACKMAILED BY HER BULLY

BLACKMAILED BY HER BULLY

Sam Crescent

Copyright © 2019

Chapter One

Running was never in Ava Marshall's book. But there was no way she could stay in Crow Valley, not if he was back. Why had he come back? She felt sick to her stomach as she rushed into her home. Her parents had left it to her in their will after an unfortunate accident.

With her hands shaking, she couldn't get the key into the lock. Closing her eyes, she took several deep breaths and started again. She had to focus, to be in control.

There was no way she could allow herself to make a mistake.

Once the key was in the lock, she turned it, clicking it open. Rushing inside, she slammed the door closed, throwing each bolt across the door before heading up to her bedroom. She'd never moved into the main bedroom. Her parents had been dead for five years, but she'd stuck to her old room.

She went straight to the closet, grabbed her suitcase, and started to fill it. How long had he been in town? She didn't know when he got back, but if he was here again, then it wouldn't be long before *he* followed. People were talking about *him* like he'd been a missed member of society.

Working at the library, she rarely got any updates from anyone, but then, no one really liked her.

She felt sick to her stomach just thinking about it.

With most of her clothes crammed into the suitcase, she closed it, using as much strength as she could. Next, she grabbed her passport, money, and any paperwork she'd need.

If *he* didn't stay long, she could come back. She loved her family home, and even though Crow Valley had never accepted her, not after what she did, it was at least home.

With her bag and case in hand, she ran downstairs, nearly falling in her haste to get away. Holding onto the railing, she felt another wave of sickness, and she had no choice but to sit down. Letting go of her bag and case, she spread her thighs, putting her head between them and taking several deep breaths.

"It's fine. I'm fine. I'm going to be fine." No matter how much she repeated the words, it seemed she was lost to the fear.

"I'm shocked at just how sexy he looks," Martha, one of the stepmoms who attended the crafting class at the library, said. "I haven't seen him in years, and do you know what I heard?"

"What?" Nancy asked.

"He's loaded. Like, ridiculously wealthy. I've heard it's not all legal either. He's dangerous."

"Please, if he does that, why did he come back

here?"

"No one can pin anything on him. He's like a crime lord. Or a drug one. I tell you, you should have seen those smoking hot eyes of his. He could do whatever he wanted to me," Martha said with a sigh. *"It would beat having to figure out sewing a damn Halloween costume."*

"Why did he have to leave again? It has been what? Twelve years?"

"About that. Logan Stanford and all of his buddies had to leave because of her."

The moment she heard that name, Ava knew she was in trouble. No one had said that name to her in years, or the other name, but they didn't need to say *his* name, for her to know he wouldn't be far behind Logan. Tears filled her eyes, and she lifted up, breathing deeply.

"She's the one who accused him of sexual assault."

Instead of arguing with Martha and Nancy about what actually happened twelve years ago, she'd left the class. There was no point in teaching gossips. They came to class to bring more meaning to their lives, but all she ever heard from them was how boring it was being a stepmom and trying to make a family work.

The sickness passed, and she got to her feet and went straight to the kitchen. Logan and his friends were never supposed to return to Crow Valley. She was promised *he'd* stay far away from her. Opening the fridge, the ink she had on her arm caught her attention. *Never Forget.* Two words, in fancy writing, and in a border of red roses.

Dropping her arm, she covered the marks as a fresh wave of tears filled her eyes. She shook a little. But this was useless.

She'd be able to get food on the road. There was

no point in waiting around. The longer she lingered, the more chance of *him* coming for her, increased. He'd promised her one day, he'd find a way to get to her. To make her pay. She'd stayed in town, determined to make a life for herself. He shouldn't be back, but with Logan back, *he* would be arriving soon, she just knew it.

She should have been safe.

Grabbing her bag and case, she stepped out of her house, locking the door. She turned to see a man standing at the end of her garden. Her parents hadn't been wealthy. They'd been able to buy this place outright after they got married. Both her mother and father had been city kids, but wanted to raise a family in a small town. Crow Valley being the small town, and well, there hadn't been any more kids.

Her mother hadn't been able to have any more after her.

She remembered the yearning she always had, and they'd not considered adopting. Instead, they had put all of their love and hope in her.

Now she was alone.

"Ava Marshall?" the man asked.

Fear tightened around her chest.

"Who is asking?"

"I am. Are you Ava Marshall?"

The man was tall. She noticed the ink on his neck. Across the street was a black four-wheel drive. She'd never been good with makes or models. It stood out on the street. Most of the people drove family cars, but this one, it looked like the kind in gangster movies. Now she felt silly.

"No," she said, the lie dropping from her with ease. There was no point in prolonging this meeting. "Excuse me." She tried to step around him. This man worked for Logan; he had to. Did it mean *he'd* given

Logan instructions to bring her in? No doubt about it, and she had to get as far away as possible.

The man, he laughed. "You know, he said you'd try to run. I didn't think you'd be that stupid." He grabbed her arm.

"Let me go." She tried to pull away from him.

"Not going to happen. I have strict instructions to take you in."

The man was strong and a lot bigger than she was. She felt the tears fill her eyes and fear grip her as he started to pull her toward the car.

"No! Stop it. Let me go."

There was no one else around, and if anyone was twitching their curtains watching, they didn't make a move to come and help her. She was, for all intents and purposes, on her own. She didn't want to panic, but she felt it rising up inside her.

Her heart raced, and she felt sick.

As they got to the black car, he slammed her up against it, holding her by her neck.

"You know, he said you'd be difficult. I didn't realize how much. Don't worry though. I like it when you fight me. It makes me feel all … hot." He pressed his pelvis against her, and she cried out, hating what he was doing to her.

"Stop it."

"Then you're going to get in the car and you're not going to cause me any trouble, are you?"

"Who are you?" she asked. Tears filled her eyes.

"You're going to do as you're told, aren't you?"

She wanted to rebel. To tell him to fuck off. To leave her alone, but to do that, she'd be risking him hurting her even more, and she couldn't handle that.

"I'll do as I'm told."

"You're going to be a good little girl, aren't

you?"

"Yes. I'll be good."

He smiled, and she hated the wickedness within his gaze, which she saw in the reflection of the car window.

She hated to relent. Giving up was never in her nature.

But you did.

This is why you're where you are.

The door opened, and he shoved her inside, putting the seatbelt on. She cried out as he grabbed her hands and secured some rope around her wrists.

"If you think you can get away from me, I'm not giving you a choice."

The rope was tight, and the first tear fell.

"I like to see you cry. You know, I've been told a lot of things about you."

She jerked away from him as he touched her cheek. "Let me go."

"No."

"Are you at least going to tell me your name?" she asked. "You know mine."

He smirked. "That I do. You know what I find strange. I've seen at least three curtains twitch and there was even a man walking a dog, and not one of them tried to stop me. There is no love lost between you and these people." He tutted. "You must have been a very bad girl."

Another tear fell, joining the last one.

"Keep on crying, sweetheart. It's not going to do you any good." He stepped back, and she sank into the seat. There was no point in fighting or arguing. "The name's Hunter." He slammed the door closed and climbed behind the wheel.

"No more questions?" he asked.

"Will you answer them?" She didn't look at him. She didn't want to give him the satisfaction of knowing she was terrified, and she was.

It had been a long time since she was this terrified.

Over twelve years.

She closed her eyes, hating how weak she felt.

"Someone has been waiting a long time for you," he said.

"Why do you work for him?"

"Do you even know what he's capable of?"

"Yes, I do."

"Then you should know a man that powerful has my loyalty. He has bought it."

"So you can buy loyalty these days?" she asked. "You can be taken by the highest bidder."

Hunter laughed. "Normally, I can. But you see, there's a thing about Logan, he managed to earn my respect and my loyalty another way, and now, I'll do anything for the crazy bastard. Even if it means abducting a woman for him."

"How fun," she said.

"You have no idea. At first, I didn't think he'd go for it. I know he's capable of a lot of things, but you see, I had no idea you're the reason he's the way he is."

She looked up to see Hunter staring at her. Every now and then, he'd glance down at the road, but his focus was on her, and she hated it.

"I didn't do anything."

"No, you didn't? We'll see. Maybe your memory is fogged up, but one day, you will realize all of this is your fault."

She lifted her tied hands and wiped away the tears.

Logan was supposed to stay gone, along with his

other friends. She didn't know what Logan had done to be cast out, but she'd been told all of them had gone. *He* wasn't going to come back to Crow Valley. She'd been promised that.

He'd been one of the star boys. The little rich kid who could have anything he wanted. Only, she'd not bowed down to him. She'd fought him then, and she'd continue to fight him, every step of the way, until he was taken down.

"What's he like now?" she asked.

"Ah, has curiosity raised its ugly head?"

She looked back at him. "I want to know what I'm up against. Exactly *who* I'm up against."

"I think you know. Logan has told me he hasn't changed much. He's gotten older. A little meaner, maybe. He's powerful. Rich. Any other woman would be flattered at the kind of attention he's bestowing on you."

She felt sick. She didn't know what Logan would want with her, unless he was acting on behalf of his friend. "Please, take me home."

"Not going to happen."

"I didn't do anything wrong. I did what I was supposed to."

He laughed. "I'm sure you did. You better relax. Where we're going, it's not going to get easy for you. Believe me, it's going to get very hard. Logan's been planning this meeting for a long time."

The radio was turned on, and she closed her eyes, letting the tears fall.

She should have left Crow Valley when she had the chance. After her parents died and she was left all alone.

Tugging on the rope, she tried to pull her hands free, but it was no good. There was no fighting this hold. She gritted her teeth and pulled again, trying to find the end. If there was a chance of getting out on the road before they even got to wherever Logan wanted her, she'd take it. Would *he* be with Logan?

She'd not seen *him* since the day he'd paid an impromptu visit to her home. Her parents had been at work, and she'd decided to be home-schooled. There was no way she could go back to school. Her locker had been defaced, and her life had become unbearable. She had no choice but to finish her education at home.

He'd promised her. Looked right into her eyes and told her there would come a day, he'd be back, and when he did, he'd pay her back. They would be even. All this time she'd known he'd be back, and she only hoped he would never find her.

This was her mistake.

She would have to live with it, but why would Logan want to hurt her? She had done nothing to him.

****

Staring out across the expanse of his lawn, Logan took a long draw on his cigarette marveling at the fake beauty before him. A real garden wasn't tamed. It didn't have gnome ornaments or statues of semi-clad women. At the click of his fingers, he'd be able to have real women, standing naked, waiting to amuse him.

He preferred the wildness, the chaos, danger to all the fake and preened lawns. The gardener had promised to stay on, to help maintain the grounds. He'd fired him on the spot. True beauty was seeing what lay beneath. To Logan, it wasn't about masking nature, but seeing it grow. Seeing the real world, and being inspired by it. He looked forward to seeing the grass grow, the weeds coming up out of the grounds, surrounding their fake, ceramic gnomes and poised sculptures.

Throwing his cigarette to the ground, he stamped it out, blowing out another puff of air.

Gripping the cold cement railing, he breathed in the night air. It was nothing like the city. No lingering toxic car fumes, or the stench of decay. Walking down the street, he'd be able to get a good whiff of rotten food, animal piss, and the unmistakable scent of desperation. He couldn't get any of that now.

The air was clear, crystal clear.

Just like his feelings. He was more than ready for what he planned to do.

For twelve years he'd bided his time, preparing, getting stronger, throwing away the shackles that had once bound him, and taken over. He was no longer caged for a crime he didn't commit. The moment he stepped foot in the small town, he made sure the Sheriff knew who the real boss was. Before Logan had kicked out the previous tenant, he'd laid down the law. If the Sheriff even thought to interfere with his plans, Logan would make the Sheriff's extracurricular activities public. It wasn't his fault the man liked to go and visit gay bars, and also have a hand at underage children, boys more specifically. Logan remembered being in those bars, and the Sheriff had tried to lure him in. He'd tried to blackmail Logan, to get him to confess, and also tried to scare him. When the man tried to touch his dick, even then, Logan had been strong. At eighteen years old, he'd been bigger than everyone in his high school. No one could take him. He'd been a tank, unmoving, unyielding, but Ava, she'd taken him down. She'd crushed him to his knees, and now it was his turn to reciprocate. Her lies and hatred had ruined his life, or at least, ruined a few years of it. She'd had him incarcerated, punished for no reason at all.

The town, from his research, wasn't behind her.

No one would save her.

He smiled. This was exactly what he'd hoped.

If there was someone in town who cared for her, who hoped to save her, the Sheriff would look the other way, which was exactly what Logan wanted. Everyone could do whatever the hell they wanted to do so long as none of them interfered with his plans.

The door opened, and he didn't bother looking.

There was only one man who would interrupt him. His other men were on guard. Being powerful came with a lot of enemies.

"She's in your office."

"She came willingly?" Logan asked.

"I wouldn't say willingly, but she didn't exactly put up much of a fight."

Logan chuckled. He finally turned to his friend. Hunter had been the kind of guy who jumped from job to job. He only worked for the man who paid the highest price. Logan didn't even have to offer him money or a job. He simply stopped the man from dying. He'd been severely beaten and left for dead, with broken bones, bullet holes. Rather than leave him in the dumpster to die, Logan had taken him home, and made sure he received the best medical care and rehabilitation to help him.

Having shattered legs was no easy feat, and well, Logan needed a man who was able to walk on both of his, and Hunter was the right man for the job.

There were times he was sure the man didn't even have a soul.

"That's not like her. Ava always put up a fight."

"She knew you were here," Hunter said.

"Of course she did. I made sure I was seen around town. It's a small place."

"She was going to run. Were you prepared for it?"

"I'm disappointed she didn't make this easier for

17

me." He stepped into the house with Hunter hot on his tail. He got to his office and paused.

Every single year he'd been away, he had one of his men take pictures, to follow her for a couple of days a month. He hadn't seen her in the flesh in twelve years.

"You'll stay here," he said.

"Logan, do you really think this is the best idea?"

"Yes."

Hunter was a close friend. He wasn't just an employee, and Logan valued what he had to say, most of the time. Right now, wasn't one of the times he wanted the other man to speak. He wanted silence so he could do what needed to be done.

Stepping into the office, he closed the door and took in the woman tied to a chair. Hunter had even gagged her. There were tear stains from her eyes. She hadn't been able to wipe them away.

Ava never cried.

She saw him, and for a split second, the air stilled. He watched her, seeing the hazel of her eyes once again. She'd changed. Her hair was much longer than before. Back in high school, she'd always worn it to her shoulders. The blonde locks had been a tease even then. He couldn't get a good look at her body, but he saw she still had her curves.

Her tits were still nice and big. He wondered if Hunter had purposefully tied the rope to highlight just how big they were. He imagined his friend did. Hunter would want her to be on display. His friend had promised time and again to help him.

Facing his past wouldn't be easy, or at least that was what he'd been told.

One look at her, and he knew it was good to be home.

She started to struggle against the ropes.

Stepping into the room, he crouched down. "Well, look at you. All grown up. I like what I see."

Her voice was muffled. He stared at her. She didn't look away. Her gaze was focused on him. He couldn't bring himself to not watch her.

Twelve years was a long time to find closure.

The room was silent, and he didn't want it to be.

When he reached out, she flinched away from his touch, and he grabbed her face. "The first thing you're going to learn is not to do that. Do you understand?" He tightened his grip, and she nodded her head. "Good."

He removed the gag, and the moment he did, she started to scream. He raised a brow as she opened her mouth again and screamed.

"Are you done? No one can hear you. Not that anyone would come running."

"Fuck you," she said. Her voice sounded shaky.

He laughed. "You've still got a mouth on you, I see."

"Stop it. Let me go."

"Not going to happen. You can waste your energy screaming if you like." He moved to the back of her chair and started to open the ropes.

"What are you doing?"

"You're not very trusting, are you?"

"You got your goon to grab me from my house. You haven't given me a reason to trust you!"

He lifted up, his lips right next to her ear.

"You're alive, aren't you? I'd say I can get points for that. Besides, you deserve everything you've got coming to you. The lies you told."

"I didn't lie."

As the ropes loosened, she got to her feet, trying to make a run for it. He grabbed her hand, hauling her back. Banding his arms around her, he felt just how

19

curvy she was, her nice plump tits, curvy ass, and juicy thighs. He loved her curves, always had.

"Keep on moving. Keep on wriggling. I've got all night."

At his words, she slumped in his arms, and he smiled. This was Ava through and through. First, she'd fight, and the moment she thought she was giving him what he wanted, she'd give in.

He let her go, and again, she didn't disappoint; only this time, he let her leave the room.

He stepped out, to find Hunter had her in his arms. Only his friend had a hand across her mouth, and the other cupping her throat.

"You let her go?"

"Nope. I didn't let her go. She's fun to play with, and she does everything I expect her to." He folded his arms across his chest. "Bring her back into the office. We've still got to have our little chat."

Hunter pulled her, wriggling and fighting, into the office. He threw her to the floor.

"Do you want me to stay?" Hunter asked.

"Sure, why not? I'm sure Ava will love an audience. Especially for what I've got planned."

"I don't know what it is you think you're going to get out of me, Logan. I can't change what happened."

Hunter was no longer holding her down.

Ava sat perfectly still on the sofa, her accusing gaze on him. Her hands were up as if to protect herself.

He smiled. "This is one of the many things I like about you, Ava. You think you're the one in control, but you're not."

Sitting on the edge of the coffee table in front of her, he stared into her eyes. He'd thought about them so often. Soon, they would be filled with pleasure. She was going to accept his bargain, and she'd be all his.

Everyone in town would know her for the liar she was, and he'd have his revenge upon every single person in town who'd dared to harm his reputation.

"You know, sexual assault is a hard reputation to come out of. Did you know that?"

Ava frowned. "What?"

He smiled. "You can play dumb all you want, but I know the truth. You, Ava, are a fucking fraud. You think I didn't know what you wanted, even back then. I knew you wanted me."

"I have no idea what you're talking about."

He put his hands on her knees, and she captured his wrists.

"Stop it," she said.

"You see, Ava, there is only one way this is going to go."

"I don't know what you think I did, Logan. You've got it all wrong."

He laughed.

"Shut her up," he said.

Hunter was there, hand over her mouth, holding her back.

"There, that's better. Let's see, yes, Ava, I've decided I'm not going to hurt you. Believe me, I can if I wanted to. I'd even be able to hide the body afterward. Trust me. There's so much I can do to you." He stroked her knee. "You're going to be my fuck toy, Ava." She shook her head and tried to talk. "You see, when I left Crow Valley, I did so with the knowledge I'd come back. They put me in prison, threw away the key. I had to serve time for your lies. Did you expect me to be there for life? I was a good boy in there, Ava. I knew how to lay low. I made some connections, and I knew it would only be a matter of time I'd deal with you. I believe Luke told you I'd be back. He did give you a warning. You're still here, and I know it's time for you to pay up for what you did. The tarnish you attached to my name. No matter what I do, I cannot remove that little label from my life, but you see, you're going to help me with that. You're going to prove to the town how you lied. You're going to be at my disposal, whenever and however I fucking like. You're going to ride my cock, and beg me for more. I'm going to capture every single moment of it. If you're a good girl, only you and I will ever be able to see it. The town will know you belong to me. Let go of her mouth."

Hunter shrugged.

"I would never do that. There's no way, I'd be … that for you."

He smiled. "You seem to think I'm giving you a choice."

"I don't know what kind of sick game you think you're playing, Logan. I don't want it. I'm not part of this. I didn't lie. I don't know what you think you know. Sexual assault—"

He didn't give her a chance to finish her sentence.

"I suggest you be careful how you finish that little sentence. Do you understand me?" He had his hand wrapped around her neck, silencing all protest from her.

"Stop," she said, muffling out the word.

"I rather like this. You seem to think you have a choice, but there is no choice." He squeezed her neck a little more before finally letting her go.

He listened to her gasping for breath. He watched her as she grabbed at her throat, but he made no move to help her.

Staring at her now, he looked forward to seeing her relent. To finally getting a taste of her body.

He'd liked her back then. Even as he'd bullied her every single day, not giving her a reason to even look at him, he'd taken advantage of every moment to touch, to feel her.

Pushing those thoughts aside, he stared at her now.

She really was a beautiful woman.

"What makes you think I'd ever agree to something like this?" she asked. "You've got to be completely crazy if you think I'd ever allow you to do anything like this."

He smiled.

"How about now?" He pointed at the television and pressed "Play."

Loud and clear the sound of fucking filled the air, and Ava's face paled.

"Do you see anything you like?" he asked. "I see a whole load of things."

"How did you get this?"

"I happened to know a few people. It would seem your parents weren't as squeaky clean as you'd think. No, they liked to fuck a lot of people, and believe me, their medical bills show a great deal. Did you know they enjoyed many a weekend with other people?"

"My parents are dead," she said. "You can't hurt them."

"But this would hurt their memory, but what about you?" he asked. He clicked the forward button, and next, he didn't exactly like watching this one, but seeing as he set it all up, he made himself watch it.

"Grant?" she asked.

"Oh, he's an employee of mine. You know, the one who always had to go away on business. The hotel I own, and let's just say, I made sure every single corner you were exposed to."

He looked at her, seeing the tears in her eyes. "If you want any of this to go public, walk away. Leave. You can go right now."

"Why are you doing this?"

"You know why. I'm not even going to justify that question with a fucking answer. You owe me, Ava, and you're going to pay up one way or another. So, what will it be?"

Chapter Two

Sixteen years ago

Ava cried out as she was slammed into her locker.

"Well, well, well, if it's not little fatty!"

The pressure was pulled away from her. There was no mistaking Luke, one of the most popular guys in school, who was also one of many guys who liked to bully her.

She grabbed her book and closed her locker, turning to see his little crew. There were three other guys.

"Be careful, she might eat you, Luke," Riley said.

There was a round of chuckles.

"Nah, she won't eat me. She only eats stuff with real flesh on. You'll be the one in trouble, Logan. The guy's huge. I bet she'd choke on him."

They all started to laugh.

"Are you done?" she asked.

They crowded around her, and she hated it when she became the center of attention, even when it was bullying. She hated attention of any kind.

Her hands shook, but she held onto her book in the hope none of them saw just how nervous they made her.

Logan stepped forward and pushed her hard. His hand was large; even at fourteen he was the biggest guy in school. He pushed her against the locker. "I suggest, little girl, you be careful who you talk to."

"We're the same age. That hardly makes me little." She shoved against his hand.

"Ah, so you like it rough. Is that what you're trying to say?" Logan asked. Both of his hands went to her shoulders, and she let out a gasp as he pushed her hard against the locker, making her wince.

"Logan, man, we've got to go. Principal is heading this way," Marvin said.

"Then I guess, we better go." Logan made no move to release her.

She glared at him, refusing to break eye contact even as her heart raced. Out of all of the guys, Luke terrified her, whereas Logan confused her. She had noticed Logan stared at her. It was like he was trying to figure her out, or whatever the reason he had for staring at her.

He was bigger than she was in every single way. Before he left, he pushed himself against her, making her very much aware of who was stronger between the two of them. There was nowhere else for her to go. She was at his complete mercy.

"Until next time." He gave her a final shove before walking away.

Without waiting around to be questioned by the principal, she quickly darted across the hall and turned the corner, heading toward her next class. There was no way she could tell on Logan or the others. They were the stars of the school, and if she did, it would make her public enemy number one. All she hoped to do was get through high school and leave town. It was all she really wanted.

****

Present day

"I can't believe this," Ava said.

The movie was on pause, and she saw how naked she was. Hunter and Logan were able to see. There was no way for them to stop looking. There she stood, in all of her naked glory.

This can't be happening.

Only, it was.

Logan would release the footage of her parents. She'd had no idea they were into orgies or any of what she'd caught a glimpse of. With regards to Grant, she'd met him in a bar a few years ago and they got close. He'd asked her out on a date, and she'd taken it. They'd dated for a couple of months before they actually had sex. When he'd taken her to a motel room, she hadn't thought much about it, seeing as he said he moved around. She'd used Grant in an effort to move on, to find a way out of the pain that was her everyday life.

All this time, he'd been working for Logan, and only doing as he'd been told. There hadn't been any feelings for her.

"I hate you." The words spilled from her lips with ease. She did hate him, just not as much as she hated *him*.

Glaring at Logan, she wanted nothing to do with him. There was no way she could make this choice. Not fair in any way. Her parents didn't deserve to have their memory crushed because he wanted revenge. What was the deal with him calling sexual assault? That wasn't her, and now she was more confused than ever before.

It doesn't matter.

Logan chuckled. "I'm not going to need you to like me in order to fuck me." He stepped toward her, and she took one back. With each one he took, she kept on moving away until his desk was in the way, and she was trapped. He put his hands flat on top of his desk. She felt the hard ridge of his cock pressing against her stomach. This wasn't the first time she'd been in this predicament, not with Logan. There were a few times, so many years ago, almost a lifetime ago, when it was different. When he'd trapped her in a school classroom and wouldn't let her go, not until he had one taste.

She pushed those memories aside and instead focused on trying to get out of this.

27

"I'm not going to sleep with you."

"You want everyone to know what you get up to in your spare time? How you look when you come? You want the entire town, if not the world, to see."

"You can't do that," she said.

"Oh, believe me, I can. I wonder what people will think when they see miss squeaky clean all dirty and more than happy to have a cock inside her pussy. It won't be as easy to convince people of your innocence."

"What do you want?" she asked.

"For you to beg."

"Let me go. Be the bigger man and forget all about this."

He laughed. "Do you really think I came back to this piece of shit town for the views? No. I came all this way for you. To right a wrong *you* committed. Everything that happens from here on out is all because of you. Now, either submit to me, or pay the price. Either way, you're not getting out of this squeaky clean."

She glanced over his shoulder, staring at the television. It taunted her.

"I thought he cared."

"Oh, he did. For the big paycheck heading his way when I got what I wanted. He's got no problem starring in your little porn show." Logan lifted his hand close to her face, and she couldn't help but flinch as he touched her.

He tutted. "Don't worry, sweetheart, I have no intention of hurting you. At least, not where anyone else can see. You won't get any black eyes from me. I'll make sure of it. Your time is running out. I will pick for you if you take too long."

She hated this.

Why had it come down to this?

Why didn't you leave town when you had the

chance?

So many questions whirling around her head, but none of them could be given an answer. Not until she dealt with this little problem. She hated feeling like this. Trapped. Unable to move. But it wouldn't have mattered if she left town. Logan was clearly determined to find her.

The evidence of Logan's excitement pressed against her, and what was more, she wasn't offended by it. What the hell was wrong with her?

"Five!"

"Wait, what? No, you can't count down."

"Four!"

"Stop it." This couldn't be happening. Her time was being taken from her. There was no way for her to think past the panic. It was all happening too fast.

"Three!"

"Logan, please, stop this. I get you're angry with me. I know you are." The entire town was, but this wasn't the way forward. It couldn't be. There's no way she could accept this as being all she had to—

"Two!"

"No, please, give me more time. You have to understand you're wrong about a lot of things. So very wrong. Please, Logan. You have to see reason."

"I like hearing you say please. Believe me, you're going to be begging for a lot more by the time I'm through with you." The fingers that had touched her so gently traveled to her neck, and he wrapped his hand around her throat, giving it a gentle squeeze. He didn't cut the air off, but the threat was there. He was the one with all the power, while she was powerless to do anything.

"One!"

There was no time. She couldn't let him make

such a life-changing decision.

"Yes!" She cried out the word. The moment she did, she wanted the world to open her up and swallow her whole.

This couldn't be happening.

But with each passing second, there was no denying exactly what was going on. Logan was going to use her. One of the men from her past had used her for Logan. Nothing she had with Grant was real. She'd wondered what had happened to him. He traveled a lot with his work. At least that was what he said to her. After she slept with him, they continued dating for a couple of months before he broke it off, and it was the end of their relationship. The end of everything.

"Yes?" Logan asked. He gave another squeeze to her neck before finally pulling away and letting her breathe.

"Yes, I will do whatever it is you need me to do. Just don't release them. Please, destroy them."

"There is that tiny word again. It means so little to a lot of people. Please. You never said it to me before," he said. "I rather enjoy hearing you say it now." He took a step away from her and glanced up and down her body.

She wore jeans and a shirt, but from the way Logan looked at her, she could be naked. Stripped bare for his pleasure.

"Strip!"

"What?"

"If you think I'm going to allow you to head home, knowing you had plans to skip town, you've got another think coming. You're here. You're mine, and I'm not letting you go. Now fucking strip."

"Logan, please."

"That word again. It was nice, but now, until I

want to hear it, it's gone."

"Gone?"

"You're not allowed to say it or you will be punished."

"I don't know what sick kind of revenge you want—"

His hand was once again around her throat. "Let's get something straight here, sweetheart. You're not the one in charge here. I am. I say what goes, and what I say goes right now, is you stripping off your clothes and doing as you're told."

She looked toward Hunter. The other man stood by the door, looking as if this was a regular nighttime activity for him. It wasn't something she was used to on a Monday night.

"Don't look to him for help. In fact, don't look to anyone for help. The sheriff won't come for you. No one in this town will, and the first person who does, I'll kill them."

"Is that what you are now, a killer?"

"I'm a lot of things. I've had to be in order to survive. Maybe one day you'll see some of my new sides. Now, enough small talk. Strip."

He stepped away from her.

She covered the space around her neck. He'd held onto her just a little too tightly. It had been on the verge of pain, but now, she was free. Would his marks still be with her come morning, or disappear?

Pushing those thoughts from the back of her mind, she kicked off her shoes. She hadn't exactly paid attention to the best kind of running shoes. These were slip-on ones, and at the first sign of trouble, they wouldn't last. Not to run in. Next, she didn't know what to do. Her jeans or her shirt? Either one would expose her underwear to his gaze.

"Hurry up. I'm not wanting to wait around forever for you to make a necessary decision." He tapped his watch.

It didn't matter which one she removed. They were both coming off anyway. She went for her jeans first, unsnapping the button and trying to ignore both men standing in the room, watching her. Were they watching her?

She didn't make a habit of getting naked for anyone, and yet here she was, doing exactly that for two men. Her previous lovers, she'd been with some time and always expected her time with them to last a lifetime. Relationships had always been important to her. She had hoped to get over what happened to her, but the men in her life hadn't lasted. Nothing had worked.

Again, they were thoughts she really didn't need nor want. This was all on her.

Tucking hair behind her ear, she played with the hem of her shirt.

"Time's wasting away here."

She pulled the shirt over her head, throwing it to the floor.

Hoping he wouldn't make her go completely naked, she stood before him. She wore underwear that had seen better days. She wasn't made of money, so she only replaced her underwear when it was really necessary. It hadn't been so at the last mall shopping trip.

"Nice try. All of it."

"Why have you turned into this person?" she asked.

"Being falsely accused of something and having your reputation tarnished will do that to you, oh, and going to prison."

"How? What did you get slapped with that has you taking this out on me?"

"Shut the fuck up and do as you're told. Your innocent act is not going to wash with me."

"I don't know what it is you think I've done, but you're wrong."

His hand was around her throat. "Enough talking." He spun her around, and she had no choice but to put her hands on the desk or be smashed against it. Logan grabbed her panties, and without waiting, tore them from her body. The sound of the tear echoed around the room, shocking her to the core.

This was all a little too much.

She didn't know what to do.

Heart pounding, she felt his hand run across her ass cheeks.

"Such a nice, plump ass."

She cried out as he squeezed one of the cheeks before giving it a slap.

"What do you think, Hunter? Perfect to be hit. To be spanked."

"It has got a nice curve to it. Spread her cheeks. I wonder if she's ever had anything but a stick up her ass."

She tried to push him away, but he trapped her against the desk. The hard edge of the wood dug into her body as he pressed her against it. He gripped the curves of her ass, spreading them.

"Stop it!" It was on the tip of her tongue to beg him to stop. To plead with him, but she pressed her lips together.

"Look at this." His finger stroked between the lips of her pussy.

"Is she nice and wet?"

He cupped her with his entire hand, one finger sliding between her slit, going from her clit, down to her entrance. He pushed a single digit inside, then a second one.

"Soaking."

"She tight?"

"Yes. So very fucking tight. How long has it been since you let a cock inside here?"

"Leave me alone."

"Aw, she thinks she can scream and curse." His hands stopped touching her.

She screamed as he slapped her ass, three times, giving a final fourth. The pain was instant, harsh, and humiliating.

Hunter saw it all. She'd heard his questions. He was in on this with Logan. There was not going to be any saving from him. They were both working together, and she was the object.

Nothing more.

Logan lifted her up, spun her around.

"You can play the victim all you want to here, but I see the evidence. So does my friend here." Logan ran his fingers across her lip. "Taste yourself."

She wanted to deny him, to be defiant.

He grabbed her hair, making her gasp, causing her to open her mouth, and she had no choice. He slid his fingers inside, and she tasted herself.

"For a woman who claims to be afraid, you're wet, Ava. We're going to have a lot of fun with this. You know that, right?"

He let her go, and she had no choice but to use the desk to help keep her on her feet. Her legs were like jelly.

"The rest of it."

She reached behind her, flicking the catch of her bra open, and letting it fall to the ground. She wanted to cover herself, but there was no use in doing that.

"Nice tits," Hunter said.

"Leave us," Logan said, and she looked up.

Hunter didn't question him. Simply opened the door and left, closing it behind him.

"You're the one in charge?" she asked. "You can command anyone to do whatever you want? They don't care what it is you're doing?"

"You're asking a lot of questions, and I've got no interest in answering them. Spread your legs."

She opened her mouth, about to ask him another question. He let out a tut, and put a finger against his lips.

"If I was you, I'd be careful what you asked me. I'm growing rather impatient, and you're boring me. Spread your fucking legs or get on your knees. I'm sure your throat can take my cock, and swallow a nice big mouthful of cum."

She opened her legs. There was no way she'd be able to handle being on her knees.

"That's a good girl." He stepped up toward her and touched her thigh. She let out a little gasp.

Logan stared into her eyes. His were so dark. They were brown but almost black. In the past, whenever she had looked at him, he'd been watching her. She didn't know why he was, only that he'd always been one step ahead of her. She couldn't stop him from doing anything. He'd been in charge, and she merely at his mercy.

"What are you going to do?" she asked.

"What I should have done all those years ago. I mean, after all, I did back away before it went too far, but you still went screaming."

"Logan?" He continued to accuse her of something she hadn't done.

"Shut up!" The tips of his fingers traced up her body. He moved past her pussy, going up to her tits. He caressed over them, over each tight nipple, then back down again. Each time, she expected him to go for her pussy, but he didn't. He was the master of control.

Always one step ahead of her.

"Do you know it is harder for a man to see when a woman is aroused?" he asked.

She didn't respond.

"For a guy, everyone knows. A nice, hard dick. It's hard to hide." He chuckled. "Get it, hard to hide."

"I get it."

"But a woman. Unless you touch her pussy, for the inexperienced, it's not that easy, but for me, you see, I know women. I've studied them. This little flush on their skin. So easy to believe it's the result of a blush and not the evidence of a very aroused woman." He went to her nipples. "The air isn't cold. It's nice and warm in here. I made sure of it, and these hard nipples, another sign. Again, a woman can claim to be cold. I know you're not cold. I feel how warm you are."

"You have me naked, Logan."

"Do not try to pretend you're cold. I know you're aroused by me." His hand cupped her pussy, and he plunged two fingers inside her. "The evidence is right here. Soaking wet, tight, and ready for a nice, hard cock. You want to keep on fighting and claiming you're a sweet, little innocent woman, go ahead. I know you're getting off on what is happening here. You have no control over what happens here, whereas I have all of it. Every single scrap."

In and out he pushed his fingers inside her, working her pussy.

She closed her eyes, and he pinched her clit, making her open them.

"I didn't give you permission to close them. You keep those beauties on me at all times, understood?"

"Logan?"

"Do I make myself clear?" he asked.

"Yes."

He was the one in charge.

Staring into his brown eyes, she waited, expecting him to hurt her, but all he did was play with her pussy, preparing her, getting her nice and wet. He drew her to the peak, to the edge of arousal, making her stay at the precipice, not letting her push over, keeping her precariously there, waiting, expecting, and when she thought he was going to let her come, he took a step back.

She watched as he licked his fingers, the evidence of her arousal glistening on his hand.

"Go to bed. Hunter will show you the way."

"But?"

"You think you deserve an orgasm? Nah, you're not going to get one that easy. You're going to earn it. Now, get the fuck upstairs, and don't even think of getting your clothes. You're not wearing them. Consider it another privilege you need to earn."

He took a step away from her, and she watched him go to his liquor.

"Logan, can't we talk?"

"No. No more talking. You seem to think you're the one with the power here. You're here to do as I wish, unless you want this to go viral by the end of the day."

She left the office and looked at Hunter, who smirked. She didn't want to cover herself, but it took every single ounce of strength not to. She would make Logan pay. He would see how wrong he'd gotten this, and when he did, he'd be fucking sorry. Very sorry.

****

The following morning, Logan stood outside on his back porch, staring at the perfect garden once again. Only this time, it was light and he got to see just how perfect everything was. He hated it, but he wouldn't have anyone do anything to it. Not yet, not ever, probably.

He wanted it to overgrow, to be surrounded by mess.

His parents had once demanded perfection, and he'd been a huge disappointment to them, or at least he thought he had until they had squandered their fortune trying to help him. They'd wanted to prove his innocence, but all the judge had wanted to do was to lock his ass up. He'd been painted as an entitled little rich boy who was used to getting what he wanted. When his parents died, they'd done so, broke. The Stanford Legacy had been shattered. They'd died while he'd been in prison. They hadn't seen the man he'd turned into, but then, he imagined they would be disappointed after all. He wasn't a model citizen, not anymore.

Stepping out onto the lawn, he looked up at the French windows that were open. He saw her. She was wide awake, using the curtain around her to try to hide her nakedness.

Taking a long draw on his cigarette, he blew out the smoke.

She saw him. Her hazel eyes were right on him.

There had been so many times throughout his life he'd thought of those eyes. He'd watched her all the fucking time, to no avail.

She stepped back into her room, closing the doors, but he wasn't ready to end their little staring contest.

Throwing his cigarette to the ground, he stamped it out, heading inside. On his way to the stairs, Hunter crossed his path.

"What's on the agenda for the day?"

"Nothing. Have your fill of entertainment on the town."

Hunter grabbed his arm. "I know all about

vengeance, my friend. Maybe you should come with me. I saw a lot of women more than willing to grace your bed."

"I don't want any of them."

"This woman, Ava, she's more than the reason for your imprisonment, isn't she?" Hunter asked.

This man before him was the closest he'd call a friend in recent years.

"You don't need to know a single detail about her."

"Don't let her consume you."

"Did I ask for your opinion?" Logan asked.

"No. You didn't. Force of habit. I will give you one final piece of advice though."

"What?" He was growing tired of this conversation and had far more important details to work through than what his friend wanted.

"Find out what it is you want to do with her, and make a decision before you do something reckless. Ava clearly still has power over you."

He grabbed Hunter's jacket, drawing him close. "She is nothing."

"She's something to have you reacting this way. Just think about it. It's important for you to know how you feel in the scheme of things. It's you I care about, no one else."

Logan let Hunter go and turned back to the stairs.

Walking up them, he stopped at Ava's door. He'd had this room specially decorated for her.

He spared no expense. There was no way for her to get out. He had the key, which was currently in the lock right now.

Opening the door, he found her, with the curtains wrapped around her, sitting on the edge of the bed.

He closed the door, key in hand, and locked the

door.

"I'm a prisoner now."

"Yes, but don't worry. I'm not going to lock you in the basement or behind bars. I'd say your room is rather comfortable. You have a nice, comfy bed. A bathroom."

"And I'm guessing there are cameras, right?"

There weren't, but she didn't need to know that. He wasn't an idiot. Of course he'd have loved to have the ability to watch her when he wasn't there, but to do that, he would risk others watching the two of them together, and that he couldn't have. The only room in this house with cameras was his office.

"What do you want, Logan?" she asked. "I don't know what I ever did for you to hate me this much?"

"You don't? Still playing up the innocent act, I see." He removed his jacket, putting it on the chair beside the door.

Next, he started on the buttons of his shirt.

"What are you doing?"

He kicked off his shoes and removed his pants. He was careful to push past the hardness of his dick. He was so fucking hard for her, it was unreal.

"Logan?"

She stood up as he did, to his full height.

Compared to him, she'd always been a small little thing. During their high school, girls had thrown themselves at him, but he hadn't been interested in any of them. Sure, he fucked a few of them. Why not? He was one of the most popular guys in school and could have his pick of the best of them.

Ava never threw herself at him. She did everything to avoid them.

"Did you touch yourself?" he asked.

She opened her mouth, closed it, and looked

away.

He laughed. "I figured you would. You were all nice and wet, fucking my hand. Desperate for it."

"Please stop."

"It's what you wanted, wasn't it? To come?"

"Why are you doing this?" she asked.

"Because it's so fucking easy. You're this little goody two shoes who thinks she's better than everyone else."

"I don't."

"You don't?"

"You don't know me."

"Oh, but I do. You're nothing but a coward that runs at the first signs of danger." He took a step toward her, and once again they were playing this cat-and-mouse game. One step forward, one step back.

There was nowhere else for her to go.

The wall, this time, stopped her.

He slammed his hands on either side of her head.

"You couldn't handle what I did to you, and rather than tell me, you ran to the Sheriff. Do you know what it's like to be arrested? To have your rights shouted at you? Or better yet, to be tarnished as a sexual predator? Or how about being locked up? To be surrounded by fucking filth and disgust? Having your rights taken from you all because of lies?"

She shook her head. "I didn't report you for that."

"I read the file. The Sheriff was more than happy to oblige when I told him what had happened. That day, in the classroom, you were more than ready for me."

"Logan, please, it's not what I—"

"Shut the fuck up. I don't want to hear your excuses." He stared into her eyes once again. "I then had to hear it at my trial. Every word you'd said about me." He wouldn't allow her gaze to affect him.

So many times he'd been enraptured by them, dreamed about them. Of course, there were times when he didn't want to hurt her, but after what she did, he felt nothing *but* the need to hurt her. To make her pay.

"Seeing as you took care of yourself without me, it seems only fair, you now get to take care of me."

"Logan?"

He put his hands on her shoulders and pushed her to the floor.

She didn't put up a fight.

"Grant told me about how he taught you the best way to suck a cock. You wanted to please him, to make him come back for more. Now I want you to show me just how good you are at sucking, and then, maybe we can talk about something else."

"Pl—Logan," she said.

Wrapping her hair around his fingers, he gripped the back of her neck.

"Open your mouth. You don't really believe Grant was telling you how to suck a cock for him, do you?" He laughed. He'd hated listening to every single second of her time with Grant, watching it even, but he'd done it to learn her. To watch her.

Grant was the guy he sent to women. He had this power over them. He made them think he was a good guy, a nice guy.

The man was a monster. Loved fucking women. Loved hurting them as well.

Logan had made sure Ava wouldn't be hurt, just primed and ready, and of course, the movie he had of the two of them also helped his cause.

She touched his cock, flicking the head with her tongue.

"Yeah, baby, that's right. Get it nice and ready. You taste my pre-cum, don't you? I'm going to fill your mouth with every single drop."

She licked the head, moving her tongue down the long vein at the side before gliding back up and taking him in her mouth.

He grabbed her head, jerking her back so she had no choice but to look at him.

"If you think to hurt me, use your teeth, I will make you pay. I will punish you. You think stripping in front of Hunter is bad, I've got a whole team of men who will do anything for me, and your body is just a vessel for pleasure, understand?"

She nodded her head. "I won't hurt you."

"You'd better not."

He still held onto her hair, and she took his cock back into her mouth. She didn't use her teeth, but he didn't imagine she would.

Ava would never know what he'd be willing to do or how far he was willing to go. He'd learned long ago to not tell his secrets, to keep his own weaknesses to himself.

She took the head of his cock into her mouth, bobbing up and down, not taking too much. He wouldn't be able to choke her on his length.

She covered the length of him in saliva, and he liked watching her like this, on her knees, at his mercy, having to do whatever he told her to.

This was what he'd wanted.

She let out a little moan, and it traveled the length of his cock. Did she know she was enjoying it?

Watching her, he felt his balls tingle, but he wasn't some teenage boy getting his first blowjob. He was an expert, and he wanted this to last. He'd imagined it enough times, even as a young man, having her at his mercy like this.

This was by far better than anything he could

have imagined.

As he pumped his hips, her eyes opened and she stared up at him. He didn't stop even as her hand squeezed the length of him that wasn't in her mouth.

He hit the back of her throat, and he held himself there, letting her get used to him.

Her nostrils flared.

"Take it all," he said.

She didn't nod or give him a signal.

Ava moved a tiny fraction on his length, and he watched as she gagged on him, but didn't stop. She moved a little more, and he pushed past her throat. There was a panic in her eyes, and he pulled back.

Again, her nostrils flared, but she didn't try to push him away. Not that it would do her any good. He was the one with the power, not her. He got to say what she did or didn't do.

Letting go of her hair, he stroked his fingers through the length before fisting it once again. This time, as he fucked her throat, he didn't let up. He gave her everything, and he didn't give her a chance to question him.

"When I come, I want to see it in your mouth. Don't swallow until I tell you to. You're going to show it to me." In and out, he thrust, feeling the stirring within his balls. The moment he was close, he pressed his cock to her lips and filled her mouth, making her take it all. Only when she'd milked every ounce did he pull away, and as he did, she closed her mouth. "Let me see."

She glared at him but tilted her head back, showing him the creamy jizz he'd thrust into her mouth.

"Good, now swallow."

He was curious what she would do, if she would spit it back at him or take it like a good little girl.

She swallowed him down. He watched her throat

work. It took her two swallows to finish.

"Show me."

She opened her mouth, and he smiled. Was that so hard?

Chapter Three

Fourteen years ago

Sitting at the back of the library on the floor, Ava flicked through the history book, not finding the answers on the last world war she needed to finish off her essay. History wasn't her strong suit, and she had to work twice as hard in order to get a decent grade.

History didn't give her a thrill. It was boring, tedious, and she just didn't enjoy it.

Once she'd flicked through the small pile of books she had at her side, she got to her feet, reading the labels to put them in the correct order.

"Well, well, well, look what we have here."

She froze, turning to see Luke a few feet away from her. Without talking to him, she went back to looking on the shelves, seeing where the book would go. The last one was on the bottom of the shelf. She leaned down, sliding it into place, and gasped as Luke grabbed her by the hips, and there was no denying what he had pressed against her ass.

She tried to wriggle away, but it only served to press her up against the shelves.

Opening her mouth, she tried to scream, to do anything that would make him leave her alone, to make him move, but he didn't budge. His hand covered her mouth, muffling any sound from coming out.

"Let me go!" She tried to tell him, but again, his hand stopped her. She was completely powerless beneath him.

His lips brushed across her ear.

"I can't hear you. But I have to say, I see what all the fuss is about. I mean, I just figured this was a fat ass, but there is a lot of cushion with it." He gripped her ass tightly. She would have bruises where he touched her.

Tears filled her eyes, and she was terrified.

"What do you say I take this fat ass out and show you what you're supposed to do with it?"

He bit down on her neck, and she let out a squeal.

"You don't want to play with her," Logan said, interrupting the moment.

Luke sighed. "Until next time." He whispered the words so she didn't know if Logan heard them or not. Logan didn't give any indication that he had, which she hated. "You have your fun with her, buddy. She's on the large size. I need a girl who'll feel my dick."

She was shaken, but she couldn't let weakness show.

This was the first time Luke had ever cornered her. His touch revolted her, and she couldn't bring herself to look at Logan.

He and Luke were best friends, and that had to say a lot about the man himself.

Hands shaking, she went to walk away, but Logan captured her arm, pulling her back.

"If you want a piece of advice, don't be left alone with him."

He held her close, one of his hands moving to her stomach, and she became very aware of how close they stood together.

"I have no intention of it."

"He doesn't want you."

She tried to wriggle away. There was no chance of it. Logan was the strong one. It was the only time in her life she felt small, gentle even.

He had her tightly though, so she was only getting away when he saw to it.

"I don't want him."

"Every girl wants him."

"I don't."

"Then that's your mistake." He let her go, and without looking at him, she rushed to the back of the library, grabbing her bag and notebooks, leaving it without trying to find him.

****

Present day

Staring at her reflection in the mirror, Ava couldn't believe she'd sucked Logan's cock. Her face looked normal, apart from the red blotches on her cheeks. Her body didn't show any marks at all, not even bruises from his firm grip.

Pushing her hair out of the way, she stared at the locks, wondering if she could cut it off to stop him from touching her hair. She didn't want him to use her in any way to further his own pleasure.

"It's going to be okay," she said, releasing a breath.

After he'd come, he'd let himself out of her room, locking the door behind him. She was a prisoner.

No clothes.

No food.

She'd just been used for sex, for his personal pleasure, and it humiliated her to know he knew she'd taken care of herself. Having his hands on her, it had ignited a fire within her she didn't know she had.

Staring down at the sick, she scooped up some of the cold water and splashed it on her face.

"I'm fine." She spoke between each face wash.

She wasn't talking to anyone. Just herself.

When her face was thoroughly washed, she stepped back. She'd already taken a bath, but there was no bath towel and she had no way of drying herself.

The room was warm.

Leaving the bathroom, she paused as she saw Hunter in her room. He sat on the edge of her bed, smiling.

"He wants you downstairs," he said.

"For what?"

"For breakfast."

"Why didn't he come and get me himself?" she asked.

"I like how you think you can ask any question you want."

"Are you his friend?"

"One of them."

This made her pause. "He has other friends?"

"Of course he does. He's Logan Stanford. He has a great many friends. Just not all of them are nice."

She gritted her teeth. This was impossible. "Do I get any clothes?"

"No. Until Logan wishes it, you're here, naked, doing as you're bid. Be grateful he doesn't have you walking around town saying 'I'm Logan's cum dump.'"

She refused to let him see how his words were affecting her. There was no way she could fall. Squaring her shoulders as best she could, she followed Hunter downstairs.

Men were posted at the door. She couldn't bring herself to look them in the eyes. They all saw her.

Logan certainly knew how to hurt her. There was no coming back from this.

They walked down a long corridor, going toward a door that opened up into a dining room. Logan was already there, eating breakfast, reading the newspaper.

Hunter grabbed her arm, marching her toward where Logan was and pushing her into a seat.

She noticed a towel had already been placed on the seat for her.

Small mercies at least.

There was no food for her to eat. No place

setting.

"I've got to go to work today," she said, thinking about the library.

"I've already called ahead. I've told them you'll be having a few weeks off."

"You can't do that."

"I did." He took a bite of his waffle.

"I like working."

"You'll go back to work when I'm ready." He held out a piece of waffle for her to eat. "I suggest you eat it. You're not getting anything else. Everything you eat or wear will be earned. I figured with all that cum warming your belly, you needed something a bit more substantial."

She hated him.

There had been moments over the years she'd not liked him, but hate was an emotion she wasn't familiar with. She didn't like to feel anything too strongly, but it was next to impossible not to feel something.

"I hate you," she said.

"Still sucked my cock dry this morning. Hate is a very good motivator. I guess you know all about that. Trying to ruin my life for a long time now." He pressed the fork to her lips. "Come on, eat up."

She could spit the food at him, and refuse to cooperate, or she could live to fight another day. Keep her strength up rather than starve herself. Opening her lips, she took the waffle he offered, chewing on it.

Hunter giggled. She ignored him.

For the next ten minutes, Logan continued to feed her, offering her up tiny bites, which she took, in between feeding himself.

When breakfast was done, he allowed her a cup of coffee, which she took with a thank you. Again, it would be easy for her to cause a fight, but she decided against it. She would only pick battles she knew she could win.

"I've never seen you this … docile before," Logan said. "Rather intriguing."

"You want to school together, right?" Hunter asked.

"I did. There was a time Ava Marshall was one of the most intelligent women at school. She was smart. Everyone went to her to be tutored. It was the only way they were getting out of the shithole of a town. Being with her, got the grades people wanted."

"What changed?" Hunter asked.

"I don't know what changed. Why are you here, still working at the library?" Logan asked.

She turned her head to look at him. "You know why."

"What makes you think I know?"

"You came to town with all this wealth. You did your research."

"That's right. After little Miss Righteous here falsely accused me of sexual assault—"

"I didn't—"

"No one in town wanted anything to do with her. She had to be homeschooled. She still got the grades to go to colleges, but Luke's parents, they paid people to make sure no one would ever accept her into a good college. Money speaks, and me being Luke's friend, they wanted to help. She's all alone. No one will touch her. Isn't that right?"

She closed her eyes, gritting her teeth. "You've got it all wrong."

"I have, have I? You see, I don't think I do. I've got it just right." Logan folded up his newspaper. "You're nothing. The people in this town don't care about what happens to you. It didn't even take much from me to get the good sheriff to turn his back. No one here will step in my way. You're mine, Ava. To do with as I see fit and the way I see it, I'm going to make sure you pay for the lies you told." He swiped his hand in the air. "Take her back to her room. I don't want to look at her anymore."

She didn't fight Hunter as he lifted her up.

Glancing back at Logan, she saw him still looking at her. No, not looking, glaring. There was real hatred in his gaze. He hated her.

That was okay. She wanted him to hate her. It would make fighting him every single step of the way easier.

Hunter opened the door, and she stepped inside. For a prison cell, it wasn't too bad.

"If you take advice…"

"You seem to be offering a lot of it. I thought you were his friend."

"Oh, I am his friend. I know Logan better than he knows himself. There's something going on that I'm not sure of. Why don't you tell me?" Hunter said.

"I didn't accuse him of sexual assault."

"What *did* you accuse him of exactly?"

She stared down at her hands. "That's the thing, I didn't accuse Logan of anything."

Hunter laughed. "You expect me to believe that?"

"It's the truth."

"I've seen the words on the papers, sweetheart. You're not innocent. You accuse Logan of everything. Raping you. The entire scene the way it played out, is in full black and white. I've seen what you've said, and believe me, he has a right to be pissed."

"What are you talking about?" She truly had no idea what was going on.

"You're a good actress, I'll give you that. Did

you always want Logan to notice you, is that it? Do you like playing hard to get?"

"What are you talking about?"

"This conversation bores me. I actually thought you'd tell me the truth. After all, what do you have to lose? Nothing." He slammed the door closed, and she rushed toward it.

"Let me out! I'm not lying. Get me out of here. You fucking bastards! Let me out." She slammed her hands against the door, hurting herself in the process, but she didn't care. She had to make them listen to her. She had to leave.

No one came.

She tried the handle on the door.

It wouldn't budge.

She was once again trapped and alone. Sliding down the door, she didn't know what was going on. She had gone to the police but not to tell on Logan. He'd been brought up, only because he was a friend of the man *she* had gone to report. A man she hoped to never see again.

This wasn't the first time she'd heard people accuse her of reporting Logan, nor the sexual assault allegations, but she'd never justified her actions, never needed to because she had thought *he* had been dealt with. What the hell had Logan done? Whoever reported him, it wasn't her. She had proof with her witness statements. Only now she was starting to wonder what the sheriff had done, and why Logan had been taken away in the process. She'd never been told what had happened to Logan, only that he'd been arrested. The sheriff had advised her parents to send her out of town, and she'd gone to stay at a small resort until after the trial. The sheriff had said he'd take care of anything so she didn't have to deal with the trauma.

Whatever had happened, she'd been caught in the crossfire, and now there was no way out for her. No way whatsoever.

****

The town was the same, even after twelve years.

Logan stopped off at the coffee shop, ordered himself a bagel and a coffee, which tasted a little on the burnt side no matter how much cream they'd tried to add in to hide it. He was aware of the curious looks and glances his way.

He was a catch, always had been.

Hunter had taken over the rumors and gossip.

Once he'd been seen, he made his way toward Ava's house, letting himself inside with the key Hunter had stolen for him.

He had the few possessions she'd packed into the suitcase, money, and her passport.

She could have been so much more. There was a time she had dreams of being out of Crow Valley, of having a life writing or in journalism. She'd told him all about it one day when they'd been locked inside the school gym.

It was a prank one Halloween, and they'd stayed there the whole night, talking. It was the first time he'd stayed with her for a long period of time, listening to her talk, and taking the time to do the same. She listened to him as well.

He told a few jokes, to which she'd laughed. It had been fun. He would never have guessed what was to come afterward, or at least a few months after.

Stepping into her home, he was a little taken aback. He never got to see it when he was younger. She didn't invite him in, and it wasn't like he was a regular visitor at Ava's.

Closing the door behind him, he pocketed the

keys, and breathed it in.

It smelled like her.

Fresh.

Open.

Warm.

He refused to think of her as warm. She was a first-class bitch. The only difference was, she chose to hide it whereas other women were more than happy to show their true colors.

He checked out the dining room, seeing the pictures on the wall of Ava and her family. She never had any brothers or sisters to keep an eye on her. She was an only child, like him.

Running his fingers across the dining room table, he saw some old cup stains, letting him know the table hadn't been changed.

Ava wouldn't have changed a thing. This was probably a shrine to her parents. Every last cup and step. She wouldn't have made changes, and it was knowing this that he had to wonder why she would do the shit she had done to him, to his friends.

Running a hand down his face to clear the fog from his mind, he looked at each image. They weren't fake.

Ava had come from a very happy family.

Logan had watched them enough times. Her mother would pick her up from school when she could, take them out for pizza. Her parents always showed up for parent-teacher nights, and never missed anything important for their daughter.

His own family hadn't been the same. They couldn't give a shit unless it was to win some kind of trophy for them to put on the wall, or some medal. They only liked what he could provide them with, or at least that was what he'd thought until he was arrested. His parents did care. It was just when it came to his schooling, they'd gotten reports on him as their lives were too busy to wait around to talk to his teachers. In their way, they cared.

If they saw him now, they'd be happy, but like her family, his were dead as well. He'd stood by their graves without shedding a single tear whereas Ava had sobbed. He knew because he had people watching her at all times.

She'd been his intended prey for a long time now.

Tapping his fingers on his side, he stared around him, getting a sense of the loneliness she'd felt.

Good.

He'd wanted her to be alone. Whenever a guy tried to get too close, he made sure his men diverted him. He always planned to come back to make her pay, and well now, he didn't have to go far to find her.

She'd stayed in Crow Valley. It was the only real disappointment he'd felt. She hadn't made chasing her too hard.

After checking out her kitchen, living room, and the small room that looked like a laundry room, he headed upstairs. Sure enough, the main room was a shrine to her parents. The bed was still made. Pictures left untouched.

If anything, it looked like she cleaned and dusted the room but tried to keep everything in place. Opening the closet, he saw the clothes were still there, neatly pressed.

The girl had some serious fucking moving on issues.

He wouldn't let her dwell in the past too long.

Closing the door behind him, he went to her room. There he saw the twin bed against the wall, a small vanity table, and the closet door, which was open.

Nothing of any real value.

Again, more pictures but this room he didn't have a problem with doing a bit of digging.

Going to her vanity table, he opened up drawers, looking for something, anything. She rarely wore makeup, but she had a couple of lipsticks, some mascara, and a few other items.

The vanity table housed her underwear, which had seen better days. Clearly the library didn't pay all that well, or she had guilt over buying herself some pretty things. No problem. When he was ready to have her dressed, she'd be in the best clothes money could buy.

He went to the closet, clicking on the light and looking inside. In her rush to get away from him, she'd knocked over a couple of boxes.

Lifting one out, he tipped the contents over her bed, seeing lots of pictures spilling out of some of the shoeboxes and books.

He glanced through them. They were random photos. Some were of scenery, the beach, her parents. A couple were of school, and he paused when he caught sight of a couple of himself. Then of the group he'd been in.

Luke, Riley, and Marvin. They'd been inseparable growing up. Each of them had been strong in their own unique way. He did notice one thing odd about all the pictures, Luke's face had been cut out or scribbled out, which he found interesting. He didn't know when these were taken, but either way, he was going to find out.

Gathering them all back into the box, he went to lift them when his cell phone rang.

Hunter was calling him.

"What is it, you couldn't wait until I returned

home?" he asked. He'd wanted to take his time, explore the town, to see if anything had really changed.

Nothing had. It was still the same as ever before.

He hated it on sight.

When he was done destroying Ava, exacting his vengeance, he'd move on, and leave this town to rot. There was no one here who offered him anything.

"They're here. They've arrived and want to know when the fun starts."

"They're early."

"It's Luke, you know how he gets."

Logan looked down at the picture. Something didn't feel right to him, and he couldn't figure out exactly what it was.

"Make sure they leave Ava alone. When she meets them again after all this time, I'm going to be the one in charge."

"Will do. Do you want a guard on her door?"

"No. It would only draw attention to where I've got her. She's nowhere near their rooms. Keep an eye out but don't say anything."

"Is there something else going on here?" Hunter asked.

"No. It's fine. I'll be home soon." He ended the call and stared at the picture he'd placed on top.

Why would she cut out all trace of Luke? It made no sense to him.

Putting the photo back, he closed up the box and carried it out to the waiting car. Putting it in the trunk, he ignored the women staring at him, climbing behind the wheel. He took off, heading back to the house. It was on the outskirts of town, large, and surrounded by acres of forest. Beyond the forest were metal gates, and it provided enough seclusion that if Ava got away, she wouldn't get far. If his men didn't find her, his dogs would.

The metal gate opened up, and he drove down the long driveway, seeing one car parked at an angle in front of the doors.

Luke, as always, was unpredictable. He liked to think of himself as the leader of the group, but to Logan, he was just another tragic case of too much money and no attention. Unlike himself, who didn't rebel due to a lack of caring, Luke liked to be the center of the party. He wanted all eyes on him, and of course, Logan was more than happy for people to think Luke was the king, when in fact, he wasn't.

Entering his home, he heard the noise coming from the office. Hunter was at the stairwell, typing on his cell phone.

"How long have they been into my good whiskey?" he asked.

"From the moment they arrived. Luke's the one who has been asking if you've gotten her. If she's here. He wants to know when he'll get to see her."

"He's interested?"

"Won't stop talking about it."

He handed Hunter the box. "Put these in my room and let Ava know her presence will be needed for dinner."

"What do you want her dressed in?"

"Nothing," he said. "She hasn't earned her clothes yet."

"Do you think it wise bringing her down for your friends to see?" Hunter asked.

Logan had started to walk away. He paused and stepped back, going toward his friend.

"Did I in any way give you permission to think you could tell me what it is you're thinking, or your judgment?" Logan asked.

Hunter was a close friend, even closer than Luke, Riley, or Marvin had been in recent years, but that didn't mean for a single second he wanted to hear what Hunter had to say. This wasn't about him.

In this, he was an employee, nothing more, nothing less.

"I apologize."

"You should. Now, go and get my dinner guest."

He turned his back and entered his office to find Luke already sitting in the boss's chair behind the desk, drink in hand, as well as a cigar.

"Well, well, well, the man of the hour has finally decided to grace us with his presence. Whatever should we do?" he asked.

Riley and Marvin moved toward him, shaking his hand, slapping him on the back. Part of him had to wonder why he even dealt with Riley and Marvin. They were all part of his life and had been there for him in their own way, but he'd been more distant with Riley and Marvin. They'd gone separate directions.

"How you doin'?" they each asked.

"Does no one give a fuck about progress here?" Luke asked, getting to his feet. "I don't know if you lazy fuckers have forgotten, but we're not here to make a social call. We're here for one purpose only, and do any of you really know what that is?"

"What is wrong with you?" Logan asked.

"Did you find her? Was she still in Crow Valley like you said?" Luke asked.

He stared at his friend, and for the first time since being back home, he felt a wave of need to protect Ava.

Luke wasn't a good guy. He'd never been good. He always expected stuff handed to him on a plate. His family was rich, and he never liked to be told no, or denied. Logan had grown up with him and was more than used to his brattish ways, but something didn't sit right with him. As far as he knew, nothing had gone on between Luke and Ava twelve years ago.

To Luke, Ava was always too fat. She was a big girl, curves in abundance. For Logan, he liked her curves, enjoyed using any excuse to feel them against him, but Luke always liked skinny girls, not that there was a problem.

They each had their own personal preference.

His was Ava.

Luke was everything else.

"Do you have her?" Riley asked.

"It's all the bastard has been talking about," Marvin said. "How she's supposed to pay for not keeping her mouth shut."

"She had nothing to keep her mouth shut about," Logan said. "I've got her. She's in a room upstairs. Don't worry. Hunter's going to make sure she's our guest for dinner." He moved toward the whiskey and poured himself a small glass. He was incredibly thirsty. The show would be beginning soon, and he needed to be ready. Luke, Riley, and Marvin weren't supposed to join him for at least a week. They were ahead of schedule, and now he had to deal with Luke's impatience, but he'd warned them all. *He* was the one who paid the price, and he'd be the one in charge. After all, it was his money, his power, and the fear people had of him was the reason they were here.

Chapter Four

Thirteen years ago

Ava should have expected the trip. As she passed Luke and his cronies, anything could happen. She'd already seen three other guys take a tumble. With the girls, Luke had felt their asses. She was more than happy to be tripped. Rather than hitting the ground hard, she fell into a body.

"Well, well, well, you better be careful now," Logan said.

Her body was pressed flush to his, and she quickly pulled away, feeling the blush rise in her cheeks.

"I'm sorry." She didn't know why she was apologizing. There was nothing for her to say sorry for. She'd been tripped.

"Logan, you saved us all from a cave-in. Could you imagine her body hitting the floor? It would create a giant sinkhole." Luke burst out laughing. As if on cue, the others did as well.

The only person who didn't was Logan, besides herself of course.

She grabbed her books and squealed as someone touched her ass. Getting to her feet, she spun to see Luke with a smirk on his face. "I just had to see if you could feel it past all of your fat."

"Don't touch me," she said.

He gave her the creeps.

When she turned back to Logan, he had the rest of her books. She thanked him and quickly tried to leave, but Luke grabbed her again. He tugged her close, and she stumbled against him with a cry, the books once again landing on the floor.

He had her shirt in his grip, and if he wanted to, he'd be able to easily tear it from her body. She'd be standing in the school corridor naked, and she didn't want that to happen.

"You seem to think you're in charge here. I will touch you if I want to. You don't get to tell me what to do. You're nothing but a fat, fucking cow who needs to be taught a lesson." It looked like he was going to hit her.

She didn't know what happened next, only that she was pulled from Luke. Leaving her books on the floor, she rushed toward her class without a backward look. Later that same day, she expected to find her books in the trash, only to discover them neatly placed in her locker.

Whoever had done it, knew her combination, which sent a chill up her spine. She would never leave anything personal in her locker again.

****

Present day

Being alone in a room all day was making Ava stir-crazy. She sat on the edge of the bed, running the tips of her toes across the soft ground. Back and forth, up and down, back and forth.

She hated being bored. There was nothing to do unless she wanted to make herself come all the time, or go and take a nice, long bath. She didn't have a towel.

She'd yet to hear from Logan. Whatever he had planned for her, it wasn't good. She didn't want to be here.

Tucking her hair behind her ear, she glanced over at the windows. Would it be a long jump? Would she hurt herself? If she did jump and broke her leg, would he take her to the hospital? It was pointless. He'd already told her the sheriff knew exactly where she was and hadn't come to see her.

What she didn't like was knowing something had gone horribly wrong twelve years ago. She understood

Logan being angry with her, but he got it all wrong. He had to. She hadn't tried to hurt him. He'd never done anything wrong to her.

No, she hadn't falsely reported Logan, but for some reason, he seemed to think she had. She didn't know what the sheriff had done, but it wasn't what she'd told him.

Taking a deep breath, she tried not to panic. There was no way she'd be getting out of this alive by panicking, even though it was the first thing she wanted to do.

You've already had his dick in your mouth ... and you liked it.

Running fingers through her hair, she tried to not think about what she'd already done with Logan and it hadn't caused her any fear.

She wouldn't allow *him* to win, so every single time she'd been with someone, she had pushed the memory of *him* to one side and focused on living. On surviving. On not giving up. It had helped her so many times over the years, and it would continue to do so.

Her bedroom door opened, and there stood Hunter.

He seemed a little off, which was strange.

Staring at him, she waited. There was no point in making demands. She'd gotten the message, crystal clear. She was on her own.

"You're needed downstairs," he said.

Getting to her feet, she walked toward him. She still hated being naked in front of him, but she was determined not to let it show.

"Do you take advice?" he asked.

"You always seem to want to give it. I guess I don't have much of a choice in taking it."

"Don't screw this up. Don't piss him off."

"Why would I do that?" she asked.

"You'll understand when you're down there."

"Hunter, what's going on?" For him to give her a warning, it couldn't be anything good.

"You're going to need your strength. Don't fight, and listen to him." Hunter grabbed her arm and led her out of her bedroom.

She suddenly wanted to go back to the quiet space of her room. She had no desire or wish to mingle. "I can go back to my room," she said.

"It's not an option. Come on."

She wanted to fight his touch, but she couldn't do it. Hunter was much stronger than she was, and as he led her downstairs, she felt the panic she wanted to keep at bay rising up.

She expected them to go into the dining room for dinner.

It was dinnertime, right?

The passing time didn't exactly register to her anymore. There was nothing to do, so a minute could feel like an hour.

They stood outside of Logan's office, and she heard noise from inside. Conversation. More than one man.

"What's going on?"

Hunter entered the room without knocking, and, looking over his shoulder, Ava could only see Logan.

"Don't be shy, Hunter, show our guest in."

Hunter grabbed her arm, only this time it wasn't viciously, just firmly.

He pulled her into the room, and she came up short.

It couldn't be happening.

Breathe.

Just breathe.

It was like stepping into the room of her past.

Logan was there all right, but he wasn't alone. Marvin and Riley sat on one sofa. Logan stood near the drinks, and Luke, he sat on his own, with plenty of space.

"You may leave now, Hunter," Logan said.

Hunter had taken her into the devil's lair, and now there was no way out.

She wanted to run, to get out of the trap, but her feet couldn't move and she stayed perfectly still, not wanting to draw attention. She was naked.

In a room of four men as Hunter closed the door, bare for them all to see.

She wanted to cry.

Instead of looking at the men, she stared straight ahead. Spine straight. Trying to focus on not falling apart.

This was all too much.

Her heart raced. Her hands felt sweaty. She wanted to scream at Logan, tell him to get her out of here, but one quick glance, and she saw he was enjoying this. He liked seeing her humiliated.

Hands clenched at her side. She tried not to panic.

You can get through this. You don't need to be scared. Nothing is going to happen.

"I can't believe she was fucking stupid enough to stay in town after what she did," Luke said, getting to his feet.

She tensed up, ready to run if she had to.

He stepped close to her.

Don't let him fucking win!

Turning her gaze to his, she stayed into his cold blue eyes. One day, she would hurt him. She was determined to do it.

"What can I say? She clearly thought the sheriff would protect her. She got sloppy, but that's okay. She's mine now."

"I have to say, I'm loving the outfit," Luke said.

She flinched away as he went to touch her.

He tutted, and she cried out as he grabbed her around the back of the neck. "Do you really think you have the power here, whore?" He spat the words at her.

She screamed as he touched her, and she fought against him.

The years hadn't changed. No matter how hard she tried to get away, he was much stronger than she was.

"Let her go," Logan said. "She's not here to amuse you, Luke. She's here for me."

Luke let her go, and she felt herself shaking. She had to stop and get herself under control.

He'd done something twelve years ago. She knew it deep in her heart. He'd made a deal with the sheriff, and instead of Luke going down for his crimes, Logan had paid the price somehow. How was it possible for Logan to have gone to jail but Luke not? *Had* Luke gone to jail? The sheriff had told her Luke had been taken care of, and would be serving time, and she'd never have to deal with him. She'd been sent away while the trial happened as the sheriff advised her parents it was the best course of action. She wouldn't need to read out any statements, and it would all be handled. She heard all kinds of rumors, and for the most part, she ignored them.

The sheriff had told her she'd be safe. Not to worry, so she'd believed him. Why doubt him?

He'd been lying all along, and now, she had to get those fucking statements some way. Would there even be a point of getting them?

"Come here, Ava," Logan said.

She wanted to scream at him to go and fuck himself. To run as far and as fast as she could. There was no way she'd get away. With the men around the house, she'd be killed before she got her freedom.

Logan was the safest out of all of the men in the room, or at least, she figured he was. She'd never experienced an encounter with Marvin or Riley. Both men always seemed rather indifferent to what was going on around them.

For now, she wouldn't worry about them, and instead, focus on trying to make it out of all of this alive. She had to stay alive.

Stepping across the room, she was careful not to get in the way of their feet. She wouldn't put it past them to hurt her in some way. To make her pay.

Standing in front of Logan, she waited.

"Touch yourself," he said.

"What?"

"You heard me. I want you to put your hands on your pretty pussy. Let's see how wet you can get."

She shook her head.

"You're thinking of defying me. Do you need me to remind you of your place?"

The tapes? Would it be so bad to have them released into the world? Sure, they'd follow her everywhere, but that wouldn't matter, not to her.

Logan leaned in, his lips brushing across her ear. She didn't dare jerk back or stop him. "Let me paint a little picture for you, if you don't start to finger your pussy, I'm going to make you suck every single dick in this room, and thanks to Grant, you know how to deep throat. I've heard this is one of Luke's pleasures."

She jerked back, hating him so much.

Sliding her hand between her thighs, she found herself completely dry. She wasn't aroused or turned on.

This was more than embarrassing and humiliating. She didn't know how she was going to keep up the charade of being able to stand in the same room as Luke. He was the worst kind of person. There was no reasoning with Logan. All he saw was what he wanted to.

She was alone.

"Does she even know what she's doing?" Luke asked. "I thought this was supposed to be some kind of show. If she can't even do that right, pass her to me. I'll show her how a real man handles her."

She wasn't aroused, and hearing Luke wasn't helping.

"Don't," she said. "Please." Sinking to her knees in front of him, she reached for the belt of Logan's pants. Sliding it open, she started to pull them down, taking his boxer briefs with them. His cock sprang out, and he was hard. Wrapping her fingers around the length, she looked up at him.

"This wasn't what I told you to do," he said.

"Will you turn me down?" She slid her tongue across the tip, and he let out a little moan. She took him deeper into her mouth, making sure she gagged on it.

"You will touch your pussy, Ava, and you will come in this room, with them watching."

Logan grabbed her hair, pulling her off his cock. She had no choice but to follow him. He made her sit on the edge of the sofa where Luke was.

She should have stayed standing, letting them watch. Logan had kicked off his pants and his cock stood within her grasp, but she didn't reach for it. She was too aware of Luke, staring at her.

Logan grabbed her legs, and even as she tried to fight him, he spread her legs open wide, letting them all see her bare pussy.

Tears filled her eyes.

"For a fat whore, she has got a pretty cunt, hasn't

she? Is she tight?"

Luke's voice filled the air, and she wanted the world to swallow her up.

"She's dry," Riley said. "She's not aroused at all, Logan."

Staring at Logan, he glanced back at his friend, and she jumped as he touched her pussy.

His brown gaze went back toward her.

She didn't make a move.

His fingers stroked between her slit, going inside her. She winced a little as he touched her.

"She will," Logan said. He moved in such a way she couldn't see Luke or the others.

His cock was close to her lips, but he didn't make her take it. She stared up at him as he worked her pussy.

She wanted to fight him, to tell him to go and fuck himself, but that would be pointless. There was no hope for her. Not even now. Hunter wouldn't help her. She had to sit and take what he was doing to her.

Watching Logan, she knew there was only way one to get out of this room and that was to please him.

Luke, Riley, and Marvin wouldn't make a move unless Logan told them to. She had to survive this, and to do that, she needed to come. To do anything but let them believe they had won.

For now, Logan thought he was the victim. Whatever had happened twelve years ago, they believed she'd been the cause, but it wasn't true. The sheriff had done something, and she was determined to find out the truth, one way or another.

****

The last time Logan touched her, she'd been soaking wet. Now, he had to blank out the room for her to even get a little wet. She wasn't feeling it, or into it.

With Luke breathing down his neck, he was

growing even more pissed off.

This wasn't his show; it was Logan's.

Sliding two fingers inside her, he used his thumb to stroke over her clit. Pumping his fingers in and out of her, he pulled them out, spat on them, and used his spit to help lubricate her. She rocked against him, but he saw, she wasn't into this.

Staring into her eyes, he saw the tears, and they turned him on. He wanted her to hurt, to share in the pain.

"Close your eyes," he said.

At first, she didn't, but something must have changed within her, because slowly, her eyes closed, and as they did, he pressed a kiss to her lips.

The pictures of Luke, something had gone on there, and he had to find out what it was.

Why the fuck do you care?

She hated Luke, so what?

He's still your friend. He still stood by you through thick and thin. He's helped you every single step of the way when he could have turned his back on you.

There was nothing to find out. Logan's obsession with Ava was the problem. Not his need to understand her hatred of his best friend.

Kissing down her neck, he went to her nipples, sucking on each one.

"Yeah, I bet the slut likes that," Luke said. "Bite them, Logan, make her feel it."

The tears she'd been trying to contain, spilled out, and he watched her, but he didn't give up. Sucking on each nipple, he flicked his tongue back and forth. Her pussy had started to grow slick as he worked her body.

She wasn't nearly as wet as he imagined she'd be, but it would do. Kissing down her body, her legs still spread, he replaced his fingers with his tongue, tasting her. She was sweet and juicy.

Sliding his tongue from her clit down to her entrance and back up again, he felt her start to get into it. She began to rock against him, and he worked her body the only way he could.

Over and over, he drove her wild. She moaned his name, whimpered it in the air.

All of it was caught on camera. The proof she wanted this. She hadn't pushed him away.

When she came, it was a beautiful sight, and this time, he didn't use her. He didn't fuck her as he wanted to.

He licked her pussy, pushing her into a second orgasm. Everyone heard it in the room as she came, screaming his name, begging for more, but he was done. He'd gotten what he wanted.

"If you'll excuse me, gentlemen," Logan said.

Grabbing Ava's arm, he pulled her out of the room. Her body was shaking, and he heard the sound of a slap. Glancing back, he saw Luke smirking and rubbing his hand.

"Couldn't resist giving that fat ass a beating."

Without another word, he pulled her from the room, and Hunter was there, waiting, typing on his cell phone. He stood up, but Logan pushed him off. There was no reason for the two of them to take her to her room.

"Logan, what is going on?" she asked.

He didn't answer her.

Once they were inside the room, he slammed the door closed, locking it, and putting the key high where she wouldn't be able to reach it.

He let her go, and she pulled away from him.

"What is this? Why are you doing this to me?" she asked, screaming the words.

"I'm done with the dumb bitch act."

"It's not an act. I'm not a dumb bitch."

He pushed her hard and she landed on the bed. She cried out as he joined her, grabbing her hands and pushing them above her head, keeping her in place.

"Let me go."

"There you go again, thinking you've got any real power here."

"I know I don't. You've proven it to me, time and time again. I'm nothing. There's no point me fighting, right? No point me screaming out, begging to be let go. I'm useless to you, to all of you." She continued to wriggle to get away.

She wasn't a match for his strength. It wasn't even hard for him to lie on her, keeping her in place.

"Then why are you still trying to fight me?" he asked.

"I can't stop it. I have to get away. I don't know what it is you think you know, but it's lies. All of it."

This time, he threw his head back and laughed. "Everything I know is lies?"

"Yes."

"You're so full of shit."

She sobbed and collapsed.

"Why weren't you aroused?" he asked. "Just last night you were soaking wet and begging for my dick, and now you've gone all coy and soft."

"Fuck you!"

He moved his pelvis so she would realize he was very much naked, and he could do exactly that, if she didn't shut up.

She froze.

"Tell me why you weren't turned on."

"Do you think it's easy for me to get aroused in a room full of guys who bullied me growing up? I hate them."

"You're able to get wet for me, and last time I checked, I was just as much of a bully as the rest of them. You had no problem getting wet with Hunter in the room."

"Maybe I like him. You ever thought about that? Maybe I like seeing him watch me." She pressed her lips together, and he knew without a shadow of a doubt she was lying.

"You're a bad fucking liar."

"You don't know anything."

Keeping her hands locked above her head underneath the grip of one of his, with the other, he reached down between them. Gripping his cock, he placed the tip against her clit and stared into her eyes, watching her, waiting. She wasn't as wet as she had been last night, but he'd made her come twice with his mouth, so there was something for him to play with.

Up and down, he watched her face as he slowly worked her body. He wanted to slam deep inside her, but he held himself back. There would be a time and a place for fucking her hard. For now, he wanted to see what her problem was.

She stared up at him, and he bumped her clit. Her teeth sank into her lip, and she tried to stop herself from making any noise.

It wouldn't work with him. Sliding his hand up, he cupped her face, running his thumb across her bottom lip. She opened up, and he took possession of her mouth, kissing her. Plunging his tongue inside, he heard her moan, and she started to wriggle against him, her legs wrapping around his waist. He didn't fuck her.

He stayed sliding across her slit, bumping her clit with each thrust. Gripping her hip, he followed the curve of her thigh that was up on his waist. Cupping her ass, he groaned. She felt so amazing. There was no denying how much he wanted her. It had been part of him for so long, it was like second nature to him to want her.

This was the challenge to him, to punish her, to make her pay without falling for her. He had to do it. There wasn't going to be a future between them. Not ever.

She would pay for everything.

Pulling back, he was done waiting. He'd never fucked her before, and he had to see his own man do the job just to get the leverage he was going to need. With his dick at her entrance, he sank in deep, hearing her whimper.

Grant had told him she was tight, and the man hadn't been wrong. Logan was big and even though he'd made her come, she would be uncomfortable, but he didn't stop. He pulled out of her, slamming in deep.

He broke off the kiss to stare into her eyes.

"You feel so fucking good on my dick. This is how it's supposed to be. Wet, soaking, and ready to ride my cock. You're such a good girl, Ava," he said.

She whimpered, and he grabbed both of her hands, lifting up, and he started to pound her pussy. Staring down at where they were joined, he watched his cock. It was slick but not dripping wet as he would have liked, but that was okay. There would come a time, she'd be exactly as he wanted her.

Driving in deep, he couldn't look away. He didn't want to. He fucked her hard, wanting more of her, desperate to feel her come, but tonight he wasn't going to have the time. His balls tightened up, and he was so close, there was no way he was going to be able to hold back.

When he came, he pushed in deep, making her take every single inch of him, and he groaned as his cum spilled from the tip, shooting into her cunt.

There was no time to linger, and after he'd given her every single drop, he pulled out of her.

Ava lay on the bed, legs spread, his cum leaking from her pussy.

"Get some sleep."

He left the room without another look and locked the door behind him. Hunter was waiting for him, with a pair of pants and a new shirt.

"I figured you'd want these to cover yourself up."

"I can feel your judgment all the way over here," Logan said. "Whatever you've got to say, say it. I don't want to play games with you."

"Then I will keep my opinion to myself."

"You promised me, you had my back."

"I do."

Logan pulled on his pants and looked at his friend. They'd been together for some time. He trusted Hunter. It was the reason he made Hunter go and collect her and not anyone else.

"Then tell me."

"Luke."

It was a single word, and Logan sighed. "Your genuine dislike of a guy doesn't make him a bad person."

"You're right, I don't like him, but you ever wonder what is going on with Ava? I saw the pictures, Logan. It doesn't make it hard for me to say something bad happened between Luke and Ava."

Logan ran his fingers through his hair and looked at the locked door. He had suspicions, but this was Luke, one of his best friends.

"This is what she does, Hunter. She makes you believe something is there that isn't. Don't let her get under your skin. You'll be playing right into her game."

"It's a game now?"

"It will always be a game to her. She's smarter than you give her credit for. She will hurt you and spit you back out. You have to be careful."

Hunter laughed. "You're making her sound more like one of your drug enemies than a woman. I saw her reaction to Luke."

"She was naked in a room of four guys."

"And yet I never saw that kind of reaction to her when she was walking around this house with me," Hunter said. "Be careful with what you're pushing to one side. It may harm you later on."

He let out a breath. Logan didn't want to think. He'd just been in the tightest pussy of his life, and above all else, the pussy he'd been craving for most of it. "I don't have time for this. I've got guests. If you really want to check things out, talk to Ava. Also, get her some clothes. They're hanging up in my closet. A pair of jeans and a shirt. No underwear." She'd earned them after all.

"Logan," Hunter said, stopping him.

"Yes."

"Be careful. We may be wrong about this, and Ava may be the brilliant actress you paint her to be, but there is also a chance there is something there, and if it's the truth, then you're going to be hurt."

"I won't be hurt. Luke is a lot of things, but he'd never hurt me." He was sure of it. Leaving Hunter to give Ava her present, he joined his friends in the office. They were still drinking, but now they had some food. One of the maids who worked for him was sitting on Luke's lap. She was thin, beautiful, and looked at Luke as if he was a god. This was what Logan remembered from their high school years.

Not a single girl ever said no to Luke. He had a way with women. They flocked to him. Maybe it was power thing, Logan didn't know. He'd watched Luke for years with women, and knew there was no reason for him to use force, or to hurt them.

"Look what I've got, Logan. She has promised to be my bed companion tonight, haven't you, Daisy?"

The woman's name wasn't Daisy, but rather than correct him, she gave him a smile and a giggle.

"Go and wait in my room. Naked, not a stitch on. You better be ready for some serious, hard fucking."

"You know I pay them to work for me," Logan said, taking a drink of whiskey.

"I do, and I pay them to fuck me. It's a win-win."

"When was the last time you actually fucked a woman without money of some kind being exchanged?" Riley asked with a smirk.

Luke laughed. "The trick is to give them treats up front. You show them what you're willing to give them, and then anything you want, is on the market. Don't get me wrong. Some women still play hard to get, but a nice shiny jewel and you'd be surprised at just how quickly they'll sink their hot little asses on your cock. Even hurting themselves to get it." Luke clapped his hands, holding imaginary hips as he pretended to ride whatever woman it was in his lap. "It's always the hard-to-get ones that are the real gems."

"Hard to get?" Marvin asked.

"You know, the ones that think they're better than you. Who look down at you and treat you like you don't matter. Watching them squirm. There is a real reward in that."

"And you've had experience with this kind of thing?" Logan asked, intrigued.

"I have. They're all designed to take a cock, and it's their place. I don't have any room in my life for prim and prissy. The key is to teach them what they got to have, not what they think they should. It's where you're going wrong with your little captive, Logan. You're not the one in control—she is. But then, I think she always has been when it comes to you."

Chapter Five

Thirteen years ago

Licking her ice cream cone, Ava walked across the street, passing a darkened alley as she made her way home. Crow Valley at nine o'clock at night was just as safe as if it was seven o'clock in the morning or even lunchtime. The crime rate was low. In fact, the only real danger came in when it was around Halloween and a couple of kids fancied themselves a pumpkin. They'd go out to Old Ford's field and take the biggest one they could find. No one ever found the culprit, but it was known roughly who did it.

Crime just wasn't a big deal.

Just as she rounded a corner, she came to a stop when she saw Luke, Riley, Marvin, and Logan all heading her way. Even though they weren't seniors yet, they were still the most popular kids in school. Rather than cower and run, she tried to cross the street. It didn't work to avoid them, as they followed her, still heading toward her.

She stopped, and so did they.

This was pointless.

"What do you want?" she asked.

"Your ice cream," Luke said.

Stepping up to them, she handed them the ice cream. Vanilla wasn't her favorite anyway. She wanted to get home without having to deal with them.

Luke took the ice cream, and before she knew what was happening, he'd pressed it against her chest.

She cried out as the cold sank beneath the fabric of her shirt.

"What are you doing?"

"I don't want anything your mouth has been around, and let's face it, you don't need the extra fat." He grabbed her hard and shoved her against Logan, who captured her. His grip was firm, almost to the point of pain. She tried to wriggle free, but he wouldn't let her go. He held onto her, and she watched as Luke smirked.

"Lift her shirt up," Luke said. "Let's see if her tits are really that big or they're just fat."

Logan didn't make a move to lift up her shirt.

"Nah, I don't want to see a fat girl's tits tonight. Frankly, I'm bored, and I'm in the mood for ice cream." Logan shoved her to the ground, stepping over her.

Within seconds, they were gone, and she was shaking.

Getting to her feet, she walked as fast as she could to her home.

Letting herself inside, she collapsed against the door, hand to her chest, trying to catch her breath.

"Everything okay, sweetie?" her mother asked, coming out of the kitchen carrying a large bowl of popcorn.

She nodded her head. There was no point in scaring her. "Yes, of course. Nothing to worry about."

"You want to join us for the movie?"

"Yes." She would gladly do anything that didn't involve her remembering her encounter with Luke. Each time she was in his company with his three other friends, he always had a reason to try to get her naked, and it scared her. "I've just got to go and change my shirt."

****

Present day

Luke was there in the house somewhere. Panic flooded every single part of Ava as she held the blanket against her body. She'd just had sex with Logan as well.

What the hell was wrong with her?

He was her captor, the very reason she couldn't leave town, and she'd enjoyed the sex. She hadn't achieved an orgasm, but it had been very close. Pushing her hair out of her face, she stared across the room.

What were they doing right now? What was Luke trying to convince Logan to do to her?

She didn't want to even think about it. There had to be a way to leave.

Her bedroom door opened, and she sat up, keeping the blanket to her chin. It wouldn't protect her. She was no match for any of these men. Hunter entered the room, carrying clothes.

He closed the door behind her and stared at her. Was that guilt she detected in his gaze?

"Clothes for you to wear," he said.

"So I've finally earned them?"

"Logan did tell you you'd be rewarded for good behavior."

"Then tell me how I get out of here?" she asked. "What exactly do I have to do to be free?"

Hunter stared at her. He didn't answer her. Rather than look away, he kept on watching her.

"Are you going to talk, or is this a staring competition?" she asked.

"I saw the records," Hunter said.

"Records?"

"Yes. What you reported. I know you had Logan arrested and sent to prison."

"I didn't," she said. "Logan had never done anything to me."

"Then why is it *his* name all over them?"

"I don't know what it is you think you saw, but I didn't report Logan. He was a bully, sure. He hung out with that piece of shit, but he never hurt me, not really. Not until now." She pressed her lips together.

There was no way she could trust Hunter. He worked for Logan, and in doing so, he could be working for Luke. She wouldn't underestimate any of the men that had currently fallen into her life. They were all in their own ways, monsters.

"You're lying."

"I'm not lying. You seem to think you have some gift to tell when I am or I'm not. Show me what you think you've read. I know who I reported, and it wasn't Logan." She tilted her head to the side. "You don't like this, do you? It's why you're here."

"I'm here for my own reasons."

"Yeah, but you want some information. You don't like Luke, do you?" She was hopeful. "Do you like any of his friends?"

"What I think and feel is none of your concern. The clothes are there for you to use, and I suggest you do." Hunter took a step back from the bed.

"Am I getting out of here alive?" she asked.

"Logan has no plans to kill you."

"Just to ruin me?"

"The same way you ruined him, but with a touch more elaboration."

"Whatever it is you think you know, you're wrong."

"I don't know anything." He laughed. "Try to get some sleep."

"How long are they staying?" She didn't want to have to show weakness, but while Luke was in the house, she feared for her life and if showing it to Hunter helped her in any way, she was willing to do it.

"Who?"

"His friends."

"Yes. They'll be here until Logan needs them elsewhere."

Hunter walked to the door, opening it.

"Who exactly is in charge?" she asked.

Hunter closed the door again, turning toward her.

"When we were in high school, Luke was the one who called all the shots. Who told people how it was going to be and what he was going to do. What about now? Does Logan still do as he's told?"

"Logan is the one with all the power and all the money. He's the one running the show."

She smiled. "I guess we'll see."

Hunter stared at her for a couple of extra minutes before leaving.

Once she was sure he wasn't coming back, she climbed out of bed and scrambled to put on the clothes. She tugged up her pants and pulled on the shirt. There was no underwear, but at least she now had clothes on.

Climbing back into bed, she put the blanket up to her neck, staring across the room. It was dark outside, and her heart raced as the sounds of the night surrounded her. Every little bump and creak, she had to wonder if Luke was coming after her.

She hadn't seen him in twelve years either. The man had sent her pictures throughout the years. There was never any return address, but she knew they were from him.

Taking a deep breath, she closed her eyes.

If she had to face them again, she was going to need her sleep.

The hours ticked by, and still, she didn't sleep. Every now and then, she'd nap for a couple of minutes, but the fear would come back, threatening to consume her. She couldn't just fall asleep. She had to be on alert.

At the first rays of sunlight, she climbed out of bed, made it, and went to the bathroom. After using the toilet, she washed her hands and splashed water onto her face.

Logan hadn't even provided her with a toothbrush

or toothpaste.

She cupped some water, sipping at it, swilling her mouth and spitting it in the sink. She was going to have to ask for some of the simple pleasures in life.

Lifting up, she found herself once again staring at her reflection.

"You can get through this. It's nothing."

The entire town had left them alone. If they knew where she was, no one was coming for her. Her parents were already dead, and she hadn't made any connections with people nearby to her.

Whatever was about to happen, when it did, they wouldn't care. Logan could kill her, throw away the key, and no one would care. She was all alone in this. She thought about Grant. It was so stupid to even be thinking about him at this moment.

Did he know where she was? Did he even care?

Why are you even thinking about him? What connection you had to him was long gone. He used you for his boss.

Don't forget, everything he did was a lie. It was all a ploy constructed by Logan.

With her face now drying, she went into her bedroom, only to stop as she saw who was waiting for her.

Luke.

He smiled as he saw her, closing the bedroom door.

She heard the lock click into place.

"Do you have any idea how hard it is to check every single room in this house? I must have opened fifty doors and not one of them was full. There are so many rooms just waiting to be filled. Even the maids didn't know where you were being kept. I have to say, you're staying in a sweet place."

"What do you want?" she asked.

"I see he finally put some clothes on you. A shame, really. I rather liked being able to see you. Still got the famous curves Logan loves, but they've matured. I can see why his dick is hard for you. I wonder if he knows."

"Get out," she said. She tried to keep her voice firm, but standing across from this monster, she felt nothing but fear.

Luke laughed. "You want me to leave. It's a little after six. People are still wandering around, doing their chores. Did you know Logan's a late sleeper?"

She didn't know anything.

Right now, she was trapped, alone with one of the cruelest men she'd ever known. Crow Valley was low on crime, sure it was. When she reported what happened to her, no one knew what to do. That was how nice it was supposed to be. She soon learned, there may not be any crime rate within town, but that didn't mean evil wasn't lurking around, waiting to snap people up, one by one.

Luke stepped into the room, and she stayed where she was, in the doorway leading to the bathroom. There was no lock on the door.

She was at the mercy of Luke once again.

Her hands shook.

Her entire body trembled.

There was no pleasure in knowing what could happen.

The way Luke looked at her, it didn't matter if she was wearing clothes. He saw what he wanted to, and she had no way of stopping him.

Just like last time.

"He doesn't know, does he?" she said. "You did something, didn't you?"

Luke laughed. "You think I'd still be here if

Logan knows what I own? What I can still feel if I close my eyes, and remember how tight you were. How you screamed when I fucked you?"

Tears filled her eyes, but she didn't want to give him the satisfaction of crying. There was no pleasure in this. Only pain.

Glaring at him, she waited for him to finish with his gloating and leave.

He stepped close, and she couldn't take it.

As much as she hated to show any kind of weakness in front of her enemy, she took a step back, and Luke laughed.

"You know, I love to see you scared. All shaken up and making sure there's distance between us. It's really cute."

"Leave me alone."

"I don't want to leave you alone. There's no reason for me to." He laughed again. "Do you really think I've spent the last hour opening every single door I could find just to taunt you?"

He reached out toward her, and she swatted his arm away.

The moment she hit him, he backhanded her. She fell against the tiled floor, the sting shocking her to the core.

Luke didn't stop.

He grabbed her by the back of the neck, picking her up and pressing her against the wall. She cried out at the pain. His grip was tight, and he hurt as he held her in place. His hand cupped her between the thighs, bruising even with a layer of denim to stop him from touching bare flesh.

"I'm going to make sure I get to fuck this pretty pussy again. Logan likes to share—did you know that? We share everything. I'm his best friend, and I'm going to make him share you. He knows what you did, and I'm going to enjoy every single second of it." He moved, gripping her ass. "Only this time, I'm going to take your ass. I wonder if he's already had a taste of your ass. I'll fuck you so hard and make you gag on my cock, tasting yourself. I'll have every single kind of virginity you have to offer."

She gritted her teeth. Revulsion traveled through her and she wanted nothing more than to hurt him, but she could do nothing.

"You won't get anymore from me. My ass has already been taken and owned. You should see Logan— he sent the guy to get me ready." She spat the words out.

"Whore!" He pulled away and slammed his fist against her ribcage, winding her.

He lifted her up by her hair, and she cried out.

"You won't win this. You don't have the power to win anything." He spat in her face, and she closed her eyes. "This isn't over."

She didn't know why he let her go, only that he did, and she kept herself upright. She listened as the door opened and the lock clicked back into place.

Rushing to the toilet, she wiped the spittle from her face and threw everything up. There had to be a way to escape.

There had to be.

****

Logan had all the pictures of Luke splayed out across his bed.

Some of them were from the past and Ava could have easily taken, but he recalled some as recently as six months ago. He picked up one of them all in a nightclub. A couple of women were sitting in their laps, and Luke had told someone passing by to take a photo and handed the stranger the cell phone.

The snap had been instant. Staring at it now, Logan knew there was no getting away from it. Something had gone on between Luke and Ava.

Why would one of his best friends send pictures like this?

More importantly, why would Ava scribble out Luke's face or deface them in any way?

The answer had to be right in front of him, but there was no way to see it.

There was a knock on the door.

"Come in," he said, gathering up the pictures and putting them back into the box.

"It's nice to see you up and all," Luke said. "What happened to the nights you were passed out cold?"

"I'm not a teenager anymore. I can handle my liquor. What do you want?"

"What? A friend can't come and see an old friend?"

"I know you, Luke. You have the pick of maids, and rather than getting your dick wet, you're here talking to me. Are you wanting to suck my dick?"

"Hardly. You should get your resident whore to do it."

"I don't have one."

"Please, you're still pining after Ava when she did what she did. Reporting you for sexual assault, when let's face it, the girl was probably begging for you to touch her."

Logan thought about the time in the classroom. It was the last time before he'd been arrested. He'd done a jail term for the accusations thrown at him, and he'd been put on the offenders' register, and for five years after leaving prison, he had to report to his case worker. That hadn't been too hard, not after he'd earned his way to the top of the food chain. He'd still been kicked out of town he'd grown up in, and asked not to have any contact with Ava Marshall.

His father had the best lawyers at the time.

Everything he and Ava had done, she'd been a willing participant. Knowing what she had said, it had driven him to have power, wealth, and people afraid of him.

Luke liked to think he ran the show, but he couldn't wave his hand and have a man kill at his whim.

Logan could.

The money was all his.

People didn't fear Luke. He was a small fish in an ocean full of sharks.

"Do you still have the hots for this girl?" Luke asked. "I mean, I figured your tastes would have improved."

"Ava is exactly where I want and need her to be. Why are you in my room?" he asked.

"I was wondering if your sharing spirit was high on your list today."

"Sharing?"

"You know, I could have Ava for the day. You could pass her around. I'm sure Riley and Marvin would love to have a turn with her."

"You want to fuck her."

"I want to hear her beg. I know what she did to you, remember? What she did to all of us."

"None of you had your life taken away. You all had your lives. You left town, but you could have stayed."

"We're your friends."

"I've already got plans with Ava today. It's time the town saw how afraid she is of me, or how not afraid, depending on your point of view. You can amuse yourself with whatever and whomever you see fit."

"You think you can just boss me around now, is that it?"

"I don't *think* I can do anything, Luke. This is my house. This is my call. I told you that. You got a problem with how I handle things, I can have you back in your cozy little apartment within the hour." He stepped up close to Luke. He was taller, stronger, and bigger than Luke. "Do not interfere with my plans."

"I do have another question," Luke said, as Logan went to the door.

"What?"

"How far did you want Grant to go?"

"What do you know about Grant?"

"I know a great deal. Everything you've done to manipulate this point in time is not very hard to see."

"Grant was used for leverage."

"Did you want him to fuck her?" Luke asked.

"I told Grant to get me what I needed. Ava, she wouldn't want her sex life on camera. Not after what she accused me of. I knew it would be the only way I'd get leverage over her. Your point?"

"I was wondering if you knew he fucked her in the ass?"

Logan stared at his friend, and it was like he was seeing him for the first time. There were only two people who would know what Grant had done. One of them was Grant, and he wasn't there yet. Logan didn't want Ava to have to confront her past just yet. That would all come soon enough. Grant had told him what he'd done. It hadn't been caught on tape. He'd gone to her house and things had gotten out of control.

The only other person was Ava herself, and seeing as the two hadn't had contact in twelve years before yesterday, Logan knew for a fact Luke had visited

her.

"Why do you care?"

"I knew how much you wanted to be her first. You couldn't have her pussy. I bet she hadn't been a virgin for a long time, but her ass, that could have been your little cherry."

"Get out," Logan said.

"Have I hit a nerve?"

"I said get out," Logan said.

Luke held his hands up. "It's just a little fun between friends, right? I'll go. No need to shoot the messenger."

Logan waited for Luke to go before heading toward the security room.

Hunter was there, drinking a coffee.

"How long have you been here?" he asked.

"Ten minutes. I figured I'd come and check on a few things. None of the men had reported anything."

Logan didn't see a reason to have a man on the cameras twenty-four seven. He'd installed the security out of curiosity and a precaution.

He didn't have them in any room.

There was some privacy. The corridors, main hallway, dining room, and his study each had a camera. He'd also installed a few into the library.

Finding the screen with Ava's door, he rewound the footage.

He stopped as he watched Luke coming out of her room, smiling as he did. Checking the time, he rewound the tape showing his friend had been in the room for ten minutes.

"Why is Luke sneaking around your house to go and see Ava?" Hunter asked.

"I want you to bring the sheriff to me. Make sure Luke, Riley, and Marvin are gone by the time I return. I need to clarify a few things."

Getting to his feet, he walked out of the room.

He couldn't go throwing accusations at Luke, not when he didn't know the full reasons for it. Luke had never turned his back on him, and he wasn't about to accuse him of shit he didn't know.

Heading to Ava's room, he unlocked the door, and she stood in the bathroom doorway, staring at him.

She was pale.

"We're going out. Come on."

"Can I leave?" she asked.

"We're about to leave."

"What do I have to do to earn my freedom from you? To stop you from sending out the tapes of my parents and myself?"

He stopped and stared at her. "Do you really want to know?"

"Yes."

He stared at her. She was shaking, but he wouldn't allow himself to care.

She was a first-class bitch, and he had to stop seeing the girl from his past and realize this woman tried to ruin his life.

"You'll know all in good time." He grabbed her arm and pulled her from the room.

"Logan, you're hurting me." He got to the end of the stairwell. Shoving her up against the wall, he wrapped his fingers around her throat. He didn't like being lied to, and he certainly didn't like to have liars near him.

"This is not a vacation for you. You don't get to scream and beg, or make demands. You're here for me. For what I require of you. If that means prancing around naked, you'll do it. If it means getting on your knees and sucking my dick, you'll do it. No matter what I demand, you will give it to me, am I understood?"

"And if I don't?" she asked.

He smiled. "Ava, you seem to think I'm the guy you knew from high school, the one who didn't really hurt you. Pushed you around a little bit but helped you when you fell. Gave you your first kiss. You seem to think that's me. It's not. It's not me. It will never be me. You destroyed any chance you had of ever seeing that guy again. You want to push this, then you will get to see the real monster *you* created, and once he's out, you better fucking run."

He grabbed her arm again and dragged her downstairs. His men moved out of the way as he hauled her out of the house and toward his car. No one made a move to stop him. He could start hitting her, beating the shit out of her, and no one would move a muscle. They were his men, and he'd told them not to intervene. This was between him and Ava, and now he had a feeling the sheriff had some explaining to do.

"Try anything funny and I'll give you to my friends for an afternoon of fun." He slammed the car door, walking around to the driver's side.

He climbed in.

"Please, Logan, let me go."

She shook, and he ignored it.

Starting the car, he pulled out of the driveway and headed right into town.

"What is going on?"

"You better get yourself together. If you don't convince them how happy you are with me, I release the tapes."

"You release the tapes, you don't have any leverage over me."

"I've still got another one of you begging me to touch you. Try to beat me at my own game, Ava, you will lose."

She sat back down, and he drove into town.

"There's a brush in the drop-down. Do something with your hair. Look decent at least."

"While we're in town, I want my toothbrush."

"We'll make a stop at your house before heading back." It was on the tip of his tongue to call it home, but he stopped himself. It wasn't their home, or even his home.

Gripping the steering wheel, he pulled outside of the diner. There were already people there enjoying the morning breakfast.

"If you try anything in here other than the pleasure of my company, you'll be with Luke within the hour."

"I won't try anything."

Again, more questions. He wondered what she'd say if he offered her to Hunter.

"Wait." He climbed out of the car, rounded the vehicle to her side, and held the door open, offering her his hand.

She took it, and he felt the tremors of her body.

He gripped her hand tightly as they entered the diner.

There were a few private booths in the back, but he had no use for them. The idea was to be seen.

Sitting at the table in the center of the room, he pulled out Ava's chair before taking one himself. Picking up the menu, he already knew he was having the waffles.

"People are staring."

"Of course they are. You're sitting with the guy you accused of hurting you," Logan said. "You don't look very afraid to me."

"You're doing this on purpose."

"I'm doing what I need to do. You're just the

price I've got to pay in order to do it."

The waitress came to the table, and he reached over, plastering a huge smile on his face as he gripped Ava's hand.

"Hi, hot coffee for me and my friend here. Waffles, two plates, extra syrup."

"Logan Stanford, it has been an age since I've seen you," the waitress said. "Rebecca Driver. We took sex ed together."

"Ah, I remember." He didn't have a fucking clue. Ava had been in the same class, and he used to love watching her blush. He didn't need to know how sex worked. You bagged your dick, fucked the girl, and never during her time of the month, unless you had a blood fetish. He didn't.

"How have you been? What have you been up to?"

"Please, I'm kind of on a date right now."

Rebecca looked toward Ava, who failed to even smile. Ava lifted her free hand as if to wave.

"Oh, right. Yes, of course." She laughed. "Waffles and coffee coming right up."

"The gossip train will be flowing tonight," he said.

"Didn't you go out with Rebecca?" Ava asked.

"Not that I can remember."

"Just 'cause you can't remember it, doesn't mean it didn't happen. I'm sure you did."

"There were a lot of girls I fucked in high school. It passed the time." He lifted her hand and pressed kisses against her knuckles.

She looked so miserable.

"You better start acting or tape number one will come out to play."

She started to smile and lean in close. "You're

not going to win this."

"I already am."

"You don't know the whole truth."

"And what is that?" he asked.

She moved in close, her lips going to his ear. "I didn't report you to the sheriff, Logan. I had no reason to."

Logan pulled away, and he stared at her. "I saw the reports."

"They're wrong. I reported Luke." She pulled her hand away from him.

In the nick of time Rebecca was back and pouring them coffee. "It is so good to see you. I was wondering if you'd like to go out sometime. Catch up."

Logan couldn't remember if he'd slept with Rebecca or not. There had been girls in the past, but they'd been play toys. He'd not really wanted them, but he wasn't going to tell a girl no when she was begging to suck his dick.

Staring at Ava, he shouldn't believe her, but she was sitting, smiling up at Rebecca, playing her part.

He'd seen the reports.

She *had* reported him.

She'd accused him of rape, which he denied. He'd never hurt her. Why did she report Luke?

Their waffles arrived, and Ava took her plate, biting into them.

He noticed her trying to hide a knife in her pocket. Grabbing her wrist, he squeezed hard. "Don't push it."

Chapter Six

Twelve years ago

Being a senior should have been fun.

The final year of high school. Preparing for college. She already had several she wanted to apply to, and she been trying to prepare her request letters for the past couple of months. Her parents wanted her to be prepared and not to be floundering at the last possible minute.

She had plans, and they weren't to stay in Crow Valley.

At her locker, she put her books away. She picked out the ones she'd need for the upcoming class as she heard a cry.

Glancing across the corridor, she saw Logan, Riley, Marvin, and Luke, in a circle. They were the school bullies.

They came and went as they pleased. Their parents were some of the richest in town, and if anyone spoke out about them, they were always getting away with everything.

In the back of her mind, she couldn't help but feel a little relieved it wasn't her they were picking on. She'd borne the brunt of a few of their cruel tricks in the past week. She'd opened her locker to find tampons spilling out. Another time there had been condoms, and some of them had looked used. She wasn't the only one though. Other people, the losers as the crew liked to call them, had all been on the receiving end of their bullying.

Any other time, she'd walk away.

She didn't know why this time was any different. Sliding her books into her bag, she rushed toward where the crowd was cheering.

There was a small gap, and she saw Dillon. He

was a year younger than they were, with a face full of acne, and was short as well.

People thought this was fun, bullying him?

They'd poured what looked like acne cream all over him. Everyone was laughing as Luke shoved him down hard.

"Enough!" She couldn't take it.

Shoving herself into the crowd, she stepped between Luke and Dillion.

Why the fuck are you doing this?

It's not your fight.

"Well, well, well, look at this. Little miss prim and proper has come to save the young little pimple. What's the matter, you see it as extra food?" Luke asked.

"You're disgusting."

"I'm disgusting? Why don't you go and have a pie-eating contest where you'll be the winner?"

Ignoring him, she turned to Dillon, holding out her hand.

She wasn't exactly happy about what she was doing. She was freaking out inside, trying not to panic.

Ava cried out as she was shoved hard and landed on Dillon. She tried to catch herself but was unable to. The ground was slippery from all the cream thrown at him.

"Look at this, fatty and pimply. If they have kids I wonder if they pop?"

A round of laughter ensued.

"I'm sorry." She scrambled to her feet hoping she'd not hurt Dillon. He was so small.

She held out her hand, and Dillon took it.

When Luke went to push her again, instinct took over, and she slammed all of her weight behind the shove she gave right back at him.

He clearly wasn't expecting it and ended up on

his ass in the acne cream he'd done for Dillon.

Grabbing Dillon's hand, she didn't wait around to see what the consequences were for sticking up for herself.

When they were all clear and out in the yard, she turned to him.

"You okay?"

"You shouldn't have done that."

"Push him or help you?"

"Both."

"Yeah, I know."

"He's going to be pissed, you know that, right?"

"Oh, I know." She took a deep breath. "Believe me, I know. I can handle myself, I hope. Are you okay?"

****

Present day

After waffles, Logan made her sit with him as he finished up a second cup of coffee. People came and went. All the time, Ava felt their gazes on them.

"That's Logan Stanford."

"What's he doing sitting with her?"

"I knew it was all lies."

"That guy could have anyone. Why is he sitting with her?"

When they left the diner, she expected them to go back to the car. Instead, he took her hand, and they headed down the street. "Where are we going?"

"You have way too many questions."

"And you don't have any answers."

"I don't need to provide you with any," he said. "Remember your place."

"I want to speak to the sheriff. That's not a question."

"No, you've now moved to demands. Why do you want to speak to him?"

"I want to know what the hell is going on."

He laughed. "This is a cute act."

"It's not an act."

"You expect me to believe you reported Luke to the sheriff?"

"I did."

He held her hand a little tighter, but she didn't give him any indication it was hurting.

"I'm bored of this conversation."

They stopped outside of her house, and she looked up at it. To think she'd spent so much time being happy here.

You should have left when you had the chance.

She'd hoped to. More than once.

"Why are we here?"

"Supplies."

They walked upstairs, and she shouldn't be surprised he already had a key. The man had taken all of her possessions from her, or at least Hunter had.

Entering her home, she felt the scent wash over her, but she didn't have any way of being calm, or allowing herself to feel safe.

She was the furthest from safe she could be.

"What do you need from here?" she asked.

"Everything for a long stay. You're not coming back here for a time. Go ahead."

"You're going to let me wander free."

"Of course. Have at it." He walked into the sitting room.

Without waiting for any other excuse, she rushed upstairs. She didn't go to the bathroom but to her parents' bedroom.

She sat on the edge of the bed, which she hadn't been on for over five years. She lifted up the phone cradle and dialed the sheriff's office. She got Susan, which didn't help. Susan was in her eighties but refused to leave her job. The sheriff never found a reason to fire her, and being slow wasn't exactly a problem in a town that had so few incidents.

"Hello, Sheriff's office, how can I help you?"

"Hey, Susan, it's me, Ava."

"Ava, I've been told to ignore any and all of your calls."

Thanks to Logan.

"I want to speak to him. It's nothing serious, but could you ask him to come out to where Logan Stanford is living?" she asked. There was no point in even pretending the sheriff didn't know Logan was back in town.

"I've got to go now, Ava. You may be clogging up the line."

Before she could get another word in, the phone was hung up, and she heard the dial tone.

"So you want to speak to the sheriff?" Logan asked.

She jumped and stared in the doorway. She hadn't been paying attention to her surroundings, and now she sat alone on her parents' bed.

"Yes." She put the phone back in its cradle.

"You shouldn't keep everything the same way." He pointed at the room.

"It's none of your business." She got up, but Logan made no move to let her pass. She folded her arms, waiting.

"You're cute when you're angry."

"Why did you stop the sheriff from taking my calls?" she asked.

"Ava, sweetheart, you're an intelligent woman."

"Enlighten me."

"I've taken you from your home, blackmailed

you, and I'm keeping you for my own personal fun sport. You do the math."

"I know each of those is a criminal offense. Abduction. Blackmail. It's all a crime."

"Exactly, and seeing as you had no problems giving me up for what we did when we were kids, you can imagine why I'd be cautious."

"How did you do it?"

"One thing in my line of work, Ava, you learn people's business and mistakes."

She stared at him, really looked at him.

"What happened to you?" she asked. "I know you were always a bully. Around Luke you were a nightmare, but this, it's personal."

"Are you still going to act like you don't know what is going on?"

"I don't know anything. Look around you, Logan. I haven't changed. I didn't report you. You can think what you like, but I didn't, okay?"

"What exactly did you report Luke for then? Being an asshole. Hurting you? What could you have possibly had against Luke that was so fucking bad?" He yelled the words.

"He raped me," she said.

The words hung heavy in the air. There was no point in prolonging the inevitable. She couldn't pretend it didn't happen. Her parents believed her. When she went to the sheriff the first time, he'd thought it was a prank. It was so humiliating, but she refused to be brought down by the past.

"You're lying."

She laughed. "Whatever. You can think what you want. The only time your name came up was when I said he hung around with you, Riley, and Marvin. That's why I want to talk to the sheriff. I don't know why you were arrested, and it certainly shouldn't have had anything to do with me."

Tears filled her eyes.

"Luke had no reason to do that."

"You don't believe me."

"It's a little farfetched, even for you."

She nodded her head, and the tears fell from her eyes. She swiped them away. The sheriff had told her it wasn't nice to lie.

"How fucking dare you? I've seen the bruises. My daughter doesn't lie. Never has. She's one of the best students at school. She's telling the truth, and you better start listening."

It was really hard to give a statement about what happened when the sheriff had laughed at the start.

"Don't worry about it. You weren't the only one who didn't believe me. I had no reason to lie. I don't now, but you all seem to know what it is that's going on. I'll let you guys figure it out. You clearly all know what is best."

She stepped up close. "Let me go and finish packing."

"Ava." He reached out to touch her, but she flinched away from him.

"No, I don't want to talk." She pushed past him, heading into her room.

Logan grabbed her arm, spinning her around. "You're not the one in charge here."

"Oh, I know, believe me, I do. You're the one who has the final say on everything. Don't worry, I get it. I do." She tried to pull her arm away, but he wouldn't let her. "Logan, stop it."

He pulled her close, and his lips brushed across hers.

She tensed up, not wanting to touch him.

He pulled back.

Staring into his eyes, she could easily get lost in them.

How could I make him see the truth when all the evidence is pointing at me to be a liar to him? How can I expect him to believe me now?

She tried to pull away.

"Did I say you could go?"

"What do you want?"

"Well, to start, I want a kiss."

"Logan?"

He raised a brow. She knew it was pointless.

Why don't you just let him release the video and then you'll be free? Would it be so hard?

She thought about the few minutes she'd seen of herself with Grant, then of her parents. Would it really be so bad the rest of the world seeing the truth? The thought of others seeing her having sex sickened her. After Luke raped her, her parents paid for the therapy to help her get past her demons. She'd been able to move on, have a couple of relationships. Grant being the most adventurous of them all. She'd never told him what happened to her.

Knowing now Grant worked for Logan, she had to wonder if she'd told him, would he have reported it to his boss?

Glancing down at his lips, she kissed them. A single brush of lips against lips.

"You're going to have to do better than that," he said.

"What do you want from me?"

"Kiss me properly. Like your life depends on it."

"Why?"

"Because I want to and I'm still the boss."

Running her hands up his chest, she sank her

fingers into his hair, staring into his eyes. He was a handsome man, and time hadn't changed that.

Pressing her lips against his, she let out a moan as he traced his tongue across her bottom lip. She slid her tongue into his mouth, deepening the kiss.

Logan grabbed her ass, pulling her close, and she cried out at the feel of his cock against her.

She didn't stop the kiss or break from it. His touch wasn't brutal. Even though Luke had hurt her this morning, she ignored the bruising pain, and focused on Logan.

Even as she hated him, and right now she did, she couldn't deny her attraction to him, or how she wanted him.

You're sick.

You should hate him.

Push him away and tell him to fuck off.

She did neither.

When he pulled her away and shoved her to her knees on the edge of the bed, she didn't stop him. Not as he reached for the button of her jeans, sliding it open. He moved them past her hips, going down to her knees, dragging them off her body to land on the floor. He cupped her pussy. His fingers slid through her pussy, teasing over her clit.

She moaned his name as he filled her with two fingers, pulling them out to stroke back up to her nub.

Looking up, she saw him there, watching her.

With his gaze on her, she heard his zipper coming down. The hard tip of his cock pressed to her entrance. She cried out as he slammed in deep.

"Fuck, yes!" He growled the word out, but his gaze stayed on her. He held her hips as he pulled out onto to slam back inside her.

Over and over, he rammed his length in, and she

loved it. The bite of pain, the instant pleasure.

He pulled all the way out, but she was wet enough for him to slide in easily.

She whimpered his name as the pleasure rushed through her body, but it wasn't enough to give her an orgasm.

"Yeah, it's me fucking you, Ava. Me. It's my cock you're creaming on. No one else. Now shut the fuck up and take it."

He fucked her hard, almost bruising in his thrusts. There was nowhere else for her to go. She gripped the bed, fisting the sheets as he used her body. She watched him, and he stared into her eyes as he came. He pushed as far and as deep as he could go. She felt each wave flood her pussy.

His grip was punishing, but he didn't release her.

Time stood still. The only sound to fill the room was their breathing.

He smirked at her. "I needed that."

It was like a wash of cold water ran over her.

Crawling away from him, off his cock, she scrambled off the bed, reaching for the jeans.

"Wait, what the fuck, Ava?" He grabbed her, but she jerked out of his reach.

"What?"

"What the fuck did you do?" He looked at the bruise on her stomach, going around her ribs.

Luke hadn't hit her hard enough across the face to leave a mark. It had stung and she'd cut her lip, tasting blood, but it wasn't long-lasting.

Staring at him now, she let him see. "I'm not even going to tell you who. You know who."

****

Arriving back at his house, Ava pulled away from him and started for the stairs. Logan watched her. When she realized he wasn't following, she stopped and turned toward him.

"You're not coming?" she asked. She wouldn't look at him.

She'd not spoken to him in the car either.

"You're free to roam the house. You've got clothes, and you can wear them whenever you want. Try to escape and I'll remove the privilege. You can't call anyone nor have anyone come and visit you."

She snorted. "I don't have anyone to have visit me."

"Good." He turned on his heel and walked away.

"Why?"

He stopped and turned toward her. "What?"

"Why are you letting me free?"

Logan chuckled. "You're not free. You'll never be free. Don't try to make this more than it is."

He watched her this time, heading upstairs, going to her room.

Hunter cleared his throat.

"The sheriff is waiting for you in the library."

"Excellent." He walked into his office, going to the window, overlooking the gardens.

"You're not in a rush?" Hunter asked.

"No. That bastard shouldn't be sheriff."

"I've got all the necessary paperwork to end his employment. Just tell me when."

"I will, but not yet. I need him in place." He tapped his leg, trying to get the image of Ava's body out of his head. There had been bruises he'd not seen, not as he fucked her from behind. He'd not allowed her to come, hadn't even cared to take care of her.

"Is everything okay?"

"I want you to do some digging for me," he said. "Wait, where's the guys?" He turned, giving Hunter his full attention.

"They're at the country club enjoying women and gambling as per your request."

"You didn't stay with them."

"You didn't say I had to."

"Right." He ran fingers through his hair. "I want you to look into Luke's past."

"Why?"

"Ava said she reported him for rape."

Hunter raised a brow.

"I need to know if there's something we're missing. Some clue."

"You think she's lying?"

"I have no reason to believe she's telling the truth."

"That's a pretty big allegation," Hunter said.

He agreed.

"What do you think?" Hunter asked.

"Luke went into her room this morning, and Ava now has bruises. The way she reacted last night, she was different."

"So you think she's telling the truth?"

"I don't know. I know Luke and he's many things, but a rapist?"

"A part of you must believe it."

"He could have anyone. Why would he resort to raping a girl who didn't want him?" He remembered the time he'd been with Ava twelve years ago. It was only one afternoon, and it was a time that stayed with him forever.

Running fingers through his hair, he could even remember the vanilla scent of her and how she felt against his body. He'd not been an asshole to her then or a bully in that room. He allowed himself to have a little taste of her.

BLACKMAILED BY HER BULLY

"I don't want to accuse him, Hunter. I need proof."

"I'll go and do some digging. I'll see what I can come up with. Do you want me to start now or would you like some company with your sheriff?"

"No, go. I don't need any help with the sheriff. I've also given Ava free rein. Make sure the men know not to let her go. I want an eye on her, but I don't want her hurt. Got me?"

"Yes."

Hunter left then, and Logan gritted his teeth.

Pulling out his cell phone, he dialed Grant.

"Hello, boss, what can I do for you?" Grant was one of the best men he had at garnering information from powerful men's wives. He'd sent him many times into different lions' dens to get him what he needed, and he always made sure he was well compensated.

"Ava," he said.

"What do you need to know?"

"Did she ever talk about what happened to her twelve years ago?"

"No. She spoke of something bad happening, but she never wanted to go into details. I figured she was referring to you."

"Was there anything that happened you found odd?"

"Not really. I mean, I went to take her to the swimming pool, but she had a panic attack. She wouldn't wear a swimsuit and she doesn't go as far as I can tell."

"That it?" he asked.

"It's all I can remember. Once you had the video, you weren't interested in me learning more. You want me to come and help?"

"No, you keep doing what I need. Thank you."

"Got it."

He hung up and rubbed at his temples. Nothing was helping him right now.

Going to his whiskey, he poured himself a generous shot and drank it down in one go, loving the burn.

With his head back in the game, he headed toward the library, and sure enough, there was the sheriff. The abusive prick that he was.

He wondered if he hated being controlled rather than being the one doing the controlling.

"You see anything you like?" Logan asked. "Nah, I don't think so. None of these are defenseless little boys."

"What is it you want? I can't keep coming whenever you need me."

"Oh, you will. Believe me. Or you won't like the consequences."

"You can't threaten me," he said.

"I just did."

"I got a call. Ava tried to call. She wants to speak to me. Why?"

"She seems to be under the impression she told you something else twelve years ago. Do you know anything about that?"

"I have no idea what she's talking about."

"You have no idea?" Logan asked. "No clue at all?"

"Ava has always exaggerated the truth. You saw the statements. I took down exactly what she told me. What lies has she been spilling to you?"

He stared at the sheriff. Something was off.

"She told me Luke raped her," he said.

The sheriff burst out laughing.

Logan didn't like his reaction. It was the exact same one he'd had when she told him.

"Did you laugh at her back then?"

"Son, I don't know what lies she is spreading, but you've got to get your head out of your ass. I did what the good justice system told me to do. What happened was because of her, not me. I followed protocol."

Logan grabbed him, slamming him to the desk, lifting him up, and doing the same again.

"Let's get one thing clear right now. I don't like you. I think you're a piece of shit who gets his kicks off hurting little boys. I can't stand you. You're useful to me by the information you can provide me. But if you ever laugh again at Ava, I will cut out your tongue. Do you understand me?"

The sheriff nodded.

Letting him go, Logan stepped back.

"Look, Luke could have any girl he wanted, even back then. He didn't need to force anything. I'm not saying she and Luke didn't have something going on. They probably did, and when he got bored and moved on, she felt ashamed."

"Did she report the rape to you?"

"Yes, she reported a rape. *You* were the person she named. No one else."

"So she's lying to me."

"Yes."

He nodded. "Get out. Do your job and don't allow anyone to come here. You know the rules."

With the sheriff dismissed, he made his way out of the library, and paused. He didn't know what to fucking do.

Ava was lying, but why did she sound so convinced of it?

There was no way to talk to Hunter.

Why had Luke hit her? Was it because of what she did to Logan? Logan ran fingers through his hair, not liking being clueless to what was going on.

Making his way up to her room, he found the door open. Her closet door was open, but her clothes were hung up.

Going to the window, overlooking the back yard, he saw her walking across the field. She still wore jeans and a shirt. She didn't have any shoes on, and for a few seconds, he watched her, wondering what was going on in her mind.

Was she thinking about her next lie?

Leaving her bedroom, he headed outside to find her still standing, looking up at the sky.

"Did you get to see the sheriff?" she asked.

"You have a way of eavesdropping when it's not wanted?"

"I saw him leave."

"Yes, you did."

"What did he say?" she asked.

He stared at her, seeing the hope in her eyes. Was this still an act? Nothing had changed.

"You did ask him, right?"

"He told me you never mentioned Luke. You only reported *me* for rape."

"What?"

"Just drop the act, okay? This is all fucking boring. Nothing happened, or did it and you want to hide it?"

"What the hell are you talking about?"

"Turn on the waterworks, if you think that's going to work?"

"Are you fucking kidding me right now?" Her voice rose as she screamed at him.

"What's the problem? Truth hurt? What exactly happened between you and Luke? Were you ashamed of what happened? Is that why you dragged my ass into it?"

"Nothing happened between us! He raped me. I'm not lying."

"Come on. You and I both know it didn't happen. You reported *me*, and I got my ass thrown in jail."

She opened her mouth, closed it, looked around her and shook her head. "And you know this because you were there?"

"Luke doesn't need to force someone. And *I'm* the one who went to jail over your accusation."

"You know, I didn't think it was actually capable of hating someone, but right now, I really know how to. The sheriff is lying, and seeing as I can't find any evidence or convince you of the truth, then what's the point? Luke's in on this with the sheriff. I don't know how or why, but he changed my statements. He had to have. I can't do this. I don't want to do this. Fuck it." She pushed past him, marching her way toward the doors.

"You're not going anywhere. You step foot out of the front door, I'll release the tapes."

She turned to look at him. "You know what, it doesn't matter. Release them. I don't give a fuck anymore. I'm tired of being trapped here with trying to get over what happened to me. Tell Grant thank you. He made me realize I wasn't a victim anymore. I'm the one with the power, but I'm not going to stick around here and let Luke hurt me further. He's already sneaked into my room, and there's no way I'm allowing him to have power or you. Go ahead, let it all out. Let the world know the truth. I don't care."

She stormed into the house, and he followed her, a little taken aback by the sudden turn within her. She went straight to her bedroom, and using the bag she'd packed everything in, she shoved items of clothing back into it.

"You really want to risk this? I'm not joking

around," he said.

"I don't care. I didn't accuse you twelve years ago. I never had a reason. Our time in that classroom I was with you. You were my first kiss, and if you must know, Logan, I'd wanted you to be my first. I will warn you, Luke is not your friend. He is your enemy, and he will try to destroy you. Every single chance he can get. You'd be best to get away from him when you have the chance." She zipped up the bag.

"I will release them, Ava."

"Do it." She glared at him. "I honestly don't care. I'm … I never meant for you to get dragged into this, but I know who I reported and it wasn't you. I've got to figure out what went wrong."

He stood in the doorway, not letting her get past.

"Please," she said.

"You really want to do this?"

"Do your worst, Logan. You think I haven't survived worse? Leave me the fuck alone. I mean it." She pushed him, but he didn't budge.

He wouldn't allow her to leave, but he was about to call her bluff. Stepping back, he let her go past, and he watched her.

"Last chance," he said. She held onto the door but didn't step back.

"I'm ready for whatever comes. You'll be the one making a big mistake, Logan. Not me."

She stepped over the threshold, and he dialed the number he had. He wasn't going to be blackmailed or pushed into a corner.

Within the hour the videos had been sent to every single resident within Crow Valley, including her in his office. She wanted to push him, he could push back.

When Luke, Riley, and Marvin got back to the house, they were all stunned.

"We stopped off at the diner for old times' sake. Everyone is talking about Ava—what did she do?" Riley asked.

"She left."

"You let her fucking leave?" Luke asked.

"She wasn't a prisoner. She had a choice, and she decided to test me. Now I'll wait and see what she does. She's going to be begging me before the end of the week. No one will hire her. She will have nothing, which is exactly how it should be." He watched Luke and couldn't get Ava's accusations out of his head.

There was no way something happened between Luke and Ava. He couldn't believe it. Luke was capable of many things, but raping a girl wasn't one of them.

He wouldn't doubt his friend, not now, not ever.

"You think she'll be back?" Riley asked.

"Yes, I do."

"Okay, call me stupid, but isn't this what you wanted?" Marvin asked. "You wanted your revenge, and now you have it. Shouldn't this be the end of it? Pack up shop, move on? You know, that kind of thing."

"You'd think it would be that easy, don't you? No, I want Ava to be at my mercy. I want her broken. Not only has she tried to ruin me but she's trying to take my friends down with her. I won't allow that. She will learn her place. Are you boys ready for the next step?" he asked. "Or are you all too chicken to stand beside me?"

"I'm in. All the way. I've got your back, Logan. Always," Luke said.

"Good."

Riley and Marvin joined in, and he held up his glass, saluting them.

Ava would pay one way or another, but it would be Logan who did the final snap. He'd waited too long. She wasn't going to get away with her lies. He was determined to get his revenge in all areas.

He was a patient man.

This was twelve years in the making.

What was a couple of extra days or weeks? Ava could have done this the easy way, but she'd taken it out of his hands and now he had no choice but to make sure she suffered one way or the other.

Chapter Seven

Twelve years ago

Ava stared at her reflection in the mirror. Her mother had forgotten to pick up a witch's costume and so she was having to go to the school's Halloween dance as a bloody nurse.

"I am sorry, honey. I didn't mean to screw it up."

She laughed. "You didn't. Honestly. I'll be fine. Look, all scary." The costume was the same as last year, only it was a little shorter because she'd grown, and now she had the whole sexy, bloody nurse thing down. Her breasts were threatening to spill out of the top, but it fit. Besides, if it got too cold, she'd be wearing a jacket. "How do I look?"

"Gorgeous. Will there be any cute zombies at the party?"

"Mom, please, I don't know. Probably. It depends on what you think is cute."

"Are there any guys you think of as cute?"

"Not really." She wrinkled her nose. "Right now, they're all dumb. You know."

Her mother laughed. "I hope you have fun."

"Me too. You and Dad looking forward to your trip?"

"Yes. A weekend away and our little girl is going to a Halloween party. It doesn't seem right."

She laughed. "It is. It will all be fine. You've got to trust me. You and Dad deserve some time away."

"What did I ever do to deserve a daughter like you?"

"You learn to trust her so she doesn't have a problem with anything." She hugged her mother. "I'm going to head out. I've got my key so you can lock the doors. I'll call you the minute I get home."

"Good. I don't know if I want to leave you."

"It'll be fine."

Walking out of her bedroom, she left her parents to finish packing while she made her way across town toward the high school. The students had been let loose, and everywhere was decorated with fake spider webs, ghosts, ghouls, goblins, everything. It screamed Halloween.

The moment she entered the main hall, heavy music blasted out.

She went straight to the punch stand, pouring herself a cup and staring out across the dance hall.

It was so crowded already with everyone dancing to the beat of the music. She sipped at the drink and tasted alcohol, really strong as well. Dumping the punch into the trash bin, she walked around the school, taking in the fear. She'd helped decorate. The only reason she came to the party was so her parents didn't feel guilty about going out on their trip.

She made her way back into the main hall, and before she could refuse someone dragged her onto the dance floor. She was shocked to see it was Logan who'd done it.

He seemed just as surprised as she was.

"Sorry, Anna said she'd come as a sexy nurse. Figured you were her."

Don't blush.

Anna was one of the most popular girls in school. Most guys wanted to date her, and girls wanted to be her.

He'd thought she was that girl, which meant, he thought she looked sexy in a bloody nurse's costume.

Get a grip, Ava. It means nothing.

He's a bully.

He falls in with Luke.

He's not a good guy.

A bad one. Really bad.

"Erm, you really should go and find her."

"Why? If she wanted to be found, she would be. You're here. I'm here. I don't see a reason to change it."

"But, wouldn't she want to see you?" she asked. "You are dating her."

"I don't date."

"Oh, okay."

The song came to an end, and she pulled away. "Thanks for the dance." She quickly rushed off the dance floor, wanting to be anywhere else.

As the evening wore on, she got a little bored and decided to leave the school. She stepped outside, but it was quiet. She saw a couple of people making out, but that was no different than most Halloweens.

Just as she was about to leave, someone grabbed her from behind, covering her eyes and mouth, moving her back into the school.

She had no idea where they were going until she was dumped into a room. It was dark, and she quickly rushed toward the door but it was locked from the outside.

Slamming her hand against the door, she tried to open it.

"Let me out of here. What the fuck!"

"It's no good."

She gasped, turning around, but of course, it was pointless. It was pitch black.

"Who are you?"

He chuckled. "It's Logan."

"Do you know who I am?"

"I'm guessing from the fear, you're Ava Marshall. My friends may or may not have mistaken you for Anna once again."

"I'm never wearing this costume again."

"Shame."

She ignored him, putting her hand against the door.

"How do we get out of here?" she asked.

"When they're good and ready to let us out. It's the basement. We're not getting out of here until they let us out from the outside."

"I know what it means." She closed her eyes but didn't see the point in doing so. It was dark. It wasn't like she was blocking out the scenery. "I have to get home."

"Will your parents be worried?"

"My parents aren't home. They've gone on a vacation, but they still want me to check in. Can't you call them? Your friends. Tell them they've made a mistake?"

She was hopeful they'd listen to him.

Logan's face lit up. He was sitting on the floor with his cell phone in his hand. He put the call onto speaker.

"Hello, the awesome Luke is here, how may I direct your call?"

She rolled her eyes. It was typical he was finding some way to joke about all of this. It wasn't funny. Not even close.

Blowing out a breath, she started to pace but didn't go very far in case of falling and hurting herself.

"Stop being a dick right now. You know who it is. Come and let us out."

"No can do, my friend. You're alone, and I suggest you make use of the time."

"You do know you've kidnapped Ava, right?"

"Yep."

The P came out with a resounding pop. She turned to look toward where Logan was, or at least where she thought he was.

"Like I said, my good friend, enjoy."

Luke hung up, and Logan cursed, throwing his cell phone across the floor.

"Did you really need to do that? It's probably broken now."

"I'll buy another one. They're not hard to replace. You may as well stop pacing."

Now that she'd been in there a while her eyes were growing accustomed to the dark. Sitting down on the floor, she winced. "Do you think there're any rats?"

"There better not be."

"Great. My parents are going to be pissed."

"Why? They're not home."

"They're expecting a call from me, and I've never left them hanging like this. I don't know why your friends have picked me to play this stupid prank on, but it's not fair. I don't like it." She breathed out a sigh. "I hate the dark."

"There's nothing here that will hurt you."

"Not even you?"

"I won't hurt you. Consider it a Halloween locked in treat."

"Oh, goody." She leaned her head back against the door or was it the wall now? She didn't know. "How long have you been here?"

"About ten, maybe twenty minutes before you showed up."

"I thought these guys were your friends."

"They are."

"Some friends you got who are willing to throw you in the school basement. They're really good guys." She couldn't help but fill her voice with sarcasm.

He burst out laughing. "You're cute when you're worried."

"I'm not trying to be cute."

"I didn't say you were trying anything, did I?" He winked at her. "Still cute."

"I don't want to talk about this right now."

He laughed, humming to himself. She didn't want to be down in the basement.

"Why would they throw you into the basement and no one else? Why not Anna?"

"I don't know the mysterious ways my friends work, Ava."

The time ticked by. It felt like hours but could have easily been only a few minutes. She had no way of telling the time and had left her cell phone back at home. Now she felt stupid.

She hoped her parents weren't worried about her.

The temperature had started to drop, and she wondered if the school was empty, deserted. She couldn't help but let out a shiver.

"Come here," Logan said.

"I'm good."

"Stop being a baby. You're cold. We can warm each other up."

"It's fine. I'll be fine. So long as your friends open the door."

"They're not opening it until the morning at least. Stop being difficult, come here, and hug me."

She rolled her eyes, but seeing as she was extremely cold, she crawled across the space toward him. She touched his leg first and immediately recoiled.

"I'm not going to bite."

"Sorry."

She moved in close, and to her surprise, he wrapped an arm around her, pulling her in close.

"See, not a problem."

He was much warmer than she was. The costume

she wore was too revealing, leaving nothing to the imagination.

Logan stroked her arm, and she rested her head on his shoulder. Rather than being awkward, it was nice. A lot nicer than she wanted it to be.

"Not so hard, huh?"

"I don't know. I'm putting a lot of faith in you that you aren't going to hurt me."

"Why would I hurt you?"

"You're part of a crowd who likes to. Not just me either, a lot of people. Don't you remember Dillon?"

"Oh, please, that was just funny."

"It wasn't funny. Neither is shoving people into lockers. Do you know how much that hurts?"

"Don't know. Never been on the receiving end of being pushed into one."

"Believe me, it hurts. Not to mention all the tripping. Name calling. Do I need to go on right now?" The last thing she wanted to do was to have to go into detail with part of the school bully gang what exactly it was he'd done.

"Why not? It seems to me you've got a lot of shit to get off your chest. Talk away. Fill the silence."

"And have you throw it all back in my face? No, thank you. I rather like the silence." She pressed her lips together.

Logan didn't stop holding her.

"Are you struggling to stay quiet?" he asked.

"Nope."

"You're going to be stubborn the whole night?"

"Yep."

He chuckled. "Two can play at that game."

****

Present day

It had been two days since Logan had released the

videos to everyone in town and also uploaded them online. So far, Ava had lost her job, and no one would serve her in town. She'd been booed out of the grocery store and ignored. Someone had even thrown an ice cream cone at her, and of course, she was denied everywhere.

Standing in her home, staring at the empty fridge, she knew she was going to have to either leave town, or do something.

She'd been to the sheriff's office three times to no avail. He was either out or she was thrown abuse until she had no choice but to leave.

What Logan had done … she didn't know if he'd ever really do it, but she'd clearly pushed him too far and now she was paying the price. There was nothing she could do. The videos were out, and she was all on her own. No one was going to help her.

Slamming the door closed, she pressed her head against it.

It will be fine.

The easiest option would be to take her belongings and run. To put the house on the market and to get the hell out of town. Only … she didn't want to get the fuck out of town. It pissed her off that Luke would be winning again.

He'd already turned Logan against her.

Now the entire town was against her, not that they'd believed her in the first place, but she'd hoped they would.

Luke was a monster.

How was it she was the only one to see it?

What the fuck had the sheriff done with her original statements to have people turn against her?

Grabbing her jacket, she stormed out of her house, not surprised to see the words "lying whore" scrawled across her front door.

Ignoring it, she closed the door and rushed across the lawn, heading toward town. She kept her head down.

"Bitch, you're a lying whore."

"We saw the videos. No one had to force you."

"You're nothing."

"Get your skank ass out of town."

Random people threw insults at her as she made her way across town, going straight to the sheriff. This time, she won't be bullied or pushed aside.

There was no way she was going to let anyone push her out of her own town. Luke had won twelve years ago, and in the past couple of days. But he wouldn't win any other time.

As Ava entered the station, Susan stood with a sigh. "He's not here."

She didn't even bother listening to Susan. For a town where crime never happened, the sheriff was sure busy all the time, which was strange considering he loved sitting in his office with his feet up.

Without knocking, she opened up his office door, and there he was, alone, feet up on the desk, reading a magazine and this time, nibbling on a sandwich.

"I'm sorry, Sheriff, she barged—"

Ava didn't give her a chance to finish. She slammed the door closed and flicked the lock into place.

"Are you attempting to take me hostage? If so, I should warn you it's a—"

"What did you do with them?" she asked.

"Whatever do you mean?" he asked.

"Cut the bullshit. I know you manipulated those statements. I never once mentioned Logan, other than to say where Luke may be." She slammed her hand against the desk, leaning on it as she yelled at him.

Her anger had risen. Seeing the proof of the

sheriff just sitting there, in his chair, it annoyed her, filled her with a rage she couldn't even begin to describe.

"You need to leave," the sheriff said.

"I know my statement. I remember what happened."

"Please, nothing happened."

"If nothing happened why wouldn't you do the rape test? Why wasn't Luke arrested? Why is he walking around town as if nothing happened, but Logan is the one pissed off!"

"The accusations you have flying around right now, you better be careful. You should learn to take responsibility for your actions."

"Fuck you! You're a monster. I will find something on you and make sure the entire town knows what you did. The girls in this town need to be protected."

"Again, your lies are going to get you in trouble. I saw the videos. You think I don't know what I'm dealing with?"

"I was an eighteen-year-old girl. He cornered me. What you saw was me trying to get past everything." She shook her head. "You don't deserve to wear a badge."

Turning on her heel, she left the sheriff's office, determined to find something, anything on him, but she had no way of knowing.

Walking down the street, she headed toward her home only to stop when she saw Luke, parked and waiting.

There was no way she could stop him from approaching. If she got to her house, he'd only shove his way inside and then she'd be alone with him.

Tapping her fingers on her thigh, she nibbled her lip, trying to make a decision.

"Come on, Ava, you don't want it to be like this,"

he said.

Turning on her heel, she rushed back into town, but she didn't go into the diner. She went straight to the library. He was following her, but he wouldn't do anything if she was in a public place. He couldn't risk it.

Inside the library, she ignored the angry language from the women working behind the counter.

Logan had really messed up her reputation.

Ignoring them, she dialed Logan's number. It had been mailed to her with a card, offering her a second chance. She didn't know who mailed it, but she kept the card on her, and she held it now within her grasp.

There was no way she was going to confront Luke, not right now. She didn't have the strength to do anything.

The town was against her.

Logan hated her.

There was only one option for now, and that was to get Logan.

"Hello," he said.

"It's me."

"I'm sorry, who is it?"

"Ava Marshall."

"Now, why would you be calling me?"

She looked up to see Luke standing in the doorway of the office.

"I want you to come and pick me up. I think we need to talk, don't you?"

"Are you having difficulty already?" he asked.

"I want to negotiate." She wasn't going to talk anymore on the phone, not with people listening. "Will you please send someone to the library? It's urgent."

Luke closed the door, but he didn't say a word.

Her heart began to pound.

"Hunter is already on his way. He'll be with you

in a couple of minutes."

"Good. I look forward to seeing him." She put the phone down, and Luke grabbed her, shoving her up against the wall with his arm across her neck. "He's coming for me. Hunter was already on his way."

"You think you're so smart, don't you?"

"I think I'm willing to do whatever it takes to make sure you pay."

"How is that working out for you? I heard no one is willing to listen to you."

"Fuck you."

"One day soon, you will. Do you really think Logan is the one calling the shots? It won't be long until he's passing you around for all of his friends to enjoy."

"That day is not today," she said.

She had to find a way for Logan to see the truth. Tears sprang to her eyes, and she glared at him.

"What's it going to be, Luke? Are you still going to be here when Hunter comes? I don't think he likes you."

"Oh, please, Hunter is Logan's little lapdog, but it's me he listens to."

"You better hope so. One day, he will believe me, and then your act will be up. I don't know what it is you did to make all of my statements to go away."

Luke burst out laughing. "Well, darling, that will be for another time, won't it?" He stroked her cheek. "Until then." The pressure tightened across her throat, and she stared at him, waiting for him to end it. To kill her.

Would dying be so bad after what he'd done to her?

He wouldn't allow her to find out as he pulled away and she was able to breathe again.

She took several deep breaths, inhaling.

"We don't want the likes of you here anymore," Trudy, her old boss, said, coming to the office. "Whatever dirty call you just made, you better hope it wasn't a fortune or we're billing you."

"You've got me all wrong," she said.

"No, I don't. Once a whore, always one. I know what I saw, and you didn't fall too far from your parents either."

She didn't allow them to see how much their words hurt.

Don't show weakness.

Hold your head high.

Stepping around Trudy, she ignored the glares, walking toward the front doors.

Hunter was already walking toward her, and she rushed out.

Before she knew what she was doing, she threw her arms around him. "I'm so grateful you came."

"Does this have to do with Luke I see trying to avoid being detected?" he asked.

She pulled away and nodded.

There was no way she could trust Hunter.

"Come on." He took her hand, leading her back to the car.

She didn't know whom she could trust. The sheriff should have been the only person, but he'd lied and look how he acted now, as if *she'd* been lying the whole time.

Hunter helped her into the car, and she dropped her head into her hands.

"He's dangerous, you know, Luke is. To Logan."

"I know."

She turned to look at Hunter. "You know?"

"I see the way he looks at my boss. There's no love or happiness there. Just anger, hatred, and even resentment."

"Haven't you told him? Told Logan?"

"They've been friends a hell of a lot longer than I've been his. I don't know everything, only what I've been told."

"Luke was always the asshole. The main bully. Logan … he did things, but he wasn't as bad as Luke."

"I have to disagree. I've seen the way this town has treated you and that was all Logan. Luke had nothing to do with it."

"He had everything to do with it." She couldn't help but yell. People refused to see the truth, and she was growing tired of them believing Luke was some little saint.

"You claim Luke raped you."

She covered her ears and screamed at the unfairness of it all. Hunter didn't stop her as she screamed again and again until her voice was hoarse.

Hunter had stopped on the side of the road, and she stared out as the tears wrecked her entire body. She couldn't stop sobbing.

Everything had been so fucked up.

She sniffled. "It's fine. The only person who believed me back then was my dad. He knew I wasn't a liar."

Each word came out on a croak.

"That's a lot of work to cover up," Hunter said. "There's no rape kit."

"Because I was told I wouldn't need one. My parents were assured they had everything they needed." She laughed. "Wow, at every turn I was taken for a fucking idiot." She looked toward him. "How did you know that?"

"Logan has me looking at possible leads that would in any way indicate Luke was a rapist."

"Wow," she said. "I don't know what to do anymore. I never reported Logan. We … what we did with each other was consensual. I liked him a lot. I didn't report him. I don't know how he ended up taking the fall for Luke." She sniffled. "I guess Luke's parents had a way of manipulating the sheriff."

"What did you say?"

"Luke's parents were one of the richest in town. I think I heard something a while back that the fortune had been taken due to bad debts, not paying taxes, that kind of thing."

"No, the part about the parents and the sheriff."

She shrugged. "I don't know. Maybe his parents blackmailed the sheriff. I don't know what they could have on him. He's been sheriff for as long as I can remember. It's his job. It's who he is." She looked toward Hunter to see him frowning. "What is it?"

"It's nothing."

"You have something going on. What is it?"

"We're not besties, Ava. Not even close."

She growled in frustration. "I'm so over male ego. I'm serious right now. Have you seen the way the town is treating me? Have you seen what they painted on my door? What they've called my parents?" She shook her head. "I don't even know why I'm hoping you'd care. You'd have to have actual feelings, which you clearly do not."

"I've seen."

"Then you know I can't even drive to the store for groceries. My car ran out of gas yesterday. They won't let me fill it up, refused to let me even try." She wiped away the tears, not wanting to show even more weakness. "I don't know why I'm telling you all of this."

"I don't know why you need to either, but you are."

"I'm sorry," she said.

"Don't be."

"I'm being shoved out of this town. I didn't do anything wrong. Luke hurt me because he wanted to get to Logan."

"Why?"

"He didn't want Logan to have a … first. Once he'd taken it there was no way of him ever being able to claim that part of me."

"Your virginity?"

She sniffled and nodded her head.

Hunter sighed. "I'm not on your side. I will never be on your side. I'm working for Logan. He's the only one I care about."

"Okay."

"If, and this is a big fucking if, there's something in the Sheriff's past linked to Luke's parents, I'll find it. I'm not working for you. I'm merely doing a job for my boss."

****

Logan sat behind his desk as Ava walked into the office. Hunter held her arm, not that she had any real reason to escape from him. She had come to him after all, not the other way around.

"Now this is intriguing," he said. "That will be all, Hunter."

Ava stood, arms folded, waiting.

"Aren't you going to beg me?" he asked.

"This is what you wanted, right? Me at your mercy. You've got it. I can't even leave town. No one will help me unless I walk right on out of here, and I can't do that."

"I did warn you."

"I know." She didn't say anything more.

He stared at her. Her eyes were puffy, bloodshot,

and her face looked a mess as well. Devoid of makeup but she looked deep in despair.

"You didn't have to come to me for help, you do know that."

"I know what I do and don't have to do, Logan. I'm not stupid."

"Now you have some fire in your gut. You think you can call the shots here, is that it?"

"I don't think anything. I'm just trying to get through all of this. What is it you want?" she asked.

He leaned back in his chair, staring at her.

Women had been coming to his home for the past couple of days, begging for his attention, offering up their bodies, and he'd denied them all. There was only one woman he was interested in. Hunter had told him how within an hour of the videos being released, she'd become public enemy number one.

He got to his feet and rounded the desk, standing in front of her.

She had the prettiest hazel eyes he'd ever seen.

"I'm heading out to the city tomorrow. I want you to come with me."

"You do?" She frowned.

"Nothing is keeping you here, and I have no desire to be in such a fickle town. If you're willing to hand over your body and your life to me, I will protect you." He shoved his hands into his pockets. He'd never intended to make this kind of deal.

When he started this path of revenge, he'd planned to crush her, to destroy her, but after Hunter had told him what people did to her … he wasn't happy. This didn't give him any kind of pleasure to know her struggle.

She burst out laughing. "You expect me to believe you're going to protect me? You. You released those videos. You had possession of them." She ran fingers through her hair, turned her back to him and walked a few steps, before turning, and walking back to him. She blew out a breath. "This is so crazy."

"So is being dragged down to a station on charges that are bogus," he said.

"I've told you already—" She stopped holding her hand up. "You know what, I will make you eat your words. I will win this."

"Oh, I look forward to the fire. It's about time you start fighting back. Whatever you think it is you need to do. I'm all ears. Until then, you've got to make a choice. Belong to me or be at the mercy of a town that has turned you to shit."

"Wow, not a whole lot of choices."

He shrugged. "You should have stayed. You called my bluff, and I don't like to have that happen. I would have kept those videos private, but you pushed the issue."

"What exactly will I have to do?"

He smiled. "It's nothing illegal. You will belong to me, and in doing so, I'll protect you."

"Belonging to you? What exactly does that mean?"

"You'll do exactly as I tell you. No questions asked. Your body will be mine. When I tell you to ride my dick, you will worship it. You'll do everything I say."

"I don't want to be shared."

"If I share you, I'll be the one to make the decision."

"I don't know if I can do this."

"Then be sure to let the door knock you on the ass on the way out. You're mine. You don't get a fucking say in doing anything. Your call, Ava, but you're wasting my time."

135

"If—" She stopped, and he waited.

Time passed, and he grew even more curious as to what she was thinking or feeling. Ava wasn't easy to read.

"If there's something I can't handle, will you call a stop to it? I mean if I'm afraid and I can't stand what is going to happen. Will you force me to keep on going or will you show some compassion?"

He leaned back in his chair. "Yes."

She breathed a sigh of relief.

"I'm not a monster, Ava. I'm not going to make this easy on you though. I will have to be sure you can't handle anything. You're at my mercy, and if I think you can take something, I will make you get past your fear."

She nodded. "I don't have a choice, do I?"

He shrugged. "The options are in front of you. I will be leaving in ten minutes. Make the decision and join me out in the car."

"I haven't packed or anything."

"Don't worry, I'll buy you anything you need."

He got to his feet and headed out of the office.

Hunter leaned against the car, staring straight ahead.

"What is she doing?" he asked.

"Making a decision. This town is leaving a bad taste in my mouth, and I want to go."

Hunter nodded, opening the door.

"If she's not out in ten minutes, we leave, no looking back."

Pulling out his cell phone, he made a note of the time.

It took Ava three minutes to make a decision.

She rushed out of the house and didn't wait for Hunter to open the door. She climbed in beside him, buckling her seatbelt.

The deal was set.

Chapter Eight

Twenty-four hours later, Ava stood, arms folded, in Logan's penthouse suite in the middle of the city. They didn't come to his home straight away, but he'd taken her shopping to get her a whole new wardrobe. The price tags on everything surprised her.

He spared no expense.

She didn't want to think how he got the money. Her mind was already flooded with all the bad things he did.

Running fingers through her recently styled hair, she snorted. The length had stayed the same, but there had been layers put into it. The split ends had been removed. No dye job. Logan knew how he wanted to dress up his fuck toy.

Like now, she wore one of the sheer negligees he'd bought her. There was no reason to wear the damn thing as it didn't exactly cover anything. She'd be better off standing with her hands covering everything of real importance.

So far, he'd been too busy to make any sudden demands.

Hunter was with her. He sat at the kitchen counter, sipping at his coffee, looking at his cell phone.

"Shouldn't you be with Logan?" she asked.

"Not until he has a guard for you. I'm here to keep an eye on you."

"Does he think I'm a flight risk?"

"No. Logan has made many enemies. By bringing you back to the city, he also put your life at risk."

She turned to look at Hunter. "You're kidding?"

"No."

"Who is he?"

Hunter turned off his cell phone and spun, giving

her his full attention. She would have worn a robe if Logan had granted her one, but he said she didn't need to hide. Hunter had seen her completely naked so it wasn't like any of this was new to him.

She wanted to hide her body from him but chose not to. There was no point in trying to expend energy she didn't have.

"I can't tell you exactly who he is, but I will warn you, don't push him."

"Great, you don't really tell me anything. Just make me more nervous."

"It's for your own safety. Logan, he's powerful."

"Is it all legal?" she asked.

Hunter lifted a brow.

"Of course, you won't tell me."

She moved away from the window and sat down on the sofa in the living room, staring up at the large television with no reason to turn it on. She didn't want to watch anything.

"Is this because of what happened?" she asked. "Did he turn this way because of what Luke did?"

"Yes."

She looked up to see Hunter had followed her. "You believe me?"

"Not yet, but something doesn't add up in the sheriff's finances. I'm checking it out. I'm choosing not to upset you with claiming you lied."

"You know I was laughed at when I told the Sheriff. When I gave him my statement?"

"How long was it between the attack and you giving it?" Hunter asked.

"Erm, a couple of hours, maybe. I don't know. I … I was using the school's swimming pool. I loved to go for a swim and it was the only one in town, but they let it stay open when there was a football practice. I'd spent too long in the water when it happened. Luke was there." She stopped. "I don't want to talk about it anymore."

"Was the only other time you did when you gave the statements?"

"Yes."

She flinched as Hunter put a hand on her shoulder.

"Does Luke come here?"

"No. He's never been here alone. This is Logan's private place. He has another apartment a few blocks away from here whenever he wants to meet the guys."

"Does he trust them?" she asked.

"Logan trusts very few people. I don't even believe he trusts me. You're the first woman he has brought here."

"Is that supposed to give me comfort?" she asked, smiling.

"It should. It means regardless of what he believes, you're still important to him."

"Why are you being nice to me?"

Hunter shrugged.

"It's probably a trick. Logan put you up to it."

"No. I figure if what I think happened did, you've had a rough ride of it."

"He said no one would believe me," she said, tears filling her eyes. She didn't want to talk, but here she went, spilling the truth.

"Luke?"

"Yes. Afterward, he … I…" She pressed her lips together. "It hurt so much, and he laughed. He said I was a real woman now. He said a few other things, but he warned me. Told me no one would ever believe me. Why would he rape me when he could have any girl? He was the most popular guy in school. I don't know why I'm telling you this."

"It's fine."

"It was like he already knew, you know? That he wasn't going to be punished for what he did. He never was. All this time I thought he'd been dealt with. The sheriff told me I didn't need to worry. I'd never see him again."

"You didn't think to question where he went? What happened?" Hunter asked.

She snorted. "I was an eighteen-year-old girl. Me and my parents, we watched cop shows but didn't know how it worked. None of us did. The sheriff was to be trusted, and we had no reason to doubt him. Why would we?"

"Because that is what people do. They get curious."

"Well, guess what, we weren't. I was too busy reeling from what had happened to me." She closed her eyes, leaning her head back. "I don't want to talk about this anymore. The two people who only ever believed me are gone. You don't. I don't see what the point is. All this time I thought Luke had gone to prison. I had no idea it was Logan." She sniffled. She got to her feet, growling. "It's not fair. I can't believe how foolish I was, and my parents. We believed the sheriff, and all this time, it was Logan who paid for Luke's crimes. Even now, he thinks I'm lying—and for good reason. He wrongly went to prison for something he didn't do."

She ran her fingers through her hair and started to pace the living room.

"I need a shower," she said.

"While you're here, be careful."

"What do you mean?"

"Luke doesn't drop by here uninvited, but I don't know what Logan has planned for you. I don't even know why he's brought you here, but be careful."

"Aw, thank you, you care?"

He laughed. "Nah, I don't care about you. I care about Logan, and I happen to believe Luke is a lying scumbag, and I don't trust him." Hunter stood.

"You believe me?"

He opened his mouth and closed it again. "Let's say I believe Luke and his parents at the time may have had the power you talk about to make certain things happen. It doesn't mean I believe *you*."

Hope fell from her. There was no point in expecting him to help her. He didn't believe her. No one did.

"I need to shower." Without looking back at him, she went straight toward the en-suite bathroom. Removing her clothes, she climbed beneath the spray, turning it on, tilting her head back, and gasping as the cold jet hit her in the face.

She needed the shock of the cold to wash over her. To try to gain some control because she was so close to losing her mind and herself.

"It'll be okay."

She didn't want to talk to herself, but it seemed she was the only one in her life who believed her.

"I'm fine."

Turning her back to the shower, she tilted her head back so it got all of her hair, running her hands through the strands. When it was nice and wet, she reached for the soap. Lathering up her entire body, she started on her face before working down.

In the back of her mind was the cruel memory of Luke's taunt, of how he held her down, kept her in place as he violated her in the worst way.

She let out a shriek when someone touched her.

Opening her eyes, she saw Logan had joined her in the shower.

"What the hell?" she said.

"You don't have to be afraid. I arrived home a couple of minutes ago."

"Where's Hunter?"

Her heart raced, and she hated that with just a few memories she could be reduced to a quivering mess. This wasn't how her life was supposed to turn out.

She wanted no memory of that monster near her. Luke wouldn't win.

Logan took the bar of soap. "He's gone. Said he needed to go and do some thinking."

"Oh."

"Now, this is a pleasant surprise. You, naked in my shower. I had no idea you knew me so well."

"I was dirty. I needed to wash."

He chuckled. "Your dirty talk needs some work. Here, let me." He took her arm and turned her gently so her back was pressed to his front.

The hard ridge of his cock butted against the base of her back. She kept her eyes open, and Logan's lips brushed across her ear going to her neck.

"I've thought about you all day."

"I've been right here."

"Oh, I know it, and I love it." He bit down, and she let out a moan.

His soaped hands coming up to cup her breasts. He pinched the nipples.

"I had no idea I would enjoy having a woman's company so much, but then you're not just any woman, are you, baby? No, you're my woman."

Was she his woman or just someone he'd brought along to hurt for past sins she had no idea were hers?

She didn't know what the sheriff had done until recently.

Logan and Hunter truly believed she was lying,

143

even though she had no reason to hurt him. The sheriff had covered his tracks, and there was no way for her to stop Logan from believing the lies that had been spun. She'd been too young, too stupid to ask questions. She wouldn't make the same mistake again. Logan hadn't done anything wrong, and she didn't make lying a habit. *Luke* needed to pay.

His fingers slid down her body, going between her thighs.

Logan spun her back around so she was facing him, and he lifted one thigh up and over his hip, resting his cock at the juncture of her thighs.

"You've been thinking of me while you've been away?"

"Yes."

"Where have you been?" she asked.

"Busy, working. I can't just up and leave so easily without problems being dealt with. People needing to be taught a lesson."

"What kind of work do you do?"

"A lot of everything."

Before she could ask any more questions, he took her lips in a possessive kiss, and she moaned his name, whimpering as he slid his tongue into her mouth. She cupped his cheek, kissing him back with the same passion, feeling the tightness in her body evaporate to make way for the pleasure of his mouth, his tongue, his everything.

"Do you have any idea what it is you do to me, every single fucking day?"

"No, I don't know."

He let go of her leg, and his lips traveled down her body going to her neck, sucking on her pulse before moving further down to her nipples.

She watched him. He held her tits up in his hands

as some kind of offering before teasing over each nipple. His tongue glided over each one before he used his teeth, sinking them into the flesh.

She cried out his name, not wanting him to stop, and he didn't. No, he kept on licking and sucking at each nipple until he moved onto the next one. There was no rush to him.

He was the one in charge, and she was merely a pawn in his game.

In that very moment, she didn't have a problem being whatever he wanted or needed from her. She'd give him anything, so long as he didn't stop.

He sank to his knees before her. It was such an odd place for him to be, kneeling, looking up at her.

He took her foot, resting it on the edge of the stall. He went from her ankle, kissing up the inside of her thigh, and she couldn't look away from what he was doing.

When he got to her pussy, she cried out. His tongue went between her slit, sliding through from her clit, down to her entrance, and back up.

She closed her eyes, and he bit down hard. She cried out and looked down at him.

"I didn't give you permission to close your eyes. You're supposed to look at me, not anywhere else but at me, got it?"

Nodding her head, he waited, clearly making sure she did as she was told. It was kind of odd having him command her in the shower while he was on his knees before her, but she made no move to stop him.

His tongue went back between her slit, and she basked in his touch, wanting him more than anything.

"Do you have any idea how crazy you make me," he said. "I was supposed to be listening today to some very important details, but all I could think about was how good you were going to taste and feel. I wanted your tight little pussy wrapped around my dick, sliding up and down me. Once I've taken care of you here, you're going to be doing exactly that."

He sucked on her clit, and in that moment, she would have given him anything he wanted, without a single question asked. His tongue flicked back and forth, making her melt with every single touch. It was next to impossible not to be aroused, especially as he gripped her ass, holding her tight as he licked at her.

Logan used his teeth and tongue to create the perfect sensation, and the need built within her, becoming almost to the point of pain and pleasure, but combined it was a heady experience.

She never wanted to stop.

Not as he feasted from her pussy, drawing her so close to orgasm, but he wouldn't let her fall. He teetered her on the edge, and the abyss was so close. She could feel it.

He had all the power, but within that moment, as he held her, she knew she was safe. It was a scary thought to think the man who'd once again put her in her rapist's path could also protect her, but she knew he would. Luke would never strike while she was with Logan. She just had to find a way to reveal the truth, but there was no way of doing that, not if the sheriff had altered her statements. He didn't even get her to confirm the written statement he'd copied. Only asked for her signature. She'd been so stupid and naive. What reason did they truly have to believe he'd lie?

Pushing those thoughts from her mind, she wouldn't let them plague her right now. Not as Logan pushed two fingers inside her and started to work them in and out, pushing her to the edge, but not letting her fall over it.

He kept her poised, calm, waiting on the precipice.

"Come for me, Ava, I want to feel it."

He did something with his fingers, twisting them inside her, and she had no choice. The pleasure rushed over her. She screamed his name, not wanting him to stop as he made her come. She was on fire for more and begged him to keep on going.

Looking down at his face, she saw he was wet and the shower didn't even touch him, so all of it was from her.

He lifted up, and before she knew what was happening, he had her in his arms. She let out a cry as he carried her out of the shower. Both of them were still wet, and he laid her on the bed.

"Logan, what are you doing?"

"I'm going to take my time with you. That's what I'm doing."

He kissed her hard. She tasted herself.

"And we're going to have some much-needed fun. What do you say?"

****

Being back in the city, in his domain, was a heady experience. Logan stared down at his woman, Ava, in his bed, where she was supposed to be. Bringing her to where he was king, he could have anything he wanted. Throw her at the men, sell her, make an example out of her, and people would turn the other way, like they did in Crow Valley, only here, there were people who would do a lot worse.

At the click of his fingers, she could be anything he wanted, and there were far more willing to bend to his will.

He'd always had a cruelty within him. Even as a young kid, bringing pain, it was part of who he was.

Bullying people to get what he wanted was second nature to him and so very easy. It really didn't bother him to have people whimper and cry, to beg for him to let them go. Seeing how weak they were, he relished being the one in power. Of course, there were always limits to being a bully in high school.

For the most part, they stayed out of his way, and Luke was more than happy to take on the weak.

Logan, he enjoyed watching people suffer, but fighting the weak wasn't the appeal. No, he liked to fight the strong. To come out the victor, there was the real fight.

After he was wrongly accused, his parents had lost their fortune trying to win appeals to get him released. Their fight had been for nothing, as he'd done his time, before finally being released early for good behavior. He'd come to the city in the hope of starting a new life, one where no woman would dare spin their lies again. Only, a guy with a sexual assault charge as well as a jail term hanging over his head, no one wanted to hire him. Who would? Women were everywhere, and one look at his past, and well, he'd found life to be particularly difficult, but he hadn't stopped. Being incarcerated, he'd made a great deal of friends, and he knew how the world worked. It didn't take him long to figure shit out.

With all of his anger and aggression, he'd done the only thing he could think of doing: he fought.

Every single day, he signed his name up and made a name for himself. Underground fighting was a big deal in the city. Men and women made a lot of money off the sweat and blood of fights. The death fights were the biggest gamble, and he'd entered a couple, coming out victorious.

He'd been the most vicious, and he'd never lost a

fight.

"What is it?" Ava asked, drawing him back to the present.

She was a woman, and he'd had to fight a couple back in his day. Hurting her should be easy for him. If she'd not done what she did, he wouldn't be where he was now. He'd be back in Crow Valley.

But did you ever want that?

Did she do you a favor?

He was clearly fucked in the head because he didn't think anything she did was worth what he'd gone through.

The power.

The money.

The fear.

All of it was part of his life.

It was what separated him from the boy she knew.

He wasn't Logan Stanford, little rich boy who could do what he wanted. No, this time, he was the monster people feared. The fighter who was nothing who took down the crime lord who tried to own him.

One day, he'd tell her the story, but for now, his dick was hard, and he didn't want to go down memory lane. There was no need to.

Taking possession of her lips, he heard her moan, wrapping her arms around him. He spun her around so he was the one on the bed, and she straddled him.

"Let me feel you."

She smiled at him, and it sure as shit melted his heart. Ava lifted up, and he helped her, holding the hard length of his dick as she slowly sank down on him.

He closed his eyes, basking in the wet heat consuming him as she sat on him. When she was seated to the hilt, he ran his hands up and down her thighs, watching her.

"What is it?" she asked, another teasing smile on those curvy lips.

"It's you. It will always be you." He stroked a finger up her body, across one full breast and moving back down toward her navel and to her clit.

The moment he touched her, she closed her eyes, gasping and lifting up.

"Ride my dick," he said.

Part of him wanted to push her to the bed, spread her legs wide, and fuck her hard. Not giving her a chance to want to stop and showing her who was the boss, but he always wanted to see her naked, writhing on him, begging for more.

Her nipples were nice and hard, and as she started to bounce on his dick, he watched them, mesmerized with each drop and fall. Her tits were natural.

He stopped touching her clit, stroking his hands up her body, to cup those delightful mounds. The moment he did, she let out a moan, and he pinched the ends. She ground down on his cock, and he loved how tight she got when he applied a little pain to those peaked ends.

Without pulling out of her, he spun them back so he was the one between her thighs. He grabbed her hands, pushing them above her head, keeping her locked in place as he bit down on her neck.

He felt possessed, needing to mark her precious skin with his touch so anyone who saw would know who she belonged to.

Being back in the city, he was himself again. Not some snot-nosed boy looking for revenge. It had all been too easy getting Ava back in his life.

With a few threats and clicks of his fingers, he could have anything.

Ava, though, she liked to put up a fight, and he was more than okay with that.

He pulled out of her tight heat, staring down at her cunt, seeing how wet she was. He wanted to flood her pussy, to have her dripping with his cum. While he owned her, she would only have one cock, and it would be his. Wrapping his fingers around his length, he worked it up and down, pulling back the foreskin as he did.

"On your knees," he said.

She didn't argue with him.

"Spread those legs. Keep them wide open." He climbed off the bed and went to the bottom drawer in his cabinet against the far wall.

Pulling out a tube of lubricant, he knew there was only one place he wanted to be inside tonight.

On his walk back to the bed, he smeared a generous amount of lubrication all over his cock. Climbing back onto the bed, he squirted some over her ass, and she gasped. When she made to move, he pressed a hand against her back.

"Don't move."

"Logan."

"Did I say you can talk? Shut up before I put your mouth to good work on someone else's dick."

He wouldn't bring Hunter into the room. There was only so much of Ava he was willing to share, and too many had seen her naked already.

You released the videos, dickhead.

It didn't matter what he'd done. He couldn't undo it, even though he currently had a team removing all traces of them from anyone who could easily see them. He wasn't a total monster, and he did wish to right that wrong.

She was silent as he worked the lubrication

against her ass.

He wondered if she was aroused when Grant did this.

Not going there.

Everything he'd done over the years had brought him to this moment, and he wasn't going to regret a single decision, even if he didn't like what he'd done.

There was no stopping it or changing it. He had to live with what he'd done.

Pushing the tip of his finger against her ass, he started to tease her open, to prepare her, to get her ready for his dick. In and out he worked, adding a second finger and pushing her open, trying to get her spread for him.

She whimpered his name, and he slapped her ass. "What did I tell you about speaking?"

He didn't want to hear her voice, but for her to be quiet.

When she was silent once again, he touched her clit with his other hand, combining the pleasure for her, getting her used to the feel of his fingers, taking his time, not wanting to hurt her.

He waited until she was ready for more, when she took two of his fingers with ease and began to rock back against him.

If he was anyone else, he'd take his sweet time letting her get accustomed to him, taking weeks to stretch that tight little asshole.

Instead, he was impatient and wanted her all now, without waiting.

He didn't believe in being patient for anything, and he had no problems taking what he wanted.

With the tip of his cock at her anus, he slowly, inch by inch, sank inside her. She cried out, and he paused, working her clit so she was distracted as he took

her.

His cock was far bigger than Grant's. He'd seen the other guy completely naked to know he was no competition when it came to the length of his dick. He was the one with all the power, no one else.

As he stroked her clit, he thrust in, until he was finally seated balls deep within her. It was tight, fucking hot, and he got a thrill knowing she'd taken him all.

Gripping her hips, he waited while she got used to the feel of him. He wasn't a total monster and knew she had to be feeling a little full, but again, he wasn't a patient guy.

With his hands on her hips, he pulled out of her.

"Touch your clit, baby. I'm not going to stop and you're going to love me being in this ass, so you better start enjoying it."

He reached between her thighs, finding her fingers already stroking her clit.

"Good girl." He worked in and out of her.

At first, he started out slowly, giving her a chance to accommodate him, taking his sweet time, watching her hot ass open up around his cock.

She moaned his name, whimpered it as he worked in and out, giving her more, speeding up. His thrusts started to show his impatience as he worked her, going deeper until their flesh slapped together as he fucked her harder.

He heard and felt as she came, finding her release before him. This time, he didn't mind her coming without him, especially as he wasn't far behind her.

When he came, he did so hard, filling her hot ass with his cum.

He held himself deep within her, waiting, gaining control before he finally eased out of her.

Unable to look away, he saw some of his cum

leak out of her and he pressed a kiss to her ass cheek.

"Stay there," he said.

Climbing off the bed, he made his way toward the bathroom. He wouldn't look at himself in the mirror because he didn't want to even think about what he saw there. This was nothing.

Ava was here for his mere amusement, and it was nothing more.

Walking back to the bedroom with a washcloth in hand, he placed it against her anus and cleaned her up.

He left again, rinsing out the cloth and throwing it in the laundry basket. On his way back to the bedroom, he stopped in the doorway. Ava had moved from her position; she was lying on his side of the bed, curled up, and he saw some tears in her eyes.

Without saying a word, he climbed in behind her.

He didn't care what the tears were for.

Wrapping his arms around her waist, he pulled her back against him, but she fought.

"You can fight me now, Ava, or I can kick you out in the street for the night, naked. You can see how you fare. A naked woman like you would be easy pickings."

"I can't believe we just did that. I let you do that."

"Ava, you wanted it, just like I did."

"But, it's … even … I don't know. I'm so confused."

He sighed and reached over her head, turning on the light. She tried to turn it off, but he captured her hand, stopping her from touching it.

"I'm thinking you're needing a spank to realize your place," he said. "This isn't the first time someone has taken your ass, and I'm sure it won't be the last. Why are you reacting like this?"

"The last time … with…"

"Grant!" He was growing impatient.

It had been a long day, and frankly he was tired, sated, and in need of some beauty sleep. Not to analyze the way she'd been fucked by his orders of one of his men.

"Yes, even when me and Grant did that, it didn't end well."

Now he paused. "What?"

"I, I didn't want to do it, but he said it would help me get over my issues. It didn't help."

Now, he was angry. "Are you saying Grant forced you?"

"No, no, he never did that. It wasn't like you're saying. I'm making a mess of this."

If Grant so much as touched her in force, he'd fucking kill him. "Then tell me exactly what it is you mean?"

"It never felt like this," she said. "With Grant, I wasn't really thinking about him or what it would mean. I did what I had to in order to get the moment over. It wasn't rape. I didn't want my past to constantly get in the way, and I was tired of not enjoying anything. He helped in his own way. He just wasn't who I wanted or who I needed."

"Who was it you needed?"

"I don't know. I guess someone who wasn't being ordered to do a job. It's probably why I couldn't always allow myself to get comfortable with him. He wouldn't allow himself to because I was nothing more than a job."

Chapter Nine

Until Logan believed her, Ava had made a vow that she wouldn't bring up what Luke did to her. There was no point, but one day soon, she'd have the truth, and then it was up to Logan what he did with it.

After she'd revealed her feelings about Grant, he'd not said anything. He'd stared at her for a couple of minutes, maybe even longer, but he'd turned off the light, pulled her close, and gone to sleep.

Nothing more.

It had been impossible for her to sleep, and she'd pulled out of Logan's hold when he'd fallen asleep, which had been stupid. She'd missed his arms the moment they were gone and wish she hadn't pushed him away.

At some point throughout the night she must have fallen asleep because the next morning she woke up alone in his large bed, without a sign of Logan.

She sat up, stretched her arms above her head and tried to work out the knots in her shoulders. For the most part of last night she'd been tense.

Climbing out of bed, she padded across the floor, making a beeline for the closet to grab something to wear, and made her way toward the bathroom. Doing her morning routine, she ended with staring at her reflection in the mirror. Did she look older?

There was no grey hair she could detect, and for the most part, she looked normal. Yet, in the past few days, she'd never known fear quite like it. There only was one other time, but it hadn't been nearly this close.

She didn't think she'd ever have to face Luke again. She'd been promised it was all over, and now, she didn't know what to do or what to think.

Running fingers through her hair, she tried to

clear her mind, but it wasn't doing her any good.

Letting out another breath, she looked around the bathroom and finally decided to head into the kitchen to have a cup of coffee. This was where she found Logan still. He was on his cell phone, dressed impeccably in a suit.

"You know, I don't have a clue what it is you actually do," she said.

She wore a pair of sweatpants and a shirt three times her size. She'd stolen them out of Logan's closet. It was nice having a guy in her life who wore larger clothes than her. She didn't have a problem with her curves at all, but she liked wearing his clothes and in a completely non-weird way, having his scent completely wrapped around her.

"How do you mean?"

"Back at the library a couple of your exes were talking about how wealthy you are."

He laughed. "You sound a little jealous there."

"Not jealous."

He snorted. "Oh, I think you are. Believe me, some of the women would be pissed I picked you."

"They're married."

"Doesn't matter to some women. They don't give a shit about the men in their life and are always looking for the bigger bank balance."

"Not all women are the same."

"Again, never said they were. The same could be said for men as well, you know. We're no saints either. I've seen my fair share of men who want a woman with lots of money." He shrugged. "It's why sex can be so good."

"I don't know what it is you're talking about."

"You're telling me my wealth doesn't impress you?" he asked.

"Logan, you were one of the richest kids in town when I was growing up. I didn't care then, and I don't now. It doesn't change who you are."

He snorted. "You would be surprised at how wrong you are. Besides, the money I had back then was all my dad's. This is all mine. Earned and taken in the right way." He pocketed his cell phone. "Hurry up, have breakfast and get ready. We're heading out."

"We are?"

"Yes. I think it's time you saw a little of what it is I do."

She stepped into the kitchen. "Sure, I'd love to. What do you want? Pancakes? Toast? Cereal?"

"I've already eaten. I'll go and pick you out an outfit. You will wear it, do you understand?"

She didn't want to admit she felt a little upset that he'd already eaten without her. Pasting on a smile, she nodded. "Sure."

He left the kitchen, and rather than get her kitchen goddess on, she settled on a small bowl of cereal and a coffee.

He returned minutes later, but he didn't stand with her. He was back on his cell phone, and he took it outside onto the balcony. She watched him, eating mouthfuls of her cereal, wondering what he actually did. It was natural to be curious, wasn't it?

She finished off her food, and cleaned up after herself, before walking back into the bedroom.

The bed, which she'd left untidy, had been made, and her clothes were laid out for her. She stared at the red dress.

Picking it up, she walked back out to find Logan, who was entering the penthouse again.

"I can't wear this."

"I picked it out for you. You will wear it."

"Logan, you want me to go to your workplace. I can't wear this. It's like an … evening dress."

"You continue to question me and you're going to make yourself look stupid. I don't need to lift a finger to help you with that. This is what you're wearing. I want you to do your hair, and to look the part as my woman. Do you understand?"

"Why do I have the feeling I'm not going to like this?" she asked.

He chuckled. "You probably won't, but again, not my problem. I've given you an instruction, and you will follow it." He grabbed her arms and spun her around. "Hurry up. I don't want to be late."

She stepped back into the bedroom, holding the dress in a death grip. How was she supposed to wear this?

It was so … sexy.

It doesn't matter. This is what he's told you to wear, so wear it.

Stepping out of her sweats and shirt, she missed them the moment she took them off, but didn't make a grab for them.

She had to do this.

Even though she'd come here and she liked to believe it was by a choice, Logan still held all the power over her. He could do what he wanted.

"Let's face it, it's not a choice." She mumbled the words to herself, noting there wasn't even a bra or a pair of panties waiting for her.

She stepped into the dress, lifting it up. There was some padding in for her breasts, but nothing for her panties.

"Beautiful," Logan said, making her aware he'd stepped into the room.

"You like it?"

"Yes, I like it." He zipped up the back of her dress, and his hand lingered on her waist. "I'm going to look forward to taking this off."

"Why no panties?"

"Because, if I can't wait until we get home, I want to be able to touch you whenever I want."

She gasped as his hand slid beneath the bottom of the dress.

"And I can do that with so much ease right now. You're so wet, Ava." He kissed her temple, and before she could even get close to having an orgasm, his hand was gone.

She missed his touch, but she didn't beg.

"I'll be waiting for you outside."

Logan left her alone once again, and she was so curious about him. Who was this man?

The red strappy stiletto heels were so beautiful. She expected them to hurt as she put them on, but they were a dream on her feet.

"Let's see how we get on in a couple of hours." She ran a brush through her hair, leaving it down, and, seeing as she had no makeup, she joined Logan.

Hunter had arrived during the time it had taken her to get ready.

"I'm in shock," Hunter said, seeing her.

"What? You think I clean up nicely?"

"That you do, but I'm thinking about how fast it took you to get dressed. I've never known a woman to be able to do it with such speed." He winked at her.

"Shall we?" Logan said. "Keep your eyes to yourself." His growl was at Hunter.

She watched the exchange, not really understanding it.

"You do know you had me walking around your place back in Crow Valley completely naked, right? I didn't imagine that?"

"I know exactly what it is I got you to do. We're not back in town, and you're not walking around naked. I could have it that way if you pushed."

"No, no, it's fine."

"Good. I for one am growing tired of these little chats, Ava. If I want my men to see you, they'll see you. While you're here, you belong to me. I don't share."

"So does that mean if your friends decided to join you, I'm still yours?" she asked.

Don't think of Luke. Don't think of Luke.

She kept repeating the mantra in her head, hoping he'd answer.

"We'll have to see, won't we?"

He took her arm, leading her out of his penthouse suite. He locked the door, and Hunter was waiting by the elevator.

"I don't have a key."

"You don't need one."

"I'm trapped here?" she asked.

Logan sighed. "For your own safety. If you ever need to go out, there will be someone to take you."

"For my own safety?" She didn't like the sound of that. "Do you have a hit planned for me or something?"

She looked at Logan in the reflection of the elevator doors.

He chuckled. "No."

"Then why wouldn't it be safe?"

"My line of work, Ava, it's not always going to be … nice."

Hunter snorted.

"What does that even mean?" she asked.

"You'll find out soon enough."

Logan grabbed her arm and walked her out of the

elevator. She took notice of people stopping and staring at him. There was a mixture of arousal, lust, fear, and envy. It was like walking into the zone of several deadly sins. Didn't they know to keep themselves in check? Also, how did they know Logan. If he was so rich and his company so well known, why hadn't she heard about him?

A limo was waiting for them. Hunter opened the door, and Logan urged her inside before he followed her.

No one was waiting for them inside, and she breathed a sigh of relief. It was hard for her to relax, knowing at any moment his little friend could arrive.

What would he do when he learned the truth?

Would he still be friends with Luke?

Don't think about it.

It was always easier for her to not think about what was coming or what could happen. There was never any point in dwelling. Not long after Luke was taken out of town, which she had thought meant his arrest, her parents had told her the best way for her deal with her pain was to push it away. To stop thinking about him. He was gone, and he was never coming back. They couldn't afford therapy, so they had tried to help her in their own way. It was why she still lived with them, even when they died. The house had immediately gone to her.

Running fingers through her hair, she blew out a breath and tried to calm her nerves, but nothing was happening. She was in a state of panic, which she kept on trying to hide.

The limo started to move through the city, taking her deeper into the thick of it. She'd never been a city girl. She loved her small town, but there was certainly an appeal to getting lost within an ocean of people.

Logan was typing away on his cell phone.

The first stop was a bar.

Hunter parked the limo, and Logan stepped out, taking her hand.

"Do you own this?"

"Not yet, but I have a feeling if I don't get paid, by the end of the week the deeds will be mine."

He walked her into the bar, and it looked closed. The door had been open, and one look up and the guy behind the bar went pale.

"Where's Andrew?" Logan asked.

"He's in the office, sir. He wasn't expecting you back."

"I have given him a week." Logan helped Ava into a chair. "I think that is more than adequate time for my money. Do me a favor, Daniel. My woman will have a drink. Nothing alcoholic, and keep her entertained."

She watched as Logan and Hunter left, heading into the back.

Forcing a smile to her lips, she turned to look at Daniel.

"What would you like to drink?" he asked.

She noticed Daniel was shaking. He put the glass down gently.

"Erm, I'll just have a soda or something." She gasped as she heard a masculine scream. It was so high pitched, but it came from the direction Logan and Hunter had gone to.

She got off the stool, and Daniel reached out, grabbing her.

"You can't go back there."

"You did hear that?"

"Yes."

"Then why aren't you doing something?" she asked.

"I am. I'm getting you a drink."

He opened up a can of soda, placing it in front of

her.

She looked back at the room.

"Please, don't go back there."

She turned to Daniel. "You're afraid."

"Wouldn't you be if the guy known as 'death' shows up at your workplace?"

"Death?"

The man smiled. He was perspiring. "You don't have a clue who you're with, do you?"

"I have no idea what you're talking about."

"That's all, Daniel," Logan said.

She quickly looked behind her, and sure enough, Logan was on his way back toward her. She noticed he was wiping his hands.

"Let's go."

"I've got a soda to drink."

"And I've got business to attend to," Logan said.

Without waiting for her, he grabbed her arm, leading her out of the bar.

"What is going on? Why does he think your name is death? Or is that Hunter?"

Hunter joined them back in the limo.

"Logan, you can't keep me in the dark forever."

"I can keep you exactly where I want you."

****

The deeds were going to change hands. It wasn't like Logan needed another bar, but he had to make sure people didn't think he was going soft. The moment he started to show weakness, it was where people would take advantage.

Andrew had screamed so loud when he'd snapped his arm in two, Logan was surprised to still be able to hear. It was so high-pitched.

The bar had been struggling for nearly a year, and no matter how much money Andrew sank into the place, it was dying, and there wasn't a single chance of him bringing in the people it needed.

Also, Andrew had a little drug problem, and Logan was tired of feeding it. The bar was in a prime location. With some modifications, it would soon be a restaurant and bar to rival those already in the city.

He'd already had the plans drawn up when Andrew's drug habit had been brought to his attention. Whenever an addiction was involved, Logan rarely saw a way out for the people, and often took over.

"Logan, what aren't you telling me?"

His other little problem didn't like staying silent. After hurting someone, he liked complete silence to go over every element of his meeting. He didn't take long to dwell, just to see he'd made the right decision. He never felt sorry for any of the people he hurt. It was part of his business.

What he needed to do was to make sure he handled all of his businesses swiftly.

"Are you death? Is Hunter?"

"You need to be quiet before I put your mouth to better use." He turned to look at her, brow raised, waiting for that smart mouth of hers to get her in trouble.

She looked out of the window, remaining quiet.

Andrew wasn't the first bar he'd acquired, and it wouldn't be the last.

The next stop was one to the bank. This time, he kept Ava in the car with Hunter as he went to the meeting with John, his financial officer, who also had an addiction to being tied up and spanked. He was the owner of the bank, and like all men with power, they often needed special services from him.

Sitting in John's office, he waited for the excuses that would come.

"I will have your money back soon. I promise,"

John said. "You know how weak the markets are. Investment is not stable. It never has been."

"John, this bank is on its last legs. How do you think your customers would feel if news got out how every single Friday night you like to go to one of my whores and get fucked in the ass while someone else sucks your dick?" He pulled out his cell phone and allowed the previous visit John had made to play into the room.

"Logan, please. This is blackmail. I have done wonders for you in the past. I made a few bad choices—"

"And if I was to make a few bad choices, how do you think I'd fare with you? A click of a button and this makes headline news."

"Logan, please."

"You can keep begging. I don't care what it is you do. Tomorrow night, I want my money back or your board and all of your clients and customers will get this."

"Wait," John said.

"Is this where you attempt to beg me to stop releasing the tape?" Logan asked. "You know how I get bored with the same old shit."

"No. it's not that." John licked his lips.

"Then what is it?"

"Luke came by here yesterday."

"Luke, I didn't realize he banked with you?"

"He doesn't. His parents did."

"Is that how they lost their money? They trusted in you, and as payback, they lost their fortune?"

Logan recalled the day Luke lost everything. His parents had died, taking their own lives after losing their family fortune. By then, Logan had already become one of the wealthiest men in the city, and his friends, well, they didn't stand a chance against him.

He'd helped Luke, seeing as one of his best

friends had helped him.

"It's not how it happened. Luke … he's…" John looked around the room.

"Is someone watching us?" Logan asked.

"No, no one is watching us. Luke's parents, they had to spend a great deal to keep him out of trouble."

"What kind of trouble?" Logan asked.

"The kind that would put him in jail. Something went down when the kid was still in high school. In order to keep him from being hurt or something, they had to transfer a load of money into an offshore account."

Logan sat down in the chair. "What is it Luke wanted?"

"He wanted to know what we did with the records of what happened."

"With his parents deceased and broke, after so long, those accounts are removed as they're no longer required, correct?"

"Yes, but with his parents, days before they died, they closed the account. They wanted all traces removed."

Logan sat back. "Do you have the offshore account's name?" he asked.

"Yes."

John handed him over a slip of paper. "Luke doesn't want you to find that account."

He stared at John.

"Why didn't you call me?" Logan asked. "The moment you had this."

"I knew you were coming here today."

"Did Luke know?"

"I don't think so. You always said if something felt suspicious to me, I was to contact you. I know our business of a late hasn't been pleasant, but … I know how hard you worked to get to the top, Logan."

"We're not going to have a touching reunion. You bet on me just like everyone else. The only difference between you and them, you were far more useful to me. Get me my money. You've been granted an extra week." He got up from the chair and left the building.

Hunter stood outside of the limo, smoking a cigarette. The windows were blacked out and he couldn't see Ava, but he felt her gaze on him.

She could see him.

"You're not covered in blood, so that's a plus. I also didn't get an alert you exposed the video. I figured you were on one of your trigger-happy missions. You have days where you like to ruin people's lives."

"Get this to our tech guy. I want to know who owns the account and why Luke wanted it to be lost so badly."

"Luke was in there?"

"Yesterday."

Hunter glanced toward the car. "You think she's telling the truth?"

"I think Luke is up to something. He always has been. He has his own agenda, but I want to know what is so important he's willing to risk me finding out."

Hunter took the piece of paper. "I'll get on this as soon as we finish for the day."

When he climbed into the back of the limo, Ava continued to ignore him, staring out across the people.

Some of them were living their lives. Going to work every single day, paying bills, trying to make a life. Some had family. Others were looking for love. He'd watched the city for so many hours. He'd been king of it for a long time.

He'd stopped looking as no one impressed him.

The darkness within the city swirled like a

disease, spreading out. People thought they were living a good life, but if you looked closely enough, you started to see the cracks filtering through.

He saw the men and women on street corners. Their clothes with holes, the way they twitched.

Random men and women approaching, wanting a good time. Willing to pay a cheap sum.

The next stop may upset Ava, but he really didn't give a fuck. This was his business, and she would do as she was told.

Hunter took them down a back alley, heading toward an abandoned parking lot.

Climbing out of the car, Logan held the door open. Ava took his hand without another word, glancing around the street as she did.

"Where are we?"

He didn't answer her, taking her arm, and leading her into the main building. During his time fighting, he learned what everyone wanted. Some wanted blood, the violence. Others wanted the power, money. Each person, regardless of their sex, had a weakness, a need, and it spiraled within them like a virus. No matter how much they tried to have control, to keep themselves in check, nothing would ever satisfy them for long.

Sex was one of the biggest tricks on the market.

The cravings would consume eventually, and this whorehouse he had, catered to the wealthy. The crime lord before him had had his hands in some very deep pockets and even darker network of human trafficking, but Logan had not been interested in that line of work. The women he had on his books, wanted to be here. They had no skill other than spreading their legs, and some of them, they loved the rush of earning money this way.

Again, so long as his women and men—this wasn't just for women, as he had many guys on his books—behaved, all was well. All he required was a good work ethic and loyalty. Those who disrespected him and decided to take the easy route often found themselves dead.

As they entered the building, the heavy beat of music flooded through the walls. Sex never slept. There was always someone who wanted their dick wet. Day or night, any time they wanted, they could have it.

"What is this place?" Ava asked.

Passing down a corridor, Logan didn't need to turn left or right to see what awaited them: men and women, scantily clad or completely naked, sex a promise within the air.

Louisa stood at the desk, and the moment she saw him, a smile filled her face.

"Logan, I'm so pleased you came."

For many years now she'd been trying to get him to commit to her. To give her a chance at belonging to him, but he'd never been attracted to her. She'd been one of the fighters opposite him.

She'd been young and manipulated into the fight. At the time, she had thought it was easy money, but as he stepped into the ring, she'd been bloody, in pain, with several broken ribs.

One look at him, and she'd fallen apart. Boos had rung out. People had begged for him to hurt her, to kick her. Instead, he'd picked her up, carried her back to the locker rooms, and taken care of her. He'd never fucked her, even though she'd offered herself to him time and time again.

He had his arm around Ava, and Louisa noticed it, stopping before she embraced him.

"Who is this? Is she another girl you're going to have working here?" Louisa asked.

"No. She's my woman. Hunter, take Ava to the

bar. Keep an eye on her. Make sure no one approaches her."

He put Ava's arm in Hunter's and watched her walk away.

"She has no idea who you are, does she?" Louisa asked, a hint of jealousy in her voice.

The glare she sent Ava's back had him smiling.

"Put those claws away."

"I didn't think you were for the innocent," she said. "She looks like a little lamb, Logan. You want to hurt her?"

"Be careful, Louisa. If anyone was to harm Ava, I will hold you responsible." He walked around her, heading toward the office in the back. "We have a full house?"

"Always, you know how people get. They try to avoid coming here, pretending they're better than us, but they always come back. There was one incident while you were away," Louisa said.

Entering the office, Logan stopped and turned toward Louisa.

"What was it?" he asked.

"Luke."

He frowned. "Luke seems to be a problem nowadays. What is it?"

Louisa looked worried.

"Tell me, Louisa. I don't want to spend all day here."

"No, you want to go and pretend with your little precious."

He stepped up and slammed her hard against the wall. "You want to act tough with me, learn how to fight. Remember I was the one to save you when all the room wanted your pathetic ass dead. You came to me, remember? Not the other way around."

Louisa got up from the floor, brushing herself off. "This woman, she must really get under your skin."

"I'm growing bored of this conversation. Tell me whatever it is you want or get the hell out while I do work."

"Luke came by. He often does. He never pays for what he wants, but his requests, they were … specific."

Logan folded his arms. "Go on."

He noticed how afraid Louisa looked.

"You're scared."

"He's always been your friend. When he comes by, he boasts about how he can have anything he wants, but this was different. He was mean to some of the girls. He hit them."

This made Logan pause.

"Hit them? Did they want to be hit?"

"No. This wasn't a spank or some play, Logan. He slapped them around the face. The guys, they didn't know what to do because you have the orders your friends were to be taken care of."

"Not like that," he said. He didn't like this. This was twice now Luke's name had been brought up. His best friend was supposed to be taken care of, but he wasn't supposed to take the piss.

"Is that all?" he asked, annoyed.

"No. He wanted a woman who hadn't been here very long. A woman with standards who could pick and choose. His request was, he wanted a rape fantasy."

Logan kept his arms folded and didn't say a word.

"You're not mistaken?"

"No. Julie was the one on duty. She has never liked Luke and would always avoid him. She's hurt, really bad."

"Where is she?"

"I sent her home. I asked one of the guards to go with her. Luke left satisfied and said he'd be back."

"I want Julie's address."

Louisa nodded.

"When Luke comes in again, or any of my friends, alert me immediately."

"Riley and Marvin are never a problem. They always have a little fun, and the girls adore them. They're good guys, but they come and go so fleetingly. It's like they forget they can have anything they want. They sometimes ask about you, but it's more of a passing thought."

"But they don't like Luke," he said. There was no need to dwell on Marvin and Riley. He'd already figured out they were losing touch, like friends do. Only, he'd been trying to keep it together. What he didn't know was what he was keeping together and the why of it. If they wanted to move on, he wasn't going to stop them. In fact, it would do him a favor.

"They don't like being hurt, and Luke, he likes to hurt, Logan."

Running a hand down his face, he turned toward the television screens. There were plenty of security cameras in the building. He liked to use whatever he could to keep the men who hated him in line.

Blackmail was such a dirty word, but it got the job done.

"Then make sure you make me aware when he's here. I will take care of him." There was nothing more he could offer, not right now.

"He seems to think that's not the case," Louisa said. "He believes he's above everything. He had no respect for you, Logan."

This was not the first time he'd been made aware of this.

"Don't even begin to judge him, Louisa. You don't know why he does the things he does."

"You can't trust him."

"Again, you seem to think I'm asking your opinion on the matter. I'm not."

"Someone has to watch your back."

"Noted. But watch your place." He glanced at the screen and saw Ava sitting at the bar. Hunter stood close to her, watching. She sipped at a drink, looking around wide-eyed.

"Who is she?"

"Someone from my past. Someone who will not have any harm brought to her."

"You're being rather possessive of this woman."

"She's mine, Louisa. She belongs to me. Make sure the word gets out that if anyone hurts her, they will answer to me."

He was under no illusions his enemies were all around him. He'd made plenty of them, but he also knew how to handle himself. No one would ever be able to take his place. He'd made sure of that.

Not only did he have strength, but knowledge. There was nothing he liked more than bringing the power to their knees and watching them squirm.

Chapter Ten

No matter how many times Ava looked around her, she knew exactly where she was. A brothel or a whorehouse. She didn't know which term was the correct one, but that was what she saw. Men and women, all in the mood to fuck.

Hunter acted like it was an everyday occurrence to see … this.

"It's cute seeing you embarrassed. You're all red," he said.

"This is my first time here."

"I imagine. I don't see much of this going on in Crow Valley, that's for sure."

"I guess the city caters to everything."

"Everyone has a sin, Ava, a weakness. In the city, it's not so easy to deny. In your small town, stuff like this goes on. The only difference is, it's hidden a little better."

"Money in exchange for sex?"

"And silence." Hunter shrugged. "If only walls could talk, huh?"

"I don't care what they would say." She stared down at her drink. "So first we go to a bar where the guy tells me Logan's nickname is death. Then we stop off at a bank, and something happens there. We've made many stops, all of which everyone has looked completely petrified of him. Whenever he's around people stare but hope never to get his attention. Now we're here."

"You know who he is, Ava. You're just too scared to say the words."

"A pimp? A bully? A crook? I don't know what else to call him." She looked around, and it was like she didn't know the guy at all.

How could you know him? He's been gone from

your life for a long time, and he thought you were the reason. Stop being so fucking stupid.

"Logan is a great many things. Above it all, he's a fighter," Hunter said. "It's why he's so feared. He made a reputation for himself before he took over the rule of the city."

"His money is through illegal activity?" she asked.

"My money is through many different avenues," Logan said. "That will be all, Hunter. I'll be staying here for a couple of hours."

Hunter left without a backward glance.

"Any questions you have or you want answering, you'd best come to me."

"And you'll answer them?"

"I'll do my best. You have me pegged as this bad guy, but I'm not. Well, I have to do bad things." He smirked and signaled to the waiter.

"This is your city?"

"Yes."

"And this place?"

"This is a place where I get a great deal of revenue and where I can also help further my protection."

"You make deals through blackmail."

His brow rose. "And how did you jump to that conclusion?"

"It's how you worked with me, right? I wasn't your first rodeo. You had something on me. Sex is a weakness in everyone. I imagine you've got cameras everywhere that's important. You have rich and powerful men and women. Even their kids are probably used as leverage, am I right?"

"You're warm."

"All you need is the right footage. You have your

material, and in doing so, whoever it is you want, eating out of the palm of your hand."

"Oh, you're good."

"No, I'm not. I'm a victim of yours."

He laughed. "Victim. Please."

"I thought Grant cared," she said. "The footage you got of me. It was explicit, but it wasn't done to manipulate anyone. I wasn't cheating. I was single. Trying to find love."

"And that is your weakness. I simply wanted it. Your parents on the other hand, that was a little surprise."

"How did you get it?" she asked. She had no idea what her parents got up to on their weekends away.

"A friend of a friend."

"So you didn't set that one up?"

"No, I don't need to set everyone up. They need to fall into it." He shrugged.

The bartender placed his drink down, and Ava watched as he swallowed it.

"You hate me right now, don't you?"

"I don't know who you are. How can I hate someone I don't know?"

"You like me fucking you though, can't deny that."

"Don't bring us into this," she said.

"I'm the same guy I was last night. You were more than happy to have my cock in your ass last night."

She went to stand up, but he grabbed her arm.

"Don't even think of leaving. You're not going anywhere."

She sat down. "It doesn't matter how many times we slept together. You're not the same guy."

"And you're not the same chick." He swallowed down his scotch.

Without another word, he took her hand and led her out of the bar, toward the back stairs. The woman he'd been in a meeting with was on the front desk.

She stared at them as they passed, and Ava couldn't help but feel a little humiliated. It wouldn't be hard to guess what they were doing, or where they were going and for what purpose.

Logan must have a regular room because no one was inside as he pushed her through the doors, and pressed her up against it.

He captured her hands, locking them up above her head, and took possession of her lips. His mouth was hard, almost bruising as he took her.

He let go of her hands, but she kept them above her head. He sank his fingers into her hair, pulling her back so that she was completely at his mercy.

There was nowhere else for her to go.

He bit down on her lips, breaking from them to trail kisses down to her neck.

He wasn't gentle, his touch hard.

She should hate it, but as he sank his teeth against her pulse, she felt an answering heat awaken within her.

She didn't want him to stop. She was hungry for more, for him. She whimpered his name, begging him.

"Please," she said. And she wasn't even sure why she was begging anymore, only that she couldn't stop, nor did she want to. It felt amazing.

He lifted up her dress, and his hand touched between her thighs. Spreading her legs, he plunged two fingers inside her.

"So wet." He added a third finger, stretching her out, and she didn't argue or complain. She wanted his touch. She didn't want him to stop, not even for a single moment.

He drew his fingers up to her clit, circling the

nub.

"Take off the dress." He let go of her pussy, spun her around, and took care of the zipper.

She didn't know how he could even function. Her body was on fire, and her hands shook with the need.

He spun her back around, and this time, he went to her tits, cupping them together, pressing them close.

His tongue danced across each hardened peak before sinking down. The pain was too much, but he seemed to know when she couldn't take anymore as he eased up, sliding his tongue across each bruised tip.

He kissed down her body, and she watched him. When he got to the apex of her thighs, he gripped her ankle and lifted her leg up over his shoulder. She couldn't move, nor did she want to as his tongue traced across the slit of her pussy, over her clit, around in circles before moving back down to her entrance.

She cried out as he plunged inside her and started to fuck her. She wanted his cock, needed it.

He slid back up, sucking her clit into his mouth.

She screamed again as the pain burst through her.

Just as quickly as he was causing her pleasure and pain, he stopped, and before she knew what was happening, he had her on her knees on the bed. The silk sheets made it a little uncomfortable to stay in one place, but he kept her there.

He pushed her head down, held onto her hands, and locked her into place at the base of her back. She couldn't move or do anything. She was completely at his mercy, waiting for him to finish with her.

He stroked over the curves of her ass. She yelped as he slapped her.

"You know, I've thought about this ass a lot. I had no idea just how good it would feel being inside you, working that little puckered hole open. Fuck, I want inside you again, but this time, I want your pussy."

She moaned as the tip of his cock pressed against her entrance and began to work inside her. He wasn't in any rush.

"Yeah, look at that. Taking my cock, opening up for me. This is what this pretty pussy is supposed to do. Be ready to take me whenever I want you."

In and out, he took his time, making her feel every inch of him.

She didn't know how much she could take before he grabbed her hips and slammed inside her.

He was so big and deep, it was almost too much.

She held onto the bed. With his hands on her hips, there was nothing to stop her from moving.

Logan didn't give her a choice though. He held her in place and began to fuck her hard. He wasn't gentle or kind. His thrusts were hard, forceful, taking what he wanted.

He reached between her thighs and stroked over her clit.

The pleasure was instant, and she couldn't deny him, didn't want to.

"I can feel you, Ava. You're so close. Do you want to come all over my dick?" he asked.

"Yes."

"Good. I'm going to give it to you, and you're going to take it all."

He pinched her clit, stroking out the pain, and she came hard. It felt different with his cock inside her. She milked him, and even as she came, he found his own release.

The hot spill of his cum filled her, and afterward, she collapsed to the bed.

Logan joined her, his weight crushing her back, but she didn't ask him to leave or to stop. She didn't want him to. She rather liked having him close.

His fingers stroked up the sides of her body, tracing over her arms, then back down again.

Time seemed to stand still.

"Who are you?" she asked.

"Logan Stanford," he said.

"You know what I mean."

"Ava, don't play stupid. You know who I am and what I do. There's no reason for me to hide it."

"You're a crime person?"

"A crime lord is a good one. To different people I'm something else. A pimp, but I don't work the streets. My girls and boys are here."

She glanced over her shoulder. "And this makes it better?"

He laughed. "No, I didn't say I made it better. If my girls want to go, they're welcome to do so. From what I've learned, a pimp on the streets doesn't allow any of his girls to leave. They have to pay him everything they earn except for a pittance."

"You pay yours well. I don't know why I'm having this conversation. It's wrong."

"What's wrong?" he asked.

"I don't know. This. You're doing stuff that's illegal."

"I have legal businesses as well. I'm a wealthy man without all of this."

"Then why do this at all?"

"If I don't someone else will."

"How did this all start?"

He pushed some hair off her face. She stared into his eyes, curious, wanting to know who this man was.

"Do you really want to know the answer to that question?"

"Yes."

"I'll warn you, you won't like it."

She licked her lips. "It's about you though, right, and all of this. How did you even take over from something like this?"

"What makes you think I took over?"

"You said if you don't someone else will."

He smiled. "It's one of the many things I like about you, you're smart."

"Don't patronize me. I'm listening to you, and you're treating me like I'm stupid."

"All of this is stupid, Ava. Why do you want to know the truth?"

"I want to understand. Is that so hard to believe?"

"If you're looking for a hero, you're not going to find him in me."

"Then tell me what I am going to find. I'm not looking for a hero."

He stared at her, and she didn't know if he was going to throttle her or not. He looked ready to kill her.

Maybe not the best idea to anger a guy people think of as death.

Good going, Ava.

"I was thrown in jail, and my lawyer he said the sexual assault charge would be on my record and I was on a sex offenders' register. I was eighteen. I'd done nothing wrong, and my entire life had just been thrown down the fucking toilet. My parents were broken by what happened. They left Crow Valley behind, but it killed them. Little by little. I was angry. My rage knew no bounds, and even my friends couldn't help me. They'd given everything up for me. With no money, nothing, I started to fight. At first, they were little fights. You know, just a few punches to earn a couple dollars a night. Enough to keep me warm."

"Were you hurt?"

"They're fights, Ava. Everyone gets hurt. I started to earn a reputation. Undefeated, and a guy at one of the gyms I went to in order to train asked me if I wanted to make some real money. Underground fighting. No rules. No protection. No one to stand in my way. I took it. A couple hundred turned into a couple of thousand. Those fights you could still walk away from."

"You went further?"

"To get a reputation and to be where I am, you need to learn to kill without batting an eye."

"And you did this?"

"Yes. I'm still undefeated. Only, I wasn't just a couple of fists. I knew what I was doing. I watched who was on top. The guy who sat in this seat before me, his name was Arthur Myette."

"I've never heard of him."

"You won't. He was the biggest, baddest motherfucker in town. At first, he and I, we hit it off. I did the fights he wanted. Worked for him in security, but what he didn't know was I was more than a pretty face. I knew what he was doing, and I was calculating. You see Arthur, he had a lot of enemies, and I'm known for being a fair guy. He got greedy, and when that happened, people started to turn on him. So, one night, down at the docks, in front of all his men, I gave him an ultimatum. He gave everything up, or I killed him."

"You killed him?"

"Yes. There's no way anyone relinquishes that kind of power."

"And you never will?"

"I have no reason to. I will never allow myself to fall, Ava, you need to understand that." He kissed her temple. "And now because of everything you know, I can't let you go."

The threat was clear.

Any way out of here was death.

She understood why so many people were afraid of him.

****

The following day, Logan drove toward Julie's apartment. She lived in a nice neighborhood. The kind any young mother would be happy to raise a child. She worked for him to support her two kids, to get them through high school and off to college.

She was a thirty-five-year-old woman with a ten-year-old and five-year-old. Her husband had died in a hit-and-run, and she'd been struggling until she came to work for him.

He knocked on the door. It was a Friday morning, and he hoped the kids were in school. He didn't do well around kids.

Juliet opened the door, and her eyes went wide.

"I didn't complain. I swear."

He saw the black eye she was sporting. The heavy makeup clearly didn't hide it.

"I'd like to come in if you'd let me."

"Of course. I mean, this house is yours anyway."

Stepping across the threshold, he followed her down the corridor toward the kitchen.

"This is your house."

"I know. I will be back at work tomorrow night."

"You don't work weekends," he said.

"But I've had a couple of days off."

"I can see why." He pointed at her eye.

She touched her cheek and turned away, fiddling with the kettle.

"I did tell Louisa it was no big deal."

"What exactly did Luke want from you?" he asked, taking a seat. "Before we delve into what you're afraid to tell me, your job is secure. You shouldn't have been hurt, and you won't be returning to work until you're well. Also, this house is yours." He reached into his jacket pocket and pulled out the deeds, sliding them across the table. "Now, tell me what went down."

She reached out, taking the deeds. Her hands shook. "I can't." She closed the paperwork and left it, her hands folding. "He knows where I live and has threatened my kids. I couldn't stand for anything to happen to them."

"Luke has?"

She didn't say a word.

"Julie, you know who you're dealing with. I will tell you anything you say to me will be in confidence. I will have men put at your door with the guarantee they'll protect you."

Julie started to cry, and he didn't like tears.

He waited. Glancing down at his watch, he was so close to leaving and being done with her.

"He said you don't have a clue. That you're blind and you're not really a bad guy. You've got a weakness."

"Luke did?"

"He said a long time ago, he had a nice tight pussy. One so tight and dry, it was a struggle to fuck, but when he did, she was the sweetest victory because he had something you'd never had."

He listened as Julie told him in graphic detail what happened to her. Even as she begged him to stop, Luke kept on hurting her, forcing her, even though it went against the rules.

Afterward, Logan left her some money in the hope of helping compensate and climbed back into the car.

Grabbing his cell phone, he dialed Louisa.

"Do you have any footage from the night Luke hurt Julie?"

"No. He knows about the tapes, Logan. He had them turned off, and you'd given instruction your friends could have what they wanted."

"Okay." He hung up his cell phone and felt sick to his stomach.

Luke could be messing with him. What if it was someone else though?

Scrolling through his contacts, he found Luke's number.

Pressing dial, he waited.

It went straight to voice mail.

He dialed again.

"Dude, seriously, can't you take the hint? I've got something going on here, and I don't need you to be calling me up every few minutes."

"Why did you hurt one of my girls?"

"Did that fucking slut lie about me?"

"I have no idea what you're talking about. Louisa called me. She said you'd hurt one of the girls." Logan knew he should have talked to Luke face to face.

"I see what is going on here. Ava's got inside your head, hasn't she?"

"No."

"Please. Ten minutes alone with her and you want to act like her fucking superhero. I didn't hurt anyone. I'm sick and tired of these bitches lying about me. They don't have a fucking clue. Honestly, they want to be fucked nice and hard, and when you give them what they want, they scream rape. Don't you find it a little boring?"

Logan knew he was lying. "I've got to go."

"Dude, we're good, right?"

"Of course." He hung up his cell phone, turning over the ignition and driving out of the parking lot.

He arrived at his penthouse suite after lunch to find Hunter sitting at the dining room table, eating some kind of pasta.

"Is this what I pay you for? To sit and eat?"

"Ava's trying on the new dresses you wanted. She keeps coming out. I think the blue is more her color, but she hates them all," Hunter said. "How was your trip to Julie?"

Logan stared at his friend and his confidant.

"I want you to bring the sheriff to me," he said.

"We're talking about the Crow Valley fucker who likes little boys?"

"Yes."

Hunter slurped up the final piece of spaghetti. "Do I get a reason why?"

"Luke's lying, and I have a feeling, Ava's telling the truth." The moment he spoke the words aloud, he felt sick to his stomach. Hunter stood up.

"But you never had a reason to doubt. Why do you doubt now?"

"Hey," Ava said, gaining their attention. "I didn't hear you arrive home. So, here is the black one."

She wore a cocktail dress with a plunging neck, and she gave them a twirl. Her blonde hair hung down her back, and he wanted to run his fingers through it.

Luke raped her.
Luke raped her.

"Don't you like it?"

"It's beautiful."

"Are you sure? You don't seem sure."

"It is stunning, Ava," he said.

She nodded and frowned. "I'll go and try on the next."

He stared at the space where she stood, and he felt like the biggest fucking loser on the planet.

"What makes you think she's telling the truth?"

"Do you remember the night Luke and the boys

arrived? I had Ava come to me naked," he said. Just recalling the memory now with the new knowledge made him feel sick.

"Yeah."

"She was completely turned off, and she tried to stay as far away from Luke as possible. She couldn't stand him. When I told her what happened, she didn't believe me." Logan finally turned to look at Hunter. "So far Luke has been trying to cover old tracks and given little snippets of information to one of the women who works for me."

"What kind of information?"

"How he hurt someone years ago. Tore something from them that I could never have." He looked back over his shoulder, but there was no sign of Ava. "When I was younger, before I was arrested, Ava and I, we shared a couple of moments. They were fleeting, but I always wanted her. I never told a soul about how much I did. She was an obsession I couldn't get out of my head."

"Do you think Luke knew?"

"I do. The dates on the bank transfer into the offshore account, they were the same day I was arrested. The sheriff was lying, and if I could buy his silence and stupidity with a tape of him, what could money and power do? I bet Luke's parents knew of his love of little boys too."

"If this was the case…"

"I put Ava in front of her rapist and made her vulnerable again." He didn't even want to think of the guilt it would take for that to have happened.

She deserved more.

"Get me the sheriff. I have a feeling he'd be more inclined to tell me the truth with a bit more incentive."

Chapter Eleven

Twelve years ago

Ava tucked some hair behind her ear and looked down at the report she'd just finished.

Mrs. Little, her English teacher, was so nice and sweet, and she allowed her to use the classroom to finish her assignment as the library had been closed.

She read over the words again, wanting to ace this essay so she didn't affect her overall grade.

Satisfied with the way it read, she placed it in the file and slid it into the drawer where she'd been told to store it.

"Are you being naughty?" Logan asked.

She jumped back, putting a hand to her chest. "You scared me."

"Sorry, it's not every single day you see the town princess going through the teacher's drawers."

"I'm not a princess, and no, I wasn't stealing or trying to find answers to test scores. I was handing in a piece of homework is all."

She held her pen in her hands.

Since Halloween night, she and Logan seemed to bump into each other a lot.

"What are you doing here? Planning on stealing those selfsame notes for yourself?"

"Nah, I was looking for you."

"You were?"

"Yeah, I was."

"I doubt that."

He closed the door of the classroom, and her heart picked up a notch. He was all alone. No friends around.

"Why do you doubt it?"

"No one would know where I am." She didn't

make a habit of announcing her whereabouts to everyone. She didn't have regular friends, just acquaintances and a few people she studied with. No real connections.

"You see, that's where you're wrong. They came looking for you because I asked them to."

"And why would you do that?"

He smiled. "You're a bright girl, figure it out."

"I don't have any time for games right now."

"It's cute you think I'm playing right now. I'm not." He stepped up to the desk.

She stood on one side, he on the other.

"I don't know what is going on right now."

"Why don't you come a little closer and find out?"

"I don't know if I should." She looked past his shoulder, expecting to find Luke and the others.

It wasn't like Logan was ever on his own for long.

Not too far behind him was one of his friends.

"Ava, come here."

"Promise me this isn't some kind of joke."

"Have I given you a reason to believe it is?"

"I honestly don't know what I believe anymore." She ran fingers through her hair. She'd taken it out of the band as it had started to hurt her head.

Rounding the desk, she stepped in front of him.

"See, I'm in front of you, now what?" She wanted to be confident, to act like it didn't matter.

He stepped close, and she took a step back, only for the teacher's desk to be in the way.

"I came here looking for you. Do you know why?"

"No."

He put a hand on either side of her, and she had

no choice but to lean back.

She wouldn't look at his lips, or think about how close he was to her.

Logan pushed against her legs, and she had no choice but to open them and he stepped between them.

"Has anyone ever told you how pretty you are?"

"Logan, what's going on?"

"I've been thinking about you all day."

She gasped as his hand brushed her hip. She hadn't been expecting him to touch her, so it took her by surprise.

He didn't let her go. With his other hand, he cupped her face, tilting her head back.

This couldn't be happening.

She had to be dreaming.

Wake up, Ava.

She didn't wake up.

"I don't know what you've done to me, but I can't get these lips out of my head. I think about them all the fucking time, and it's doing my head in."

His lips slammed down, and it startled her.

At first, she didn't do anything. She didn't kiss him back, or stop him. She didn't hold him or push him away.

Logan Stanford was kissing her passionately in their English classroom.

He broke from the kiss and smirked down at her. "You haven't kicked me in the balls, so I'll consider that a plus."

"What are you doing?" she asked.

"Have you ever been kissed before?"

"No." She felt her cheeks heat up as she admitted the truth to him.

Why couldn't she shut up or stay silent?

He chuckled. "That's okay. I don't mind being

191

your first. I intend to be your first in everything."

Before she got a chance to ask him what he meant, he was already kissing her. Only this time, she didn't stay still. She kissed him back, and she touched him. Cupping his cheek, she opened her lips as he plunged his tongue inside.

She moaned, and he groaned. Each touch seemed to ignite her need for more.

For some strange reason, she'd picked this day to wear a skirt. Logan put his hands on her knees and began to push it up, but she wasn't ready.

She put her hands on top of his, and he didn't push.

Instead, he touched her breasts, and this time, she didn't stop him as it felt too good to deny. His palm rubbed across each nipple, and she gasped his name, not wanting him to stop.

"I don't know what it is you've done to me, but I can't stop thinking about you." He growled the words as he trailed kisses down to her neck, biting on her pulse.

She closed her eyes, not realizing he'd opened her shirt until it was too late, and she didn't care and was more than happy for him to keep on touching her.

"Do you want me?" he asked, gliding down her chest, going to her breasts. She didn't push him away or try to stop him.

Watching him, she cried out as he sucked on one of her tits.

Oh, my God! This is really happening.

He's got me partially naked.

When his hand traveled up the inside of her thigh, touching her, she couldn't bring herself to stop him, didn't want to. This was beyond anything she'd ever experienced in all of her life.

He stroked over her pussy, teasing her clit, and

she knew she was getting close to orgasm. It was right there, just at the point, but she didn't go over it. He kept her poised there, and suddenly, they both heard a noise.

His friends were shouting his name.

Logan groaned. "I'm going to have to stop there, but know I don't want to."

He pulled his hand away from her, helping her quickly get decent.

"I'll take care of this. Get home safely."

Within seconds he was gone, almost like he wasn't there in the first place.

****

Logan didn't linger too long.

Ava had no choice but to get dressed, feeling the spill of his arousal, and as she looked over at him, she realized something.

"I'm not on the pill," she said.

He paused, glancing over at her.

They were getting changed in front of each other, which suddenly seemed oddly intimate.

"I know."

"But you haven't been wearing a condom."

"I'm clean."

She laughed. "I wasn't thinking about you being clean. I could still get pregnant." She put a hand against her stomach. "Is that what you're hoping for? To get me pregnant?"

"I'm not hoping for anything." He wouldn't look at her.

"I don't know what is going on."

"Ava, shut the fuck up. Stop overthinking all this. It's boring and quite frankly, beneath us."

"Are you planning on killing me?"

He sighed and turned to look at her. "If I give you an answer, will it shut you up?"

"I don't know. Depends on the answer."

"Then yes, I'm planning on killing you. I'm hoping to make your life miserable and hurt you in many despicable ways. It's why I haven't shared you and have no plans to. Is this the shit you want to hear? Will this make it easier for you somehow?"

"You think I'm asking these questions to make it easy? You think any of this is in some way easy for me?"

"To be honest, Ava, I don't give a fuck."

"Well, give a fuck for me. I know you want to blame me for everything that happened to you, but you're looking in the wrong direction. You need to look a little closer to home to find that kind of closure."

"Ava."

"No. I don't want to die, and I'm not going to have you be the one to do it."

"Don't worry, I'll get Hunter to pull the trigger. Are you done? I've got places I need to be."

"And you just stopped for a quick fuck?" she asked.

"So pleased you were able to catch up with what it is I want. Now, if you want me to make an example of you, keep on talking. If not, shut up and let's go."

She wanted to scream at him, to run and pound on his chest and beg him to see reason.

If she was going to die, she'd make sure in some way, he'd find out the truth.

Pressing her lips together, she followed him out of the room. He put a hand against her back, but she didn't swat him away, even as she wanted to.

She walked with her head held high. No one stopped them.

Logan said his goodbyes to the woman on the front desk, and Hunter was outside, waiting for them.

"You know where I want to go."

Hunter nodded.

Logan opened the door, and she climbed inside, trying to tuck herself into the far corner, as far away from him as humanly possible.

Don't be petty.

What? He doesn't want me to talk.

Don't be petty. Fight the battles you have a chance of winning.

Still, she didn't speak. There was no way after his threat she'd give him the satisfaction of winning.

"Are you curious about where we're going?" Logan asked.

He typed on his cell phone before putting it away.

Glancing over her shoulder, she waited.

"You're playing that game?"

Again, she didn't say anything.

"You can talk, you know?"

She pressed her lips together and stared out of the window. As suddenly as her anger appeared, it dissipated. There was nothing there but a deep overwhelming sadness and pain. She didn't want to think or do anything.

"I know you're upset."

She closed her eyes.

"I didn't want it to end that way," he said. "I'm sorry."

Ava turned her head, resting it against the seat and stared. "Do you know what it's like to have people laugh at you? For people not to believe you?"

"Yes."

She laughed. "Of course you do. You think I'm the cause of all this, and I'm not." She released a sigh. "One day I hope you see the truth, I really do. I may even forgive you." She rested her hand on her stomach. "You've pretty much said if I'm pregnant, I won't be around long enough to even see my baby."

"It's not what I meant."

"It's what you said."

"I'm an asshole."

She smiled. "I don't like fighting with you. I hate it."

"I don't want to fight with you either." He reached across the seats, taking hold of her hand. "It's the last thing I want to do. I care about you so much, Ava."

"You do?" Tears filled her eyes, and she didn't want to give way to hope.

"I do. It's what makes everything so hard."

"You still don't believe me?"

He didn't say a word, and she knew she spoke the truth.

"Fine. It's fine. I understand. Why would you believe me when your best friend has told you the truth, right? I'm not that important. Luke has been with you your whole life. I get it."

She'd never made friends easily, often preferring her own company. Even back in high school, it had always been that way.

"Let's move on. I don't want to dwell on boring factors."

Ava had noticed they were moving away from the center of the city, going past some run-down warehouses. She noticed cars coming and going. Expensive ones. They completely stood out.

"What is going on?"

"We're going to have some fun."

Hunter parked the limo, and Logan climbed out. She didn't want him to go, and she had a feeling she wasn't going to like what she saw.

Logan opened her door and held out his hand.

She took it, seeing no point in fighting with him, not now. Not on situations that really didn't matter right now.

He lifted her out, and she offered him a smile.

There's a chance he could still believe you.

"How do you like a little blood?" Logan asked.

"I don't want to see a whole lot of blood. It's scary."

Hunter laughed.

"Come, we'll see."

Once again, his hand was at her back. They moved toward a secluded entrance, and Hunter typed in the code to open it.

"You own this place?"

"Oh, Ava, one day you will learn, I pretty much own everything."

The moment the door opened, screaming, crying, and the heavy beat of music filled the air. The lights were dim, and the noise was too much.

She squinted to try to see what was going on.

Logan led her toward a balcony, and glancing down, she saw where the light was coming from.

Two men stood in a circle made out of chalk, surrounded by men and women, screaming and fighting for more.

Money was everywhere, and even though they were up high, she saw the blood spatter.

One of the men looked like he'd already been ten rounds with a bus, and was still going strong. The other, he was on his last legs, and looked ready to drop.

"What is this place?" she asked.

"This is where it really all started for me. This right here got my name noticed. My reputation sealed, and more money than I knew what to do with."

"Even I'd heard of him, and I had nothing to do

with the underground fights. They were beneath my previous boss," Hunter said.

"Interesting conversation. I'll be back," Logan said, leaving her with Hunter as he talked with someone else.

"You're loyal to Logan now."

"I am. He saved me when he could have ended my life. He gave me a chance, and I will forever serve him."

She looked toward Logan. "I wonder if it'll be him who gets to kill me."

"Don't talk about death right now. I'm not interested in killing you." Hunter looked toward the fight and Logan returned to her side, looking happy. Hunter stepped away, giving them both space.

"Watch them. See how they want his death."

"Whose? There are two of them."

"It doesn't matter who they want. They only crave and wish to see someone fall."

She looked toward him. Now her eyes had adjusted to the darkness, she saw the happiness in them.

"You like this."

"Like this, it brings the real heart of a person out. This here, is where real pain truly begins."

"Do you like pain?"

"No one likes pain, Ava. We all deal with it differently. Pain helped me when I didn't think I could handle it myself."

"Down there, they're all champions. Some just take a few more hits than others."

She gasped as the one who looked like he'd taken on the buses and won, lifted the other man and slammed him to the ground.

This wasn't like on television. When the man was on the ground, the guy started to pummel him even more, not giving him a second to come around. This was brutal.

The other man tried to crawl away, but the other put his booted foot on his back and started to slam it down.

Once.

Twice.

The male scream had her covering her ears.

The violence, it was all too much.

Without waiting for Hunter or Logan, she rushed outside, bent over, and very unladylike, threw up.

She tucked her hair behind her ears and vomited. She couldn't stop.

During the process, someone had come out and was touching the base of her back, rubbing, offering her comfort.

When she wasn't going to be sick anymore, she swatted at their hand, stood up, and shook her head.

"No," she said.

"Ava?" Logan held his hands up. "Come back inside."

Tears filled her eyes. "Do you know what we just witnessed?"

"A victory."

"That guy may have just had his back broken, and you don't care."

"They know the risks when they come here."

"Do they? Or are you just so consumed with making money and being this big bad man, that you can't even see the truth of what the hell is going on! This was something you had to do as well?" She screamed the words, unable to contain her pain or guilt even though she had nothing to feel guilty for.

Her entire body shook. She felt disgusted, sickened, and in need of something to calm her turning stomach.

"Why did you bring me here? Is that going to be my end? Fighting?" She pointed toward the door.

"What is your sudden fascination with the end?"

"Why not? I don't know the point in all of this, Logan. You come back to Crow Valley to do what? Make my life miserable? You think I haven't had a pretty bad life the past twelve years?"

"No, I don't."

She burst out laughing.

"You've had it rather cushy. A nice little life. A house. The dream come true, right?"

She shook her head. "I was raped in the school locker room after I finished swimming. Not long after our little episode in the classroom. No one believed me. Sure, you and Luke, and the others left. I figured you'd all done something bad. I didn't pursue it. I thought Luke had gone to jail." She pressed her lips together, the tears falling down her face. At least she didn't wear any makeup. "No one in town believed me. They all … they all thought I was lying. Look at me, Logan. I didn't know why they blamed me for you, but for Luke, I'd hear the whispers and I thought it was about him. Why would he rape her? Why would he even touch her? Clearly, she's a slut and doesn't know how to handle herself. I worked at the library. I couldn't go away to college. My parents died. Relationships were a no because no one wanted me, and I struggled. I couldn't afford therapy so I handed everything as best as I could, and at times, it still wasn't enough. I'm not even comparing my life to yours. I'm just saying, it hasn't been easy, but I can't go back in there. I can't see any more of that. It's too much, Logan. I can't."

"Hunter, take her home."

Logan spun on his heel, and it broke her heart to see him walk away from her.

Hunter grabbed her arm and moved her toward the car. She climbed inside without putting up a fight. There was no reason to fight him or anyone else.

The car door slammed, but Logan was nowhere to be seen.

"Does he enjoy it?" she asked.

Hunter started up the limo, pulling out of the parking lot. "This is his world. It's what he knows, and he takes care of it."

"It's so … bloodthirsty."

"Logan had his way of dealing with his past, and so do you."

She curled up against the window, watching the city go by.

"I'm sorry. When you go back to him, tell him I'm sorry."

"You can tell him yourself."

****

The fight brought in a lot of money. The warehouse was empty, and Hunter waited for him outside. He had nowhere else to go for the time being, so he sat in a chair in the center of the ring.

The man Ava ran out on had indeed broken his back. He'd been too weak and shouldn't have signed himself up for a fight. He still earned money, just not as much as the victor of the night.

Running fingers through his hair, Logan waited for something. He didn't know what the fuck had gotten into him.

Seeing Ava throw up, it was the first time he'd felt like he'd pushed too far. She didn't need to see this, any of this, and yet, he'd forced this on her, and he hated himself for it.

The door opened, and there Hunter stood.

"I didn't know if you'd decided to leave."

"Did Ava get home safely?"

"Yes."

He nodded. "Good."

"What's going on?" Hunter asked.

"Nothing."

"You don't look like you're thinking about nothing."

"I'm not really thinking, Hunter. I'm just processing."

"Tonight was a good fight. I heard the stakes were higher than ever. People wanted more blood, more everything."

"Of course they want more blood. More everything. It's the way they are. Everything is a power trip for them. They always want more, and we always give them what they want."

"You're not happy?"

"No."

"Why?"

"I don't fucking know. All of this, it's fucking bullshit. I know that."

"You didn't expect Ava to have that kind of reaction."

"I don't know what I expected, but it certainly wasn't this bullshit. Fuck. What the fuck am I doing?"

"This started out as revenge. You finally have some sort of closure, and you no longer know what it is anymore?"

"I don't know what the fuck I'm doing, and I haven't known for a really long fucking time. Shit. This wasn't supposed to be so hard. Why the fuck does it feel hard?"

"Because you're having doubts. It was simple when you believed she was the woman responsible for sending your ass to prison. Now it's not so simple. Have you ever considered you may have feelings for her?" Hunter asked.

He glared up at Hunter. "Don't even fucking start."

"Your friends. Luke, Marvin, and Riley, you treat them well. Better than well, why?"

"They're my friends. They stood beside me."

Hunter snorted. "When I first met you, it took them over six months before I even met them, and I was by your side all the time. They're not your friends anymore and I'm guessing they haven't been for a long time, but you, you've been fighting, drawing on your past experiences. What if everything you know is wrong? If the sheriff gives you different answers, what are you going to do then? What if Ava is telling the truth and Luke did in fact rape her, but no one has ever believed her?"

"I don't want to think about that."

"You're scared she is."

He looked toward his friend and shook his head. "This is not up for discussion." He got to his feet and headed outside.

The cleaning crew would be by in a couple of hours to take care of the mess. He climbed into the back of the limo as Hunter took the driver's side.

"When will the sheriff be arriving?"

"Tomorrow."

"Saturday night is when I want to find out the truth. I've got to check on Pieces, and I'll take Ava there. Have her in the office and waiting for me," Logan said.

"You have what you're going to do all planned out?"

"I have something planned, yes." He leaned back in the car, staring up at the roof. He was so fucking tired.

The scent of cigarette smoke, alcohol, and for

some reason he felt death clung to him.

"Would you also like me to get a pregnancy test?" Hunter asked. "There is a chance she could be pregnant."

"You know I won't take her baby away or have her killed?" Logan asked.

"I know a great many things, but I'm not an emotional woman who has having a great deal of revelations and soul-searching thrust upon her. I think so far, she's handling it all well, but I imagine it's not easy for her."

"No, I guess not."

"What do you want to happen, Logan? Do you love her? Do you want to keep her? Do you want to end this charade of pain and humiliation?"

"I don't know what I want to do," he said. "I can't think right now, in all honesty. Just get me home."

Hunter was right. Unless his friends wanted something from him, he rarely saw them. He was aware of them visiting places he owned. Like the whorehouse. Using his women, never paying for the services they offered, or using their connection to him to get into bars. He'd not been clubbing with the boys in years. Not since he'd taken over and ruled the city.

Running fingers through his hair, he didn't like the way his thoughts were going or what any of it meant. None of this was how he wanted his life.

Closing his eyes, he thought about the past. One of his favorite memories was going back to the classroom where he first kissed Ava.

It was such a fucking teenage cliché.

He'd been asking around after her. He had a few guys he paid to keep an eye on her, to make sure she was fine. One of them, he couldn't even remember the kid's name, told him she was working in English class to finish a paper.

When he arrived, he stood in the doorway. She'd not heard him arrive, and he simply watched her. She was so achingly beautiful.

She was everything.

He loved to watch her, to bask in seeing her, and he wanted everything with her. He'd never spoken of his desires to have the *fat girl* as his friends called her.

To him, she'd never been fat, just perfect.

Hunter arrived at his place, and he climbed out. Logan walked inside, going straight to the elevator, clicking for his suite. He didn't look at his reflection, and as he got to his floor, he stepped off.

Keying in the code, he let himself inside.

There was no sound.

Removing his shoes, opening his tie, taking off his jacket, he made his way toward the main sitting room. There was no sign of her there, or in the dining room, or kitchen.

He went to his bedroom, and there she was, curled up. A book had dropped down beside her, and he smiled.

She was completely fast asleep. One of her hands was held up against her cheek, while the other down beside her. She looked so peaceful.

He watched her. For some reason, he felt there didn't go by a day when he wasn't watching her in some way or another.

Even as he'd tried to hate her over the years, he'd been curious about her. Letting Grant go to her, he'd been torn between murdering the bastard and asking so many questions about how she was doing.

He moved toward the bed and sat down on the edge. The moment he did, she let out a moan, and finally opened her eyes.

"Logan?" she asked.

"Hey."

"It's really late. You're only just getting back."

"I am." He took her hand and locked their fingers together. She held onto his hand, giving him a little squeeze.

"I must have nodded off. I was suddenly so tired."

"Hunter's going to get us a couple of tests. Have you skipped a period?"

"Not yet. I can't think right now. I don't even know when I'm due a period. I'm sorry. I'm all a bit ugh up there."

He smiled. "I wanted to apologize."

"Logan, you don't have to do that."

"I do. I've been around this world for so long, it's hard for me to see the flaws."

"Your world isn't flawed—it's a little bright, you know. A little scary. I don't think I can handle that kind of violence. It made me feel sick."

He reached out, pushing some hair off her face. "I won't take you again."

"The guy? What will happen to him?" she asked. "Do you just kill them if they're no good?"

"They're not animals. He's been taken to the hospital. They sometimes work for me. Hard times push them into the fighting ring, and I offer them a job. They show loyalty, and I reward them for it."

"Loyalty means a great deal to you, doesn't it?"

"Of course. Having loyal men means soldiers. My line of work, it's not for the faint hearted. My life is at risk every single day."

"Would you trade it?"

"No. Like I said, you think this is bad, but you don't know what it was like before I took over. It was much, much worse."

"How worse?"

"Human trafficking. Women being hurt. There was no order."

"What about the cops?"

"I own them."

"Wow," she said.

"I'm a fair man, Ava. I can promise you that."

"Logan, you don't have to go making me promises."

"I do."

She stared at him, lips pressed together.

"If you're pregnant, you're going to marry me."

"Wow," she said, sitting up. "That is a huge topic change." She lifted up the strap of her negligee. "Marriage? Wow."

"You don't want to get married?"

"Oh, I … I don't know. I've not really thought about marriage." She nibbled her lip. "I'm sorry. I'm all a little confused, you know."

"I get it, I do."

"I don't think you do."

He smiled. "You've got nothing to fear from me."

"You threatened to kill me not too long ago."

"And you're very much alive. I'm not going to kill you, or hurt you in any way." He held her hand again, locking their fingers together.

They were a perfect fit.

"What is going on right now?" she asked.

"We're talking for the first time ever." He looked into her eyes, and he wanted to take the pain and the fear away.

As he pulled her close, Ava moved toward him.

Cupping her cheek, he pressed a kiss to her lips. "I don't want to lose you."

"You're not going to."

"Not ever," he said. "You belong to me, and I'm not willing to give you up for anything. I've already got people working on removing those videos so no one can ever find them."

"You can do that?" she asked.

"I can do whatever the hell I want. Even if I don't capture them all, being my woman, my wife, it will stop anyone from ever thinking they can hurt you."

"No one can have that kind of power."

"You'd be pleasantly surprised." He tucked some hair behind her ear.

"I have no idea if this is a marriage proposal or not."

"It's whatever you want it to be." He kissed her again. "I'm not going to give you up."

"What does this mean?"

"It means, take a chance on me, Ava. I won't let you down. I promise."

"But you still don't believe me."

He averted his gaze and she pulled away from him, but he didn't want her to.

Holding her close, he stared into her eyes. "Give me time."

Chapter Twelve

"Give me time."

Logan rolled up the sleeves of his white shirt, shaking his head.

Hunter had already called ahead to let him know he had the sheriff and would be arriving within the hour. He had everything set up for what he was going to need.

He didn't like the sheriff and had planned to take him out. Anyone who liked hurting little boys or girls didn't deserve the kind of power he had. He wondered how many kids had passed through the sheriff's hands who had a story to tell.

Pushing those thoughts to the back of his mind, he didn't want to even think about them right now. If he did, he'd end the sheriff too quickly, and that for him, wouldn't do.

His men were silent. They knew that when he planned to hurt someone, they were not to interfere but to wait until he gave them an instruction. Nothing else.

Taking another deep breath, he felt calm and ready to deal with what he needed to.

There had been pregnancy tests waiting in the kitchen when he woke that morning. Hunter knew how to be efficient, but for Logan, there couldn't be any other way.

Checking over his tools, he was satisfied the knife was sharp, as were the scissors. He didn't need much to cause pain, or to get answers. He didn't have any elaborate tools to electrocute or to maim. Just enough to harm.

Tapping his fingers on his thigh, he glanced at the time, and finally, the door to the warehouse was open.

The sheriff had a gag in his mouth, and Hunter marched him across the room.

One look at him and the sheriff started to wriggle and try to get away. Helping Hunter with the straps, Logan tied the man to the chair. The door had been closed by one of the guards nearest.

"I see we meet again, only this time, we're in my world, not yours. Welcome," Logan said. He grabbed a chair, dragging it across the cement floor and straddling it.

He reached out, pulling the gag down. "There, that is so much better, isn't it? I can hear you now."

"What is going on, Logan?" the sheriff asked. He looked like he was going to piss his pants.

"You and I, we have unfinished business."

"I did everything you wanted. I looked the other way. No one asked about Ava. No one cared. You're free to do what you want with her. You're not going to be hurt from us."

Logan laughed.

"I had no fear of being hurt by you, or by any of you." He tutted. "This is such boring old bullshit, I tell you." Logan stretched his neck from side to side.

He loved the fear. For him, it never got old. Unlike Luke, he never got off on hurting those weaker than he was. He would openly admit to being a bully, to hurting others, but he got off on taking down those who thought they were above him.

Like the sheriff in front of him.

He was supposed to be a man of the law, but they both knew he was anything but.

"Logan, please, I don't understand."

"I want you to tell me what happened twelve years ago," Logan said.

"We have talked about this. I don't know the point of going over old ground."

"Tell me again."

SAM CRESCENT

"Is this about Ava? She is lying. It's all she knows how to do."

He grabbed one of the sharpest blades and embedded it in the man's thigh.

His screams rang out. The warehouse was empty, so his voice echoed off the walls, and to Logan, it was the sweetest music. He loved to hear the sound and would gladly listen to it all day.

Pulling out the blade, he gently laid it back on the tray.

"I've got a feeling in my gut, Sheriff. It has been festering for some time, and I don't like it. It's the feeling you're fucking lying to me. So, convince me. Tell me which one of you is the liar."

"She is. She came to me. She told me how you hurt her in the locker room. She'd gone for a swim, and she was hurting and she—" He was cut off by his screams.

Logan had pierced the other leg. He leaned in close. "The report I read said about the classroom, Sheriff." He waited, letting the words sink in.

Within a few minutes he'd already caught the sheriff in a lie. He looked over toward Hunter. The other man wasn't saying a word. There was no reason to.

"Yes, yes, of course. I'm sorry. It was twelve years ago. You know how the mind plays tricks and well, forgets."

"Really?" Logan said.

"Yes. It's a long time. A lifetime." The sheriff laughed.

Logan was laughing. He wasn't even faintly amused.

Staring at the man in front of him, he was disgusted, sickened, and wanted nothing more than to hurt him. He kept on watching him, feeling the minutes

211

tick by. Ava was waiting for him back at the bar, but he didn't need to be in any kind of rush.

This was a long time coming. He couldn't believe he'd left the town without even dealing with this little problem.

The sheriff was a monster and needed to be dealt with.

"So you're telling me, the first serious case, a rape one, in the entire history of your residency as sheriff, and you can't remember the finer details. This was a big case for you." Now looking back, Logan stared at him.

He'd been so caught up in his own bullshit and the lies surrounding him, he'd not cared about what happened back at the town. Why would he care about a town he wasn't going back to unless it was to take out his revenge on Ava?

"What did you do?" he asked.

"I don't know what you're talking about."

Logan got up, kicking the chair out of his way and wrapped his fingers around the man's throat. "I'm getting tired of all these games. I know, *Sheriff.*" He spat the words in the man's face. "I know about Luke. Now tell me to my face what the fuck happened or the next thing to cut off will be your precious dick." He brought the knife toward his dick, ready to slice it off with the single flick of the wrist. He'd gladly do it.

"Fine! Fine! They paid me. Luke's parents, they knew he was a problem and he was always getting into trouble. They wanted me to look out for him, and the moment Ava Marshall came in and told me what happened, I called them. I needed to know what they wanted me to do."

"It's all true?" Logan asked. He held onto the knife even tighter.

"Yes. They told me that Luke couldn't go down for it, and I had to pick a name."

"And you picked me?"

"No, I didn't pick you. I couldn't pick you. I didn't pick anyone." The sheriff was crying now.

He had the knife pressed hard to his crotch, and he wanted to slice the dick right off.

"Who picked me then? Did you put all of our names in a hat?"

"Luke picked you. He told me you'd take the fall. His parents agreed and set it up."

"What did you get out of it?"

"They knew what I liked. They set it up so I could have them any time I wanted."

"Them?"

"Boys. All of them. Whenever I wanted."

He stared at the man who'd arrested him, who had made him feel worthless.

"Ava never mentioned me?"

"Only as Luke's best friend. She said you had nothing to do with it. I tried to get her to change her story. She was determined to name Luke."

"So in place of all the Lukes you put my name and changed it. Settled for me pleading guilty."

"You used Luke's parents' lawyer if you remember. Your family's lawyer didn't have the practice or knowledge in criminal law."

He'd handed over his name and future to the bastard who did this to him.

"With the right contacts and money, they could do whatever they wanted, and they did. You were just caught in the crossfire, Logan." The sheriff cried out. "I'm sorry. I'm so sorry."

"Did you laugh at her?"

"What?"

"When Ava came to tell you the truth, did you laugh at her?"

"Yes. Of course. Luke could have anyone. Why would he want to be with her? It was stupid. She should have been grateful anyone wanted to look her way."

He shoved the blade into the man's dick. Without reason why, he started to hack at the man's cock, slashing him.

Blood soaked through the fabric, coating the chair, spilling down onto the floor. There was nothing left of his dick, and once he was done, his thirst for blood wasn't over.

His screams flowed out like sweet music, and he loved it, relished it.

All this time, he'd been living a lie. Helping the bastard who had brought him to this life and letting him live for free. Even paying the bastard for raping his woman.

Ava.

He stopped.

The sheriff wasn't dead yet.

"Logan, you okay?" Hunter asked.

He'd put Ava in harm's away. It was so fucking clear now. Her fear. Luke had gone to her room back at Crow Valley, had hurt her, and he'd done nothing.

"Logan?"

He ignored Hunter. Stepping back, he wiped the back of his nose. The sheriff was gasping for breath. The fucker deserved to hurt so much more.

Hunter stepped forward, snapping his fingers. "Look at me, Logan."

He stared at his friend.

"Are you okay?"

He shook his head.

"Leave us," Hunter said, calling out to the guards.

Get your shit together. You're the boss. No one else.

Shaking his mind from the fog, he realized they were alone, and the sheriff, his life was fading slowly.

"What's going on?"

"All this time, I've helped him, Hunter. I was there for him because I believed he was there for me."

"Luke hates your fucking guts," the sheriff said. "He said you were a fucking prick, losing bastard. He doesn't want you to have anything. It's why he threw you under a bus and no one else. You're nothing to him. Never have been and never will be. You're nothing."

Logan stared at the sheriff, and it was like his life flashed before his eyes. The moment he'd always mistaken as friendship and banter, turned and changed as he realized his "best friend" despised him.

"You're right, but seeing as you're into fucking little kids, I think I'm going to have some fun with you before you get the chance to leave."

****

The nightclub was amazing. Ava loved the music, the atmosphere. She smiled as couples ground together to the heavy beat of the music, and it made her think of Logan. This club was entirely legal; he'd told her before leaving her all on her lonesome.

Glancing over at the clock, she saw he'd been gone several hours and didn't want to think of what he was doing or who he was doing it with. It didn't matter.

She was having fun.

Admittedly, she hadn't gone down to dance or party. There was a guard on the door who could escort her, but if there was a person she wanted to go with, it was Logan, not his guard.

Sipping at the alcoholic drink brought her, she smiled. The little umbrella was a nice touch.

She drank a little more down, tapping her foot and watching everything below.

Logan had told her no one could see her up here. If she wanted, she'd be able to walk around completely naked, but that was never, ever going to happen. She rather liked being able to watch people without them seeing her.

Putting her drink back on the desk, she rested her chin on her hands and stared out over the crowd.

This place was all Logan.

The energy was incredible. She thought about the fight she'd seen. The violence. This was another side to him, and she really liked it. Tapping her foot on the floor, she wondered what it was like for Logan. How he was able to put aside any fear to fight and kill.

This was a whole other world than anything she'd ever known. Growing up in Crow Valley, there was nothing else.

Flicking her hair off her shoulder, she wondered if he ever thought about her.

Of course he thought about you. He planned all of this. Coming and getting you. Hurting you. This was his big plan for revenge.

Logan wanted to hurt her, and Luke, like always, got away with it.

Ava stood as she heard the doors to the office open. She hoped to see Logan. What she didn't expect to see was her nightmare standing right in front of her.

"Well, I didn't expect to see you here."

"This is Logan's office. What are you doing here?"

"Is that any way to talk to me?" Luke asked.

She stood up. There was no way she was going to allow herself to be in any kind of vulnerable position.

"You're not supposed to be here."

"I can do whatever the hell I want."

"I wonder if Logan has any idea of the hatred you have for him." She had to get out of the room, but Luke flicked the lock into place. "What have you done to the guards?"

"I haven't done anything. I know I couldn't take them. I let them know Logan informed me they could go."

"You're not the one who should give that order. Logan wouldn't have told them."

"People are stupid. They like to think they know people, but look at Logan. He doesn't even realize I can have this place wrapped around my little finger and he doesn't have to do anything but tell people to make me happy. That's all they do, make me happy. They never get in my way, and I can do whatever the fuck I want. Like tonight, I went to pay a little visit to the slut who ran her mouth, only to find she is protected. Logan's stupid. He doesn't want to believe the truth right in front of him."

"What did you do to the other woman?"

"Oh, she's safe for now. I'll handle her. The way I handle everyone. You see, Ava, you were my first."

"What?"

"Your nice, tight, dry pussy, wrapped around my dick. I was right all along. I didn't have to force any chick. I could have who I wanted, whenever I wanted. Just the click of my fingers, showing off a couple of bucks, and you wouldn't believe the kind of ass I'd get."

She hated this man. The way he talked, it sickened her.

"What I could get them to do. Um! It was a fucking dream, I tell you. Don't get me wrong. Some of them played hard to get. As they should, you know. But all it took was a couple hundred bucks and their ass was mine." He grabbed his crotch, and she felt her stomach turn.

This couldn't be happening.

"You though, you were like magic. I didn't even know what I was fucking missing until I held you down and took from you what you didn't want taken."

"You need to leave."

"I got a taste for it, and it has been so easy. No one believes a desperate woman. Not when you wire money into her bank account."

"You're a monster."

"And Logan, I mean it was a stroke of genius when the sheriff called. My parents were pissed, but I already figured out who I'd stitch up. Back then, I was the most powerful. I could have anyone do whatever I wanted. My parents were rich, and after I raped you, I knew I'd get him to take the fall. After all, I'd seen the way he looked at you. How he touched you. And I knew, he would do anything to kill you once you told those lies."

"And now I'm the richest motherfucker in town with all the power," Logan said.

Ava jumped. In the doorway, Logan stood with Hunter. How much had he heard?

From the look on his face, all of it.

They stepped through the door, and Hunter flicked the lock back into place.

"I locked that door," Luke said.

"No, I changed the locks. All you did was flick the catch and I had it installed to open both ways. You think I didn't know you were stealing from me? I knew all along. It wasn't exactly hard to guess. You always arrived, had a good time, money was gone." He shrugged.

Ava gasped as Logan removed his jacket. His

white shirt was covered with blood.

Was this it? Was this how her life was going to end?

She felt sick.

"Dude, Ava and I were just talking, shooting the shit, that's how I see it."

"Really, from where I was standing, you were taunting her with what you can get over on me. The shit you can do without me batting a fucking eye. How you had all the power when we were kids. Come on, dickhead. Keep on going. Keep on praising yourself for being the good friend you are."

"You're hearing things."

"Do you know whose blood this is?" Logan asked.

She didn't want to know. Staring into his eyes, she saw the anger and the rage shining within them.

"I don't know. Some poor schmuck? Look, Logan, what you heard. It was all bullshit. You know that. I was being an asshole."

"It's the sheriff's," Logan said, interrupting.

"What's the sheriff's?"

"This." He pointed to the blood. "All of it. Every single drop of perverted sheriff blood. You want to know why I got all this blood on my hands."

"You got really bad at throwing knives?"

"I found out the truth."

"Come on, Logan. Do you really think I'm capable of that? Please, they're messing with your head. Does this go back to that slut? She wanted it rough. She told me."

"You raped Ava. She went to the sheriff and reported it. You hurt her in the girls' locker room after she'd been swimming. It's why she can't stand to go swimming now and will never enter the locker room again." Logan took a step closer. "The sheriff had your name changed to mine, and your lawyer negotiated a deal to keep me out of jail so this wouldn't go to any judge or jury. Where Ava wouldn't have to testify and tell the truth. All this time, you manipulated this shit, and what did I get out of it?" Logan smiled. "I guess I can't complain. You're standing in the office of my club. You work for me. Your parents squandered your fortune in helping you stay out of trouble. This, is all me."

Luke's face changed. He was no longer smiling or laughing.

"What are you going to do, Logan, kill me?" Luke burst out laughing.

It was all fake.

All lies.

"I won in the end. I will still be the first man inside her virgin pussy, and you, you're nothing. I have everything, and you have nothing. You sent one of your men to capture videos of her fucking. You're not even second or third."

Ava didn't know what she was about to see as Logan approached Luke. There was a violence there.

Hunter moved toward her and gripped her.

"What are you doing?"

"What you're about to see, you can never tell a living breathing soul or you will be dead."

"You can look Ava in the eyes and know all this time, I fucking won. I fucked her. I hurt her, and no one believed her. Not even you. The precious knight you used to think you were."

Logan grabbed Luke around the throat, cutting off his air supply. Luke instantly started to choke.

"You think you're in any position to taunt me? I was never a fucking knight, Luke. I was always a bully. A worse one than you. Look around you. Look what I created in the death and blood of my victims. This is all me. Every single part of me, and you, Luke, you're not going to live to see anymore."

She cried out as Logan pulled a small knife out of his pocket, opened it up, and plunged it into Luke's crotch.

She didn't know what she was seeing or what the hell was happening.

Logan loosened his hold to let Luke scream.

"Look at her," Logan said. "Look at her and know she is going to have the best fucking life I can offer her, and you, you're going to be rotting in a gutter."

Luke was shaking. Perspiration dotted his brow.

"You will never be free," Luke said.

"I *am* free."

He plunged the knife into Luke's neck, ending his life right before her eyes.

Ava was in shock. Her body shook and Hunter tried to hide the scene from her, but it was there for her to see.

"Hunter, take her home. I'll deal with her when I get back."

She didn't put up a fight as Hunter led her out of the office. There were guards waiting and what looked like a cleaning crew, all of them ready to do what their boss had ordered.

Hunter put her in the back of the car, and she curled up in a ball, trying to escape everything she'd just seen.

"Are you okay?"

"He killed him."

"Luke deserved it. Don't tell me you're mourning for that sick fuck."

She shook her head.

"Good."

They were driving, and the city, it was all a blur. The lights, all of it. She didn't see a thing as Hunter took her back home.

Not to Crow Valley.

To Logan's apartment.

When he pulled back into the private parking space, she didn't wait for him to open the door. She climbed out and looked at the door.

Hunter was there, taking her by the hand, leading her toward safety.

The moment they entered the apartment, she went straight toward the shower. She climbed in fully dressed, turning on the hot water, scalding her flesh as she removed the dress Logan had picked out for her.

She didn't use soap or conditioner, just stood beneath the spray, letting it roll off her.

Slowly, she turned it to cold, the chill making her shiver.

She turned the water off the moment she couldn't take anymore, stepping out of the tub, and grabbed a towel. Had she really seen Logan kill Luke?

It was all too easy, wasn't it?

The blade slicing through his body. Draining his life.

It was almost too much for her.

Drying her body, she pulled on a pair of pajamas and went out to sit in the living room.

Hunter was already waiting.

"Hot chocolate soothes all pains and problems," Hunter said.

"I'm not in pain."

"No, but you have a whole host of problems, and I imagine you're pretty freaked out right now."

"A little."

She sat down, and Hunter handed her the hot

chocolate.

"Sorry, I've never seen anything like that."

"If it makes you feel any better, that was a quick kill. The bastard didn't deserve it. He should have been made to suffer more."

She laughed. "I don't know why I'm laughing. This is not something to make fun of."

"I wasn't making fun. Logan did what he had to do. Do you really think if he let Luke go, he'd disappear and live a nice life away from you?"

"I don't know what to think."

"Men like Luke, they set out to hurt and destroy people. It's what they do. They don't know any other way."

"And what about Logan? What does he do?" she asked. "What does any of this mean for us? So he knows the truth. Luke, he lied about so much. There is so much pain because of him. What do we do about it?"

"We take it one day at a time, like everyone does. We make it work, somehow."

"Do you know what the scary thing is?" she asked.

"What?"

"I don't even feel guilty about his death. Luke deserved it. Does it make me a bad person?"

"You're talking to the wrong guy here. I don't think it makes you anything. I hated Luke, so seeing him die was no hardship to me. He didn't have a right to walk free. Not after what he'd done to you and Logan. Drink your cocoa. I don't want Logan to be upset with me because I didn't take care of you."

****

Twelve years ago

"I have to say I don't see the attraction," Luke said.

Ava looked around the girls' locker room, and no one was in sight. She'd been taking late classes as the pool was open when the guys were training out on the football field. Sometimes there were cheerleaders, but there was some kind of competition and she was alone.

"This is the girls' locker room. You shouldn't be here."

"Oh, I know." Luke smiled. "I've watched him for a few years now. He thinks he's got it all covered up. No one knows his little secret, but I do."

"I have no idea what you're talking about."

"Of course you don't. Why would you know? You don't know anything," Luke stepped closer toward her.

She wrapped her towel a little tighter around herself.

"I know that you're not supposed to be here, so any kind of prank you're playing needs to be dealt with elsewhere."

"I doubt you'd be making jokes if you knew what was at stake."

Ava cried out as he shoved her hard against the locker.

"I've watched you as well, Ava. I've seen the way you are, and I'm not impressed with what I see."

"If you hate it so much, leave me alone." Her heart raced, and she had never felt so scared in all her life. She felt sick to her stomach. Petrified. This couldn't be happening, and yet, it was.

She tilted her head back, looking up at him, waiting.

"I can't do that. You see, Logan, I've got a problem with the guy. He seems to go through life getting everything he ever wanted. What he looks at, it's his within a matter of days, if not hours. Now, with you,

you're different. At first, I figured it was because you were indifferent to us. You thought you were better than us, but now I see it's not that. Logan likes you. He has the hots for you. You make his dick hard, and it confuses him. Poor guy doesn't know what to do around you other than rub himself all over you, acting like a big dog." He tutted.

"You're wrong," she said.

"Am I? You weren't alone in that classroom when he had his hands down your pants. I was right there, seeing the action. Watching you. I knew then what I could have that he never would." He gripped the edge of her swimsuit, and she grabbed his hand.

It didn't do her any good.

He pulled the suit down, and she cried out.

Fighting against him, she tried to make him let go of her, but he wouldn't do it. He held onto her tightly, and she couldn't push him away. During the struggle, he managed to pull her swimsuit completely off, and she fought him, trying to get away.

She was on her hands and knees, fighting with all of her might, but it did no good.

There, on the dirty floor of the girls' locker room, she lost her virginity. It was torn from her by Luke as he raped her, spewing about how it was supposed to be Logan's but now he had that piece of cherry all to himself, and no one else was ever going to take it from him.

Chapter Thirteen

All of Logan's clothes were burned, the mess in the warehouse and the club cleaned up. There wasn't a single trace of the sheriff or Luke near him.

He sat in the hallway outside his apartment, staring at the door.

He'd faced so many opponents over the years. Some taller than he was, stronger, fitter, wiser. He'd made sure none of them saw his fear or his nerves.

Beyond his door was a woman he had laughed at. He'd taken revenge on her for something she hadn't done.

Running fingers through his hair, he didn't move from his precious spot. He watched the door, knowing Hunter would take care of her.

The only real friend he had in his life was Hunter.

He'd already put a call out to all of his businesses, saying Riley and Marvin were cut off. They were not to get freebies and would soon be cut out of his life for good. It was the only way he could do this.

After what Luke did, he was never going to trust them again.

He didn't know the full extent of the truth his friends were told, but it was already too much. He'd deal with them, and that wouldn't take long, bringing him back to his current problem.

Ava.

The girl he should have been there for.

He'd known she'd started to go swimming after school. She once told him it helped her to think, especially if one of her assignments wasn't coming together. Luke must have found out during one of his times of watching him, trying to find any means to hurt him.

Logan sent Hunter a text letting him know he was outside.

Within seconds the door opened, and Hunter was there.

He closed the door and sat with his back leaning up against the door.

"I told you to watch her."

"I am watching her. She's inside, asleep. Curled up on the sofa, waiting for you. I gave her a hot chocolate."

"Did you drug her?"

"No. She's out cold because of exhaustion. Don't worry, I won't hurt her."

"No, you won't, and neither will I."

"Is this the reason you're out here and not in there?" Hunter asked.

Logan stared at his friend. "You hated him."

"I know."

"Did you ever suspect him of doing this?"

"No."

"You didn't?"

"I can hate men without them being rapists, Logan."

"What was it about him that you hated?"

"I don't know. It was the fact he was always there, breathing down your neck, trying to get you to do something, anything he wanted you to do. It was like he had this hold, and he knew it as well. What I didn't know was what he'd done."

"Ava told me."

"She did me as well."

"Did you believe her?" Logan asked.

Hunter paused. "I … I didn't outright believe her, but I also didn't think she was lying. I know this is complicated."

"No, it's not. She was telling the truth the whole time, but the sheriff, Luke, his parents, they're the ones who ruined my life."

"You got them both now. You made up for it."

"What if it's not enough?"

"I don't understand."

"I don't know if I can face her. How can I marry her and keep her, when I forced her to be naked in a room with Luke? To come while he watched? I didn't believe her. I thought the worst, and look what happened. She was the main victim."

"Logan, after everything that has happened tonight, you need to step into that room, talk to her. At least, do that. She deserves it after everything. Don't do anything rash or stupid. Just take your time with all of this. There is no reason to do anything right now."

"You're being the voice of reason."

"You're the one who taught me not to go breaking down walls that didn't need to be broken. Ava needs you right now. Even if it is just for a hug. You've got to give her that chance."

"I don't know if I can be all that she needs."

"She needs the man who just killed in front of her to hold her. To put aside whatever mess is between you two. Did you take the pregnancy tests?" Hunter asked.

"Fuck, I didn't even think about them."

"You were the one who wanted them. You've got to make this right. I'll be right outside if you need me." Hunter shuffled out of the way, and Logan got to his feet.

"I don't like you right now."

"Don't need to like me," Hunter said. "Besides, you and I both know I'm loyal to you and only you."

Entering his penthouse suite, Logan closed the door.

He took each step slowly, removing his jacket

and entering the sitting room. Sure enough, Ava was curled up on the sofa. She looked so peaceful.

He walked toward her, sitting down on the edge of the coffee table, watching her. She was so beautiful. Age had only deepened that beauty.

He reached out, tucking a strand behind her ear, and smiling as she moaned a little. It was a soft sound but oh, so sweet.

"Hey, beautiful," he said, when she opened her eyes.

"Hey." She didn't smile.

He saw the tears in her eyes. "Are you afraid of me?"

"No. How are you?" She sat up but didn't make a move to hold him.

He wanted to touch her so badly.

"I'm fine. Believe me, this is in no way a new experience for me."

"What is it then?" she asked. "I'm sorry. I shouldn't have asked."

"I'm sorry," he said.

"What do you have to be sorry about?"

He stared at her, and hoped she saw it.

"Logan?"

"I should have believed you."

"You didn't know."

"But you told me, and I laughed in your face."

"I'm a little fuzzy about everything," she said.

"Luke had a hold on me up until twenty-four hours ago."

"And now?"

"He's dead."

"Do you miss him?" Ava asked.

"No. I couldn't miss someone who treated me like that. His death, it was a long time in coming, and it was way too easy for him as well."

"Logan, he was still your best friend."

"Who raped you. If he didn't know how I felt about you, he'd never have been given the chance."

"You don't know that. He was a monster."

"And I'm the worst one there is. This is all based on lies." He saw the tears fall, and he reached out, gently swiping them away. "At least you're not afraid of me after everything I did to you."

"We can't change the past, Logan."

"How can you even bear to look at me?" he asked.

"You saved me."

He shook his head and got to his feet. "Everything is a fucking mess."

Ava grabbed his hand, pulling him down so he collapsed beside her on the sofa. She wrapped her arms around him and held him tight.

"What are you doing?" he asked.

"I think you need a hug."

"I'm not a little kid."

"You don't have to be to need a hug. We all need a little comfort." She didn't let him go, and he there was no way he'd complain about having his face pressed against her tits.

Get your head out of the gutter.

"How about for the rest of the night, we promise not to talk about the past. About what happened, and we pretend it's just the three of us."

"Three of us, have you taken a test?" he asked, putting his hand across her stomach.

"No, I haven't taken a test." She sighed. "I don't know the answer to that question." She put her hand over his.

"Do you want to know the answer?"

"Not right now. I think I just want to sit with you while the rest of the world ticks on by."

He kept his hand on her stomach. "Is it wrong that I hope you are?"

"What do you mean?" she asked.

"I hope you're pregnant with my child."

"Oh. You'd like me to have a child? Mine and yours?"

"Yes."

She looked down at his hands and nodded. "Let's go and see, shall we?"

"Ava?"

"If you want to know, there is only one way to find out. You *do* know it requires me to pee right?"

"I know."

He got to his feet, but when she made to lead him toward where the tests were, he stopped her, cupping her face.

"I'm going to make sure no harm ever comes to you again."

"I know, Logan."

"No, I mean it. You will always, always, be protected." He cupped her face, tilting her head back so she had no choice but to look at him.

"I love your eyes. That never stopped, not even once."

"I don't know how I feel about this guy who will talk about anything," she said. "I'm not used to you being so open to everything."

"There are a lot of things I'm going to be open to now, so you better prepare for them." He pressed a kiss to her lips. He wanted more but wasn't willing to push, not tonight.

"I can't wait to see what you've got on offer."

This time, when she took them to the kitchen, he

didn't stop her.

He wondered if her stomach was twisting and turning like his. If she was pregnant, he didn't know what he'd do.

He'd never really thought about having a child, not before Ava. His life hadn't given him a chance to enjoy the thought of a family.

With Ava, he wanted her to be pregnant.

With the night's revelations, he wanted something to be able to hold her close to him, to not let her go, ever. Getting her pregnant would be another step to being able to keep her, to hold onto her, and never let go.

She picked up a test, and he grabbed a couple more.

"How much do you think I can pee? One test should be good," she said.

"You're nervous."

"Aren't you?"

"No, I know what it is I want, and this, this is it, with you."

"Wow," she said. "Let's go and find out what is going to happen."

They entered the bathroom, and he leaned up against the counter.

"You're going to stay?"

"Yes."

"I have to pee."

"I killed a man in front of you. I think I can handle some urine. Don't worry."

"I'm thinking after this I want you to still be attracted to me."

"I will be."

"Can you at least turn around?" she asked.

He rolled his eyes but turned around.

When it was done, she put the test on the counter beside her, washing her hands. He noticed how they shook. Standing behind her, he gripped her shoulders, kissing her head. This, to him, felt right. This was what he wanted with her.

"Now we wait," she said.

The time ticked on by, and he kept an eye on his wristwatch.

"Oh," Ava said.

It wasn't time, but the test was clear. There was no going back for either of them. She was pregnant with his baby.

He wrapped his arms around her, pressing his lips against her neck.

"Hello, Mommy," he said.

****

The following morning, Ava cut into her pancake and tried not to think about what happened last night.

She was over Luke's death. Seeing him die hadn't affected her too much. She had a nightmare he'd come back from the dead, but Logan held her, and she was able to go back to sleep.

Pregnant.

She put a hand on her stomach, wondering if her unborn child knew what she'd witnessed.

Don't be silly.

She was going to have a baby.

A little human being.

Picking up her knife, she cut into the pancake and again, focused on her breakfast. There was so much to do. First, she had to go to a doctor to find out what she actually needed to worry about. There would always be worry for a firstborn, or at least, that was what she was told.

Would Logan want to raise their child in the

penthouse, or find a house? Did he even want to raise the family together? What about their future?

Their past had just been flung wide open, and now, she didn't have a clue what to do. There was so much uncertainty waiting for her that it scared her.

Running fingers through her hair, she finished her pancakes and blew out a breath. She didn't have to start making plans right away. She would take it in steps.

The first being, getting the confirmation of her pregnancy. The second … she didn't know what to do about the second.

Tests could lie.

She didn't feel sick, and women were supposed to.

"Oh, Mom, I wish you were alive today to help me out with all this. I don't think I'm ready to be a mother."

How could she take care of another human being when her own life was so messed up already?

She got to her feet as she heard the door open. Hunter hadn't stayed with her this morning, and as she walked toward the corridor, she saw Logan and Hunter heading her way.

"We've got an appointment within the hour," Logan said.

"For what?"

"At the doctor."

"We didn't even say who we were going to see," she said.

"I've got someone I trust, and they're already scheduled to see you." Logan cupped her cheeks, tilting her head back and kissing her deeply.

She closed her eyes, aware of Hunter in the background, watching them.

"What's going on?" she asked, opening her eyes

when he pulled away.

"Nothing."

"I don't know. That kiss wasn't nothing, it was something."

Hunter chuckled.

"Come on, we'll head on over now. They may see us sooner."

She stared into his eyes, wondering what was going on. Something wasn't right, but she didn't know what it was. Instead of asking him, she grabbed her coat, which he'd bought her several days ago.

Hunter took the lead, walking out of the penthouse as Logan locked it behind her.

Thrusting her hands in her pockets, she moved between the men, waiting for either of them to speak, but no words were passed between them.

She counted the floors as they headed down, waiting for something more, but still getting nothing.

The doors opened up into the underground parking, and Logan took her arm, leading her toward the car. He held the door open, and she slid inside, moving across the seat to give him room as well.

Tucking hair behind her ear, she waited. They were once again on the road.

"The city's always so busy," she said. "No matter the day or night."

"It's easy for people to get lost in it. To lose all sense of time and space," Logan said.

Awkward conversation.

She pressed her lips together, waiting for the time to pass, but it didn't, not really.

Staring out of the window she tried not to think what was going on. Touching her lips, the kiss he'd given her, it meant something, but again, she wasn't entire sure what was going on. Hunter wasn't giving away any secrets either. He seemed to be content to look outside the window.

Within thirty minutes they arrived at the doctor's office. There weren't many clients, and Logan whispered to her it was a private clinic. Hunter checked them in, and they each took a seat. There was another couple sitting opposite them. Her stomach was swollen, and the man beside her was whispering words in her ear while rubbing her belly.

They looked so happy together.

Ava wondered what it would be like to experience something like that. The love between the couple.

She and Logan, there was history, chemistry but never love. She didn't even know if he was capable of such an emotion.

They didn't have to wait long before they were seen by the doctor. Before he prescribed her anything, he took some blood to confirm the pregnancy, and also checked her blood pressure, weight, and height. He did an overall check while they waited for the blood work to return.

It would seem Logan's sway with people extended to everything. There was nothing he couldn't have. Whatever he wanted, people jumped to go and get.

They were shown to a waiting room. She was offered a green tea while Logan took coffee. She stared down into her cup. Hunter had been present with them every step of the way so far. It was odd, but having him around provided her a great deal of comfort.

"How are you feeling?" Logan asked.

"Nervous."

"Do you want the test to deny the one we took?"

"No. I don't know. Do you?"

"I'm happy you're pregnant."

"Oh, that's okay then." She rubbed at her temple, feeling the beginning of a headache. "Logan, why do I feel something's going on that you're not telling me about?"

He smiled and looked down at her lap, his hand going to her knee. "It's nothing for you to worry about."

"But there *is* something for me to worry about?"

"No."

They were called again before she even got a chance to question him further. He was confusing her.

When they entered the doctor's office, he confirmed she was indeed pregnant. She was prescribed some folic acid, advised to take it easy, and to also forgo cheese and nuts. He gave her a couple of pamphlets for her to read, and sent them on their way with an appointment in a month.

Now, as she sat in the car, she stared down at each pamphlet. Each one showed a pregnant woman, or a woman with a child, even breastfeeding.

"Should I breastfeed?" she asked.

"Do you want to?"

She opened up the pamphlet. "I have no idea. There is so much to take in."

"Didn't you ever consider having kids one day?" he asked.

She snorted. "When I was a kid, sure. I thought about getting married and having it all, but I don't know. Look at all of this. I didn't think I'd ever have kids as a grownup."

"You won't be doing it alone. You're going to have me."

She turned toward him. "Did you want kids?"

"I don't think about kids."

"You're not even curious about them?"

"No."

"I was an only child, and kids, they're a byproduct of not being properly protected or a relationship. I've not had to worry about either. I don't forget, and I don't have relationships."

"So what's this?" she asked. "Is this a mistake? It's not like you ever tried to protect either of us from this? I'm not saying it's your fault. I didn't stop you, did I?"

"This was a mistake. An error in judgment."

His admission hurt so much more.

She closed up the pamphlets, pressed her lips together, and looked out of the window. They weren't heading toward his penthouse. She'd been traveling back and forth a few times now to know the sights to see to let her know where they were.

"Where are we?"

Hunter brought the car to a stop outside of a building. It looked fancy. Old-fashioned woodwork and large windows. Dated, not decayed.

Logan climbed out of the car, holding out his hand for her to take. Still, no one spoke to her, and she followed them out of the car. If he planned to kill her, wouldn't he have taken her to a warehouse or somewhere more private?

Stop thinking about death.

You're a mistake, not a problem.

You did see him kill a man.

Why go through all of this when he could have killed me?

She wouldn't go crazy or insane.

Hunter waited back in the car, and this was new for her. She didn't know if she liked this or not.

She held off her questions as they entered the building. He walked her to the fourth floor where there were only two doors. Logan went to one, fitting a key within the lock and twisting.

He took her hand, leading her inside, closing the door, and flicking on the light.

"What do you think?" he asked.

It was a fully furnished apartment. There was no torture chair or plastic bag to capture her dead body.

Instead, it was warm. The heat surrounded her instantly.

Stepping into the apartment, she noted the large sofa, which dominated the sitting room. In the corner was a decent sized television. She wouldn't have to squint to see. Rugs covered the wooden floors, but they were nice, along with a single coffee table. A vase of red roses sat in the center.

"Have a look around," he said.

She stepped through to the kitchen and dining room. It was a nice space with modern appliances.

There were two bedrooms. One had a queen size bed, closet, and bathroom. The other was blank, carpeted, with no furniture.

"What do you think?" he asked, when she came out of the empty bedroom.

"It's wonderful place. Have you bought it?"

He held up the key. "It's yours."

"Mine?" She stared at the key, refusing to take it.

"Yes, this is your apartment. Two-bedroom, luxury." He shook the key, and she still didn't reach out. "Fine, there's more I want to show you." He put the keys down and she finally noticed a stack of files and leaflets on the table. They were all neatly placed in a pile.

"I don't know what college you'd like to go to, but I've made a selection."

"College?" She frowned, stepping up toward him.

"Whatever it is you want, all you've got to do is pick."

"I don't know what is going on," she said.

"You missed out on college, and you can do whatever you want. Any place you'd like to visit."

"Logan, what is going on?" she asked. "I know I keep asking the same question, but I'm really confused. We go to the doctor's and they confirm I'm pregnant. I thought this was good news. Now I've got an apartment, and you're offering me college. I'm thirty years old."

"So? Age doesn't matter when it comes to education."

"But what gives? This is all amazing. Don't get me wrong, I'm really grateful, but I thought I lived with you."

Logan sighed. "You can't go back to Crow Valley. Not after everything that went down. I won't allow you to, nor will I allow my son or daughter. You deserve more than what they had to offer."

"And you think this place is it? What's wrong with where you live? Are you moving in with me?"

He didn't look at her.

"You're not moving in with me."

"No, I'm not."

"Why?"

"Ava—"

"Look at me, Logan. Say what you've got to say, but you've got to look at me when you do it." She didn't like how her heart was breaking or the sick feeling twisting her gut.

He lifted his head. "Ava, this, between us, it's not going to work."

"You said you'd be here for the baby," she said.

"I will. You and I, the best way to make this work is if we only see each other when the baby is involved."

"Is this because you know the truth? Are you ashamed of me?"

"No." He stood up and made to move toward her, but she stepped back, needing the space. Right now, she couldn't handle him touching her.

She held on by a very thin thread, but if he pushed too hard, it would snap and she didn't know how much more she could hold it together.

"Then what is it?"

"I was going to destroy you. I set out to do exactly that. The video of you and Grant, it never should have made it out in the world, but I made sure it was. I fucked up."

"So, it doesn't have to mean anything? It doesn't mean anything. I can forgive you, and you're fine now. We're fine." She didn't like how desperate she sounded.

"Ava, I kill people without caring. It meant nothing to me to end Luke's life. In fact, I was pissed off because he got a swift end when he should have suffered."

"None of us get everything out of life we ever wanted. Our lives always change. Some for the better, some for the worse. We can't change what is happening. I can't—you're dumping me?"

"We were never in a relationship in the first place."

"You're feeling guilty for blaming me all these years. But you're not willing to fight for us, for what we've got?" she asked.

"What do we have, Ava? You didn't get to go to college because of me. I didn't get anything out of life I wanted. You think being who I am is what I wanted to become. No, it's not, but I'm that man. I've seen the way you react, and I'm telling you now, you and I, we're not suited to each other. We'll have a child and you'll want for nothing, but that is as far as we go. This is it for us. You and I, we're done."

"Wow," she said. "This house is mine."

"Yes. You've also got an allowance." He put the cards down on the table. "I've got to go. I've got some meetings." Ava watched him walk toward the apartment door. "I've left a cell phone with my number on the kitchen counter. If you need anything, call. Whatever you want, you can have it."

The door closed, shattering her whole world.

There had been hope inside her heart that at the very least they could try to make it together.

Removing her jacket, kicking off her shoes, she sat down on the sofa.

"I guess it's just you and me, kiddo."

Chapter Fourteen

One week later

"Has she picked a college yet?" Logan asked. He didn't look up from the paperwork on his desk. He was looking over the figures John, his finance officer, had given him. Seeing as he'd led him to finally have doubts about Luke's loyalty, he'd decided to keep the man.

Everyone had a bad couple of days or months. He'd help John through his. It was new for him, but only a select bunch of people knew of the trouble John had faced, and well, working together, he saw no reason for the downturn to continue.

"No."

Logan looked up from his paperwork to see Hunter inside his office, but also Grant. At his request, he'd demanded that Grant return.

"What do you mean no? She has had them for more than a week."

"Yep, and so far she's gone to three job applications as well. One was as a waitress. The other at the library, and I think she even tried for a museum," Hunter said, taking a seat.

Grant simply stood, waiting for instructions.

"You remember Ava, don't you?" Logan asked.

"Of course."

"I want you to guard her."

"Logan," Hunter said. "Do you think that is wise?"

"Why? Because they like to fuck one another?"

"Sir," Grant said.

"Look, I'm not trying to be a bastard. You fucked Ava at my request but I saw your dick was hard, so I don't imagine it was such a hardship to do it. She needs looking after," Logan said. He looked at the paperwork.

In his free time, he read pregnancy books. Right now, he didn't want to see facts and figures; he was curious if she experienced morning sickness. It could be nasty for some women, while others didn't feel a thing, and well, he didn't care about other women, just the one.

"Leave us," Hunter said.

Logan waited for the door to close. "Are you the boss now? Do my men follow your orders?"

"They follow the orders they know won't get them killed."

"I have no intention of killing anyone."

"What is this? I thought you wanted Grant back for a job, not for you to want to kill him in a couple of days' time."

"I'm not going to kill him."

"I know you, Logan. You want to kill him dead. Don't even pretend otherwise." Hunter folded his arms. "You push Ava aside. Have me pretty much stalk her every move, and why?"

"Because I want to," Logan said.

"This is guilt. You've got to recognize it and move on."

"And why, do tell, should I do that?"

"If not, it's going to kill you. We both know it will."

"So now you know what will and won't be good for me?" Logan asked.

"Do you have any idea how childish you sound?"

"I'm doing what is best for her!" Logan slammed the paper down along with his fist. Pain radiated up through his arm, exploding out, but he didn't give any indication he felt anything.

Hunter didn't move. "You're feeling guilty."

"I laughed at her, Hunter. I thought it was fucking jokes and lies. I was no better than those pricks. They died too easily. I had her naked in front of the guy who raped her. I'm the one who put her in front of him twelve years ago, and I did it now. Do you have any idea what it's like? She should hate me."

"I think you hate yourself enough for the two of you. Sending Grant to keep an eye on her, do you really think it's wise?"

"I'm not going to give him any instruction to sleep with her. She'll be safe."

"Ava's lonely."

"All the more reason to send Grant."

"You're making a mistake."

"We'll see."

Hunter got to his feet.

"Tell Grant he's to keep his hands off Ava and to keep an eye on her. She wants for nothing. He's her new best friend. Anything to do with the baby, he's to report back to me." He looked up. "Got it?"

"Don't you want to deal with this? To make sure he does it properly?"

"No. You like taking control when it suits you. May as well give you full reins."

Hunter didn't argue with him. He got to his feet and left.

The paperwork didn't mean anything in front of him. It was all a blurred mess with no meaning because there really was no purpose for it.

Throwing it across the room, he didn't get any satisfaction from the mess. Collapsing back in his chair, he spun around in a circle. This had never happened to him. He was doing everything he could to protect her. Why didn't anyone see what he was actually doing? It was all for her own good.

He wasn't father or boyfriend material.

The pains of the past, the revenge driving in his

blood, it had taken over, and the last thing he ever wanted to do was to hurt her.

Ava deserved so much more than a man like him. He killed so easily without caring for anyone. Seeing their life drain out of him, it was boring to him.

Luke's decisions had turned him into this monster, but it was a place he also wanted to be. With this power, no one stood a chance against him.

No one.

It's why he could never give up his crown, nor would he ever want to.

Rubbing at his temples, he wondered if Ava would fall for Grant or how she would see the new addition to her protection detail.

He didn't just use Hunter. He had several men to keep an eye on her. She was the only precious thing in his life.

****

Ava hated violence in all forms. She didn't like watching it on television, but having Grant in her living room, she wanted to slap Logan. She didn't know what game he was trying to play or even if she wanted to play along.

This was unfair.

She turned to Hunter.

"No."

"This isn't your call to make."

"So Logan doing his whole not caring routine thinks this is what I need? My ex who isn't really my ex because he was playing at it the entire time. This is what he thinks I want or need?"

"Grant's here to take care of you. You've been intimate together, but neither of you have permission to do so again."

Ava laughed. "Logan's not giving us permission

to have sex. Isn't he sweet?" She grabbed a pillow, plopping herself back down on the sofa and picking up a newspaper.

"You don't need to find a job," Hunter said. "Anything you want will be provided for you."

"Really? How about the father of my child standing before me, ready for me to slug him in the face? Will he give me that?"

Hunter didn't say a word.

"Figures."

"He's not going to allow you to get a job. The mother of his child doesn't need to work."

"The mother of his child is getting bored. There is nothing here to do, and I know I'm being followed whenever I leave." She put the paper down. "Can you tell him I need to talk to him? Anything?"

"Logan is his own boss. He's only doing what is right for you."

She snorted. "Of course. Logan knows so much already. I guess he knows what I'm thinking and feeling. No, I don't want him here. I'm sorry, I don't."

"You don't have a choice," Grant said, taking a seat on the floor. "I'm now your guardian."

Hunter's cell phone rang. "And duty calls."

He left, and she was alone with Grant. She didn't want him in her apartment or near her. He'd been working for Logan the whole time.

"You're looking good," Grant said.

"Spare me the caring speech," she said. "I don't want to hear it."

"You've gotten an attitude since we last spoke. I like it."

She looked down at the newspaper.

"How have you been?" he asked. "I heard about the tapes."

This got her attention. "Oh, so you know our time together in the hotel room was uploaded onto the internet for all to see?"

"They've been removed."

"I bet there's a trace of them somewhere and it doesn't matter anyway, the damage has already been done."

"I can't find any."

She wanted to be a bitch, but it was too much. Seeing Hunter and now Grant, she couldn't help but face the truth. She missed Logan, and knowing he wouldn't come and see her himself, it hurt and she was taking it out on anyone who dared to step in her way. It wasn't healthy, nor was it good.

"I'm sorry," she said.

"You don't have to apologize to me. I've done my fair share of crap to you. I lied to you. Hurt you."

"It was fine."

"It wasn't. I only followed his orders. I did feel something for you."

"You don't have to lie to me, Grant."

"But I did feel something. I was attracted to you. It's why I wouldn't always meet up with you at the hotel. It was bugged, and there were always cameras. I'm not a saint. I'm not even claiming to be one, okay? I'm not going to pretend there. I did feel something."

She nodded.

"Do you feel anything for me?" Grant asked.

"No, I don't. Did Logan put you up to it?"

"Logan didn't talk to me. He requested my presence, but my instructions came from Hunter. It was a new experience. Usually Logan's all over everything."

She stood up, putting the paper to one side, and walked into the kitchen.

Grabbing a cup, she placed a teabag inside, no

sugar and no milk. She drank mostly fruit-flavored teas. She filled up the kettle, the sight before her going blurry as she did.

"You miss him, don't you?" Grant said.

She put the kettle onto the stove, igniting the flame. She wiped away the tears threatening to fall, before finally looking at him.

"What do you want from me, Grant?" she said.

"Do you love him?"

"No. I don't ... no."

"You don't sound so sure."

"I can't love a man who'd do ... that to me. It's complicated. It's emotions. You wouldn't understand."

"Do you want him to notice you?"

"I'm the mother of his unborn child, so of course I want him to notice me. Why? What is with all the questions?"

"It's Friday night."

"You're getting points here for stating the obvious, but again, I don't know where you're going with all of this."

"He's at his nightclub. Logan's. It's where he goes every single Friday night. He keeps an eye on the main club, and of course any possible deals he wants to do."

"Why are you telling me this?" she asked, suspicion rising up within her.

"He's my boss and well, I did you a wrong, and I've got a feeling, you both have some unfinished business with each other. The only way to resolve it is to push you both together to face it."

"You do realize this man could kill you?" she asked.

"Yes."

"You don't owe me your life, Grant. You were on

those tapes as well."

"I know, but I feel like I've got to do the right thing here. You and Logan, you'll find out one way or the other, right?" Grant asked.

She folded her arms, staring at the man who she had once thought she cared about. "I don't trust you."

"That's fair."

"No. I couldn't do it. No. I'm not the kind of girl to go begging for attention. Logan doesn't want me, and I'm not going to force the issue. What is done. Is done." She stepped around him, going to her bedroom.

She closed the door and slid down, collapsing on the floor. There's no way she could love a man who so easily passed her up, could she? How could she count on Grant after what they'd been through in the past? It was all nonsense to her. She couldn't trust anyone.

Even still, on the floor, touching her stomach, she did miss Logan. It wasn't love, but it was something.

****

Grant stepped out of the apartment room.

"No," he said.

"You're serious, she said no."

"She won't go for it. Maybe in a short time."

Hunter gritted his teeth.

This wasn't working for his friend, nor was it working for Ava.

He had to bring them together one way or another, and he was getting tired of Logan's mood. So far, he'd not killed anyone unnecessarily, but that didn't mean they were going to have much longer before he snapped.

"You can't touch her," Hunter said. "Just be the friend she needs, but don't lead her on, and don't fucking take his place."

"You guys called me, remember? What the fuck

happened while I was busy?" Grant said.

"A whole load of shit that I don't even know how to fucking fix!" Hunter ground out through his teeth. "Just do what you need to do. When I've got a better idea, I'll call you."

He left the apartment building, pissed off.

Slamming his car door, he sat gripping the steering wheel.

Logan was his best friend. His only friend. When he'd been left for dead, Logan had helped him every single step of the way. Even after he learned who he worked for, what he did, he still stood beside him, and Hunter swore a loyalty to always be there for Logan. To be the shield to guard him. He'd protect him with his very life.

No one had ever taken a chance on him before, not until Logan. He saw the pain his best friend was in. He wished he could bring Luke back just to kill him all over again, but this time, he'd go slowly, he'd make the bastard bleed.

Neither Logan nor Ava would admit their feelings for one another.

Hunter didn't even know if they did love each other, but they had chemistry, and if he put Ava's life in danger, Logan would come running.

He wouldn't really go that far, but he needed Logan to snap out of whatever bullshit he was going through.

Chapter Fifteen

The beautiful, deep red dress left on her bed looked absolutely stunning. Ava wasn't stupid. Either Hunter or Grant had left it. She'd closed the door to take a shower, and coming out, she'd seen it.

She didn't know if she'd be able to fit into it. The material looked like it would be a snug fit.

She released the towel she had wrapped around her breasts, letting it fall to the floor. With her hands clenched into tight fists, she lifted her head. Turning to the side, she couldn't really see if she was pregnant or not.

She wasn't showing and could get away with wearing it. The fabric felt so lovely that she had no excuse not to try it on, at least once.

She stepped into the dress, lifting it up. She didn't wear any panties or a bra, and stared at herself. Someone needed to do the zipper at the back.

With no choice but to go to Grant, she opened the door, stepping out. He sat at the dining room table, where he normally sat Friday nights.

It had been three weeks since he'd suggested she go to Logan's nightclub. He'd not even offered the past two.

"Would you mind doing me up?" she asked, presenting her back to him.

"Nice," he said.

"Oh, please, I know you put it in my room."

"I did nothing of the sort." He lifted the catch.

"You're the only other person in my apartment. If anyone else got in, you'd be dead within minutes. You know Logan wouldn't allow you to go slack on the job. How do I look?" She gave a twirl.

"Stunning."

"I'm just going to go look."

The dress was amazing. She didn't feel like a slob either. For the past couple of days, she'd hung out on the sofa, eating.

She and Logan had met up for her doctor's appointment, but he'd not given her the time of day, instead tapping away at his phone, ignoring her.

He'd talked to the doctor, and it would be her next appointment she'd get an ultrasound to show her the baby. She was really excited.

Logan had left her, and Grant had taken her home.

Being ignored by Logan was the worst. Actually, she no longer knew what the worst experience was anymore. She hated it all.

Running fingers through her hair, she stared at her reflection and wondered if he'd ignore her now.

Would it be so wrong to go and visit him? To show him what he's missing?

Don't be so stupid. This is ridiculous.

It's just a dress.

You're pregnant.

You should be home, relaxing. Watching reruns of television programs, ordering Chinese food, and being miserable.

Folding her arms, she looked down at the ink on her arm.

Never forget.

She had gotten the tattoo as a reminder to never stop fighting. Even when people laughed in her face and thought she was lying, she hadn't turned away or given up. She kept on fighting.

Logan, he'd pushed her to one side, but rather than take it, she had to fight back. He thought he knew what was best for her, but the only person to know that, was herself. They were not stuck on some repeat piece of music. Their past didn't have to define them. Sure, it had fucked them each up, but she was willing to see past his flaws, if he was willing to give her the chance.

She didn't want to be without him anymore. They had already lost so much. She didn't want to lose anymore.

What if he doesn't want me anymore?

What if this was all about his own feelings and not about me at all?

It's the risk you're going to have to take.

Lying down rather than fighting for what she wanted was no longer an option.

Soon, they were going to be parents, and she wasn't going to spend her life waiting for him for the moments when they could see their child. She needed to be stronger for the both of them.

With a quick deep breath, she squared her shoulders and walked out to Grant. "I want to find Logan," she said.

Grant looked up from his cell phone. "You do?"

"Yes."

"You're not going to kill him, are you?"

"What? No, of course not. What makes you think I want to kill him?"

"It's a joke."

"It's not funny."

"Not if you're me."

"Oh, okay. Fine. I don't understand, but I will." She shook her head. Her hands were shaking. "I'd really like to go and see him. Do you know where he is?"

"Of course." He typed into his cell phone, and she waited, feeling more nervous with every passing second. "Hunter now knows we're coming."

"Wait, won't he tell Logan we're on our way?"

"No."

"But he's always with Logan. No, I can't do this."

"Hunter knows and understands, okay?"

She stared at Grant, a little confused. "He knows what? What is it he understands?"

"Your feelings for Logan."

"How can he even know when I don't completely understand?"

"I guess it's easier for us watching you guys than the two of you who are in the thick of it."

"Why am I finding you so irritating?"

"Because you know I'm right and you're pregnant and hormonal."

"That's always the excuse men make rather than see anything as being their fault."

"We're all perfect. You do know that, right?"

"I don't know anything. I really don't want to talk right now. Can we just move on, please?" She ran fingers through her hair, bunching up the curls. Pregnancy had given her a glow. The morning sickness hadn't been too bad so far. However, her nerves were really shot right now, and she didn't know if she was going to be able to handle seeing Logan.

This was all ... new for her. It was a completely new experience to have these feelings. This desire to make what Luke had done go away. He had no right to come between her and Logan.

Grant stood and grabbed his jacket. Ava didn't bother with anything and followed him out of her apartment. He draped his jacket over her shoulders as they made their way downstairs and out into the cold.

She didn't climb into the backseat of the car, but into the passenger side, strapping herself into place and trying with all of her might not to be nervous. She couldn't help the way she was feeling.

It would all be fine. She had to believe that.

"Do you know the sex yet?" Grant asked.

"What?"

"The sex? Of the baby. Have you found it out yet?"

"Oh, no. I would have told you if we knew. It's still a little early. I'm not showing all that much yet. I'll know soon enough."

"And how does it feel to know you're going to have a baby?"

She turned toward him. Grant didn't even glance her way. "Why are you asking me so many questions about the baby when you've had so many opportunities and haven't taken them?" He usually talked about his favorite movies or the books he enjoyed. Even his food preferences. The conversation was always on safe topics.

"I'm trying to relax you. You know, help you to figure out why it is you want to go and see Logan."

"I know why I want to go and see him."

"And that reason is…"

"I don't have to tell you about it." She clenched her hands into fists to stop them from shaking.

"Hunter and I, we have a different understanding as to why you want to go and see Logan."

"I bet you two do."

"We do, and it is really interesting."

"Go on, let's hear it." She couldn't think of a single reason why not to let him tell her exactly what he thought.

"We believe you and Logan are in love with each other."

This time, he had her full attention. "What?"

"Yep. Deep down we're hopeless romantics, and you guys have been apart way too much."

"I don't … that's crazy."

"You don't love Logan?"

"I…" She couldn't think of the right words to say. "No, yes, I don't know. This is none of your business."

"You're right, it's none of my business, but you've got to ask yourself, Ava, why do you cry yourself to sleep? Why did you look so happy when he arrived at your doctor's appointment only to die little by little because he didn't pay you a single ounce of attention?"

"It's not important."

"Oh, it is. You and I both know it. I've seen the way you've been, and you're denying your true feelings. Logan, he's in love with you as well."

"You don't know that."

"He loves you enough to let you go."

"Let me go? How has he let me go?"

"He's given you space. I've never known two stubborn people quite like the two of you."

"You have no idea what you're talking about."

"I know a great deal, and you're just being stubborn."

"You don't even have a clue so you can't comment," she said.

Why were they fighting about this?

"We're here," Grant said.

He parked the car across the street, and she saw the line of people waiting to get inside.

The line was so long. She went to join it, but Grant grabbed her arm, leading her straight into the nightclub. Calls and protests rang out, but she imagined that's what you got for working with the big man in charge.

The heavy music surrounded her, and she felt a little sick.

Logan was in here somewhere. Could he see her? Was he watching her?

"You don't have to be nervous," Grant said, yelling over the sound of the music.

"I'm not nervous. I'm fine."

"You keep telling yourself that. Come on. Let's go and get a drink."

"I can't have anything with alcohol."

"I know. I'm not completely stupid."

"I'm sorry."

"Don't worry about it. You're nervous. I get it."

"It's not right to be a pain in your ass."

He chuckled. "I get paid well for you to be a pain in my ass, believe me."

They made it to the bar, and Hunter signaled the waiter. She sat down in the chair, and Grant stayed close. He was her protection detail, and now they were in the lions' den, he would have to pick up his game. She'd not made his life hard at all during his time with her.

She quickly glanced around the dance floor, and then up toward the direction of the office. Was he there watching? Sitting at his desk reading paperwork? Did he know she was here?

She pushed some hair off her shoulder as Grant placed a drink in front of her.

"Drink up."

She sipped at it. Orange juice. "Thank you."

"I know. So, how do you want to approach this?" he asked. "You want to go in all guns blazing, or wait a little bit?"

"I don't know. What do you think I should do?" she asked.

"I think we should dance." He downed his whiskey, took her hand, and led her onto the dance floor.

People made a space for him, and he pulled her in

close, wrapping his arms around her waist.

"How do you do that?" she asked.

"Do what?"

"Make people move out of your way."

"It's a gift. I'm hot stuff. Don't you know that?"

She burst out laughing. "No, I don't."

"I'm attempting to charm you, and it's so not working."

"Maybe try a little harder. It'll help."

"If you want to get Logan on your side, you're going to have to do harder than that."

"What if he's here with someone?" she asked. "I've come all this way and he could be dating other people?"

"He's not."

"How do you know that?" she asked. What if she made a fool of herself for a man who didn't care about her?

He'd never made any promises to be exclusive, and here she was, acting like a fool.

"I have it on good authority he doesn't."

"How?"

"Hunter. He sees all. Stop stressing out. Relax. You know, do what you need to do. Logan is here, and he will find you. Now dance."

She didn't step too close to Grant. The idea wasn't to make Logan jealous; far from it. This was about making him see reason.

Why do you want to see him?

What is it all about?

Are you here to be with him forever?

She had no idea what the answers were, or if she even had answers for their feelings. None of this made any sense to her anymore. Did it ever make any sense? Resting her head on Grant's chest as the music turned to a slow number, she hoped she knew what she was doing for both her and Logan's sakes.

****

"Please tell me why Ava is here in my club and currently hanging off Grant," Logan said.

Hunter was by the window, looking out over the dance floor, but Logan didn't need to look out of his window to see his woman. She was right there, in Grant's arms. He clenched the pen in his hands, and it snapped from the strength of his grip.

Oh, he was pissed off.

He'd given Grant a simple instruction. To give Ava whatever she wanted but it didn't include anything intimate, and he'd disregarded his instruction, and now he was pissed off. The bastard had his hands on her waist, and he needed to get them off before Logan snapped them right off.

"I don't know where you're looking," Hunter said.

"Turn your damn head and look at the screen."

"Why? They're there. I can see them. I guess Ava wanted to go out partying, and he's doing exactly as you asked."

"He's taking the piss," he said. "I didn't tell him to let her get dressed up all sexy and come to a nightclub full of drooling men so she could get looked at."

"What exactly did you want him to do?"

"She's the mother of my child. She's supposed to be at home, enjoying a nice, hot drink of cocoa, and reading a book. Or whatever it is women like to do when they're pregnant."

"Clearly, Ava likes to dance and be held."

He wasn't going to rise to the bait. This wasn't about Ava or himself. This was about the fact Grant shouldn't be touching her, or doing anything with her. He had work to do.

Taking a deep breath, he picked up another pen, determined not to look at the screen.

"Is she even pregnant?" Hunter asked.

"Yes, she is."

"She doesn't look it."

"Hunter, stop looking at her."

"Why not? Other men are. I think they like the look of her ass."

On his feet, Hunter's throat within his death grip, Logan glared at him. "You need to stop looking at her ass."

Hunter held onto his wrist. "You need to think about why it bothers you so much."

"What?" He squeezed a little tighter before letting him go.

"You and Ava, you've been doing this dance around each other for years. Aren't you bored of it?"

"I have no idea what you're talking about."

"Oh, you do. You're not stupid. It's why you don't want her to be with anyone else, but you're not willing to take a chance and to go out and get the girl for yourself."

"You have no idea what you're talking about."

"Do you really think she's here to be with Grant?"

"I can see she's here to be with Grant."

"Wow, you really are fucking dense when you start," Hunter said. "Go ahead. Kill me. It might even help me from all the bullshit you've got throwing around."

"You better be careful."

"Or what? You're going to strangle me some more? Be careful, Logan, you keep doing it I may start liking it, and then where is your threat?"

"I don't have to put up with this bullshit. You work for me."

"Exactly. Grant and I, we work for you, but have you ever thought that we might actually fucking care about you? I know it seems a little odd considering we weren't your best friends from childhood, but look how that turned out for you. We're your friends now, and we both know what it is you and Ava need."

"And what is that? What is it you think you know better than myself?"

"You're in love with her. And even though she didn't realize it either, she's in love with you as well."

"You have no idea what you're talking about." Logan looked out toward the dance floor, and Ava was still there.

Men were checking her out, but so were women checking out Grant. They didn't look compatible with each other, far from it.

He didn't like the jealousy spreading through his body. The last time he'd seen Ava, he'd been a fucking jerk to her. Ignoring her. Pretending the only reason he was with her was because of the baby. He'd wanted to ask her so many questions, but like always, he held himself back.

"I don't deserve her. Not after everything."

"She hasn't run back home."

"I didn't give her anything to run back home to."

"Exactly. Everything she could ever want is right here, in this very room."

"No, she doesn't want me."

"And you think you know everything about her to make that decision, do you?" Hunter asked. "You know, you're starting to sound like a coward."

"Watch it."

"What? You think you can dish out beatings but

you're above these other emotions and feelings? Is that it?"

"You have no idea what you're talking about."

"I know everything I'm talking about, and all you're doing is wasting time. What will you do when Ava's in labor? It will happen, you know. I've got it on good authority pregnant women go into labor at nine months. Grant will be the one with her. What if you don't wake up to the call, or you don't make it in time? Ava has the baby with Grant in the room. He's the one who gets to see your son or daughter first. How about that? Or maybe she goes into labor when you're with her, and you do get to see your child first. What about the months and years to come? Will Grant get to be the one to see your child's first steps? His first words? Or better yet, what if he calls Grant Daddy?"

"Enough!" He bellowed the word.

He couldn't take anymore.

And there was no way he was going to watch his woman dancing with another man.

"Get the fuck out of my office," he said, leaving himself.

He was angry. There was no way he would let Grant take his place. He stormed into his nightclub, ready to murder anyone who got in his way.

Pushing people who dared to step in front of him, he grabbed Ava's arm and pulled her out of Grant's hold and across the dance floor.

Getting to her was a little blur, but he didn't stop.

"Logan, what are you doing?" she said.

He didn't speak another word until they were in the privacy of his office and he checked to see Hunter had already left.

Slamming the door, he flicked the lock into place.

"You don't get to dance with Grant, or treat him

like he was me."

"I'm not treating him like anything," she said.

"You're not? So you paw all the men who come into your world, is that it? You're fucking pregnant, Ava."

"How can I forget how pregnant I am? It's the only time I get to see you. Why can't I be with Grant? At least he's there and he's willing to dance with me. He's even willing to look at me and talk to me. What about you? What is it you're willing to do, Logan? Oh, that's right, continue typing on your damn phone. It's a device, not a person. I was right there, beside you, and you ignored me. What am I supposed to do? Wait around until you decide you want to be with me, is that it?"

"You have no idea what you're fucking talking about."

"And you have no right telling me what I can and cannot do. You're not part of my life, remember? You put me in an apartment and you put me to one side as if I don't matter."

"Of course you matter."

"If I matter, prove it. Talk to me, Logan. Or better yet, dance with me. Hold me. Do anything—but stop ignoring me."

He stared at her, and he couldn't believe they were fighting. She had tears in her eyes, and he'd been the one to put them there. He opened his mouth, closed it, opened it again, and he didn't have a single clue what to say.

"I can't."

"Do you not want me?" Ava asked. "I can't keep on going around waiting for you, Logan. I can't. I want this baby so much, and I want you, but I need to know if you want me too."

"You want me?"

"Yes," she said. "Damn it, Grant's right."

"Don't fucking mention his name to me. Not right now."

"We're standing in the very room where you killed Luke," she said. "And he's dead. Luke is gone. He's not coming back."

"I know that."

"But he's right here. Isn't he? He's the reason you put me in an apartment. Why you can't be with me. Are you ashamed?"

"No, of course not. Don't ever think that."

"Then it can only be one thing. You feel guilty."

He pressed his lips together, and he couldn't look at her.

"You have no reason to feel guilty, Logan."

"I don't? You don't think I have a reason?"

"No."

He laughed. "Wow, I came to Crow Valley to hurt you, Ava. Everything I've done has been to gain my revenge. To take it all out on you, and you didn't even deserve it. All this time, I was helping him. He took everything away from me, and I let him. I helped him fucking do it."

"But I'm right here, Logan. I'm here for you. I'm pregnant with our baby, and we're letting him win. For every single day we're apart, he's won." Tears filled her eyes, and fell down her cheeks.

"Don't cry."

"I…" She chuckled. "I didn't think I loved you. I thought I wasn't capable of loving anyone, but … I love you. I know it's crazy after everything we've been through, but I think back to that time in the classroom, when you kissed me, then our time at Halloween. I was so tired, and I rested my head on your shoulder. You never really hurt me. Sure, you said some things, but you didn't hurt me."

"I was crazy about you," he said. His hands clenched into fists.

"You were?"

"Hell, yeah. I loved looking into your eyes. Even when you were annoyed, they had so much passion and fire. You were amazing. You didn't back down or cower. You were a strength, and I wanted you all to myself. Not a day goes by that I don't regret not telling you sooner. I even stopped a couple of guys asking you out. I told them you had—" He stopped.

"What did you tell them I had?"

"Some disease that rots a guy's dick off."

"You didn't."

"Oh, I did, believe me, and it wasn't hard either."

"But why?"

"Isn't it obvious? I've never been able to handle the thought of another man in your life, Ava. Touching you. Holding you."

"But Grant?"

"Yeah, after I got him to do what I wanted him to, I sent him as far away from me as I could so I didn't kill him. I didn't think it would be fair to kill the guy for doing exactly as I asked. It's why I try to avoid being in his company. I want to hurt him."

"Oh, well, if it makes you feel any better, he's been the perfect gentleman."

"No, it doesn't, because I want to be the one with you."

"Then stop letting him win." She took a deep breath. "I love you, Logan Stanford. I didn't even realize how much until this very moment, but I love you, oh so much, and I never want to lose you. Not ever. I don't want him to take any more time from us than he already has, and I want us to make this work." She stepped up close to him, putting her hands on his chest, and he let her. "So I'm going to ask you to marry me."

"What?" he asked. "Wait, no, you don't have to ask that."

He watched in amazement as she went down on one knee. "Marry me, Logan. I love you, and I don't blame you for anything that happened. What we went through together, I forgive you, and I hope you can forgive me too, for not being stronger. For not fighting."

"You can't propose, I want to propose." He went down on one knee, but she laughed.

"No, you don't get the chance to propose. I did first."

He felt her hand shaking within his grip.

"I love you, Ava. I've always loved you, and that is never going to change."

"I hope not. I want us to live a long and happy life together. The past is staying where it needs to be."

"I can't change who I am."

"I know, and I'm not going to change you. I don't want it to hurt our child or our relationship. I love every single part of you, Logan, the good and the bad. I didn't even know I loved you until this very moment," she said, tears streaming down her face.

"I loved you as a kid, and I love you still." He pushed the hair off her face. "And I will keep on loving you every single day of my life. I'll marry you, Ava."

He pulled her in close for a kiss, and she moaned.

This was what he'd been waiting for. It hadn't been his need for revenge. All this time, it had been his need for her, and now he finally had her.

Ava was all his.

His childhood wish was coming true. Only now he knew how precious she was, and he wasn't ever letting go.

Epilogue

Ten years later

Logan checked to make sure the table was perfectly set. There were candles, flowers—roses, as they were her favorite—and lasagna baking in the oven. Hunter had stopped by to make the food for him. Logan had never been a good cook, and he wasn't about to start learning.

Ava was upstairs putting the kids to bed. They had four kids, and he still couldn't believe what a handful they were. Their first child had been his oldest son, Liam, and then they'd had twin girls, Darcy and Carla, before his baby boy, Steven, was born six months ago. He didn't think he would ever have two, let alone four. Ava's first labor had been a nightmare. He had watched her in pain, hating himself every single second.

She'd pushed out baby Liam, and he'd weighed over nine pounds.

He would never forget that night. Ava had woken up, crying out as contractions disrupted her sleep. They'd already gotten married. She hadn't wanted a big affair, and he'd taken her to Vegas to make her his. It had been the right decision as they spent their time looking for the perfect house, decorating in time for their new arrival. When the nurse put his son in his arms, it had been the perfect moment.

He was finally a father, and he'd vowed to protect his woman and son.

Less than four years later, their twins arrived. He thought he knew pain, but he wasn't a woman in labor.

Pushing the thoughts of his wife in pain out of his mind, he focused instead on being ready for Ava.

"They are asleep. I don't know for how long."

She rounded the corner, and he watched her

pause.

He held a rose, and he'd already taken off the thorns.

"What's all this?" she asked.

"This is our anniversary dinner."

"We didn't get married in October."

"No, but we did spend an entire night together on Halloween."

"You're calling our first night together when we were eighteen."

"It was one of the first moments I fell in love with you," he said.

"Your friends thought I was mistaken for that other girl. I can't remember her name."

"Anna. She didn't come as a sexy nurse, Ava. I made that up. She came as a vampire. I told my friends at the time that she was the sexy nurse. It was you I wanted with me the whole time."

"Oh. I'm not even dressed for it. I've got baby vomit on my shirt. My clothes haven't seen a washer. I'm a mess."

He walked right up to her, cupped her face, and smiled. "You're perfect. You're my wife, and I love everything there is about you."

"Really?"

"Really. Baby vomit and all."

"You know how to really charm a girl, don't you?"

"Only you. I'm waiting on you tonight. We're going to have a lovely meal, and then I'm going to take you for a nice, long bath, and if the kids stay silent and asleep, I'm going to make love to you."

She grabbed his shirt jacket and pulled him close, drawing him down for a kiss. "I love you. So damn much."

"And I you."

It was the first of many anniversaries to come, filled with love, laughter, and with their past where it was meant to stay.

The End

www.samcrescent.com

BLACKMAILED BY HER BULLY

EVERNIGHT PUBLISHING ®

www.evernightpublishing.com

www.ingramcontent.com/pod-product-compliance
Lightning Source LLC
Chambersburg PA
CBHW050720180626
46814CB00002B/525